THE MARINE'S
HOLIDAY HARBOR

THE MARINE'S HOLIDAY HARBOR

KIRSTEN LYNN

COPYRIGHT

ABOUT THE BOOK

We made a deal.

Ten years in the military, then we'd find our own home and start a family. Ten years later, I transitioned out of the Navy. Caleb Quinlin stayed in the Marine Corps and broke my heart. A year ago, life capsized again. Now, I'm a single parent to my niece and nephew doing my best to make this lighthouse a home. This holiday season is supposed to be peaceful and perfect. Instead of Santa's sleigh on the roof, a Marine almost crashes a boat on the rocks.

He has a letter giving him co-guardianship.
He says he wants us forever.
But can he call a town where his past haunts him home?
A life with him has been my Christmas wish since we were children.

Because Caleb…Caleb is my Heart.

We made a deal.

I broke it, and both our hearts. But the deal never included coming back to Camden, Maine. Anywhere but here. So, why am I risking my life sailing through a Nor'easter to a lighthouse off the coast of the one place I swore I'd never live? A letter I've been carrying for over a year in combat zones throughout the world. Two small children.

Number one reason. Brynn Reilly.
She's my first love, best friend, and the Devil Doc who patched me up more times than I want to admit.
I need her to trust my past won't stop my forever with her and the children.
Come on Christmas magic give this Marine one more chance.

Because Brynn…Brynn is my Home.

PROLOGUE

Caleb
Camp New Garm Ser (formerly Camp Dwyer, Afghanistan)

A KNOCK ON the door followed by an "It's me" turns my attention from the ceiling of my plywood palace to the one diamond in this sand pit.

"Yeah, come in." Our corpsman slips inside. I sit up on my rack and nod to the open door. "You were headed out, Hanson."

Staff Sergeant Collin Hanson cuts a glance to the corpsman and back to me. "Yeah, I wanted more pie. Is that right?"

"Whatever gets your ass out of here."

He walks by Brynn and smiles as he tugs on his utility cover and she removes hers. "Merry Christmas, Devil Doc."

She returns his smile, and a part of me hates I have to

even share that much of her with other Marines. "Merry Christmas, Hanson."

When Hanson adds some drama by trying to slam the thin door, she chuckles and focuses on me. "Merry Christmas, Caleb."

"Merry Christmas, Angel."

"The other Marines call me Doc."

I scan her from toe to head, not hiding that I'm picturing her naked under those desert utilities and combat boots. "You haven't taken the other Marines to heaven inside that body."

Her forehead wrinkles, but gold sparks shoot through her hazel eyes as they change more green than brown, a sure sign she's turned on. "You shouldn't talk about that out loud."

"I think about it every fucking second. From our first time in high school to this Thanksgiving up against that wall you're leaning against."

She pushes off the wall. "Caleb!"

I wave away her false outrage. "Sit with me, Angel."

Hospital Corpsman First Class Brynn Reilly sets the saddest-looking Christmas tree on what constitutes a desk, then crawls on the cot and sits next to me using the wall as a back rest. Brynn has been mine since we were fifteen; she became all mine when we were seventeen. If we're honest, we've been fated since our mothers had a playdate for us when we were one.

When I joined the Marines, she joined the Navy. She had one purpose for enlisting and that was to become a corpsman and go green to save as many Marines as possible. How we ended up in the same regiment, battalion, and platoon is a miracle I thank God for every day. The fact she was assigned as a corpsman for an RTC comprised of Marines from various battalions, including the 2/8, makes me wonder if somewhere, somehow I did God a solid.

I nod to the green triangular "tree" in a plastic pot. It stands about a foot tall with a few bright bulbs dangling precariously from the limbs that are more wire than fake pine now. "Where'd you get that thing?"

"It's not a thing. Don't be an asshole—it's our Christmas tree." Her gaze sweeps the room. "You need at least one decoration. Mom sent it to me, I'm giving it to you."

"Looks like the kind of tree that'd grow out here. Christmas in Hell-Man again. Bing Crosby and Danny Kaye never wrote about dreaming about this place. And people say lightning can't strike twice." Even as I grump, the words, *our Christmas tree*, seem to transform the shrub; filling out branches and making the tiny ornaments sparkle.

"Better than Ramadi, worse than San Diego."

"Helmand is not better than shit. And no comparison to our Christmas together in San Diego. Bing

Crosby and Danny Kaye would definitely dream of you in that bikini."

She caresses my cheek with the backs of her fingers, and I lean into her touch It's a tightrope we walk, but for her touch I'd chance everything I have. "Did you get any chow?"

"Aye. I loaded down. The pie just made me miss your pies more."

I smile and count it a win when she scoots closer to me. A tight regulation bun keeps her hair off her collar, but it hides the waves of chestnut silk I'd love to run my fingers through.

"Missed having you there, Angel."

"Sorry, I had to assist at the hospital. I missed sharing Christmas dinner with you, too."

"You eat?"

"Aye. Shoveled it in and came here."

"Glad you did."

She releases a deep breath. "I'm missing Christmas in Camden more than ever this year. From the smell of balsam to snow to you singing carols off-key, and Mom over-decorating until you're afraid to sit still or be wrapped in tinsel. Don't you miss home?"

"I did…and then you came to me and now I'm home." She slides her fingers between mine linking our hands. I squeeze her hand. "You better watch it, if we're caught we'll face a shitstorm."

"Hanson wouldn't say shit. And funny, you didn't care if he walked in while taking me from behind after Thanksgiving dinner."

"At that moment they could burn me alive for transgressions. I thought we weren't talking about that."

"We're both thinking about it. I gave in."

"You want a repeat."

She doesn't laugh, recognizing how serious I am. "We can't, Caleb. We seriously can never let that happen again over here, because joke or no joke, if we were ever caught that's it for our careers. And the fact you came inside me…I can't risk going home because I'm knocked up."

I rest my head back on the wall, but hold her hand like it's my only tie to earth. "Understood and agreed. It's just wicked good holding your hand."

"I hope Liz records Michael and Ella opening their gifts for us. What did you get the kids?"

The thought of our niece and nephew tearing into their gifts brings a smile to my face, and works as the distraction she wanted. Christmas through the eyes of a two and five-year-old could even bring a little peace on earth out here. "Got Little Bit, a stuffed Chesty bulldog, and for Michael a chess set. You?"

When she doesn't answer, I open my eyes. My gaze collides with hers, filled with such adoration that I shift, uncomfortable with the hero in her eyes compared to who I really am.

"You are so sweet when it comes to them. You call Ella Little Bit?"

"She's a little bit of everything; sweet, sassy, sunshine, and storm…she's *a little bit* like you." I caress the back of a finger over her cheek and catch a drop of moisture from her eyes. "Come on, Brynn, what did you get them?"

"Ella is getting Disney princess pajamas, complete with all the princesses. I can't remember her favorite. I included slippers. For Michael an Osprey model; Liz says he likes models even though he's young. Hopefully Mark will help him."

I huff a humorless laugh. "Yeah, don't hold your breath. But those are outstanding gifts."

"Thank you, but you're their hero, so mine will be tossed aside."

I frown. "What's that pouty bullshit? It's not some fucking competition."

She laughs and she might as well rip out my heart and take it. "No, it's not. And I'm not being pouty. They adore you, Caleb. You should come home on leave more and hear them. It's *Uncle Caleb does this* and *Uncle Caleb puts four spoonfuls of chocolate in our chocolate milk* and *Uncle Caleb can fight off a million alien soldiers from Pluto.*"

Chuckling, I scrub a hand over my face. "A million

aliens, huh? Might feel like it after Uncle Caleb's patrol tomorrow. And Plutoians, or whatever, might be an easier fight."

She nudges my arm and shakes her head. "Don't talk about tomorrow in Afghanistan. All of that doesn't exist right now. Dream with me a little bit longer. Let's stay in Maine a few more minutes. Do you think Liz will cook the turkey too long again?"

My frown returns at the longing in her voice. I ignore her question about Liz and the turkey; dragged out of the warm dream by a cold reality. "Why do I get the feeling you'll be staying in Maine forever once this deployment is over?"

"Stay there with me, Caleb."

"I'm where I should be, and Maine will never be home. You picked the wrong brother if you want all that, but then again, compared to Mark, I've always been wrong."

"Fuck you, Caleb, I don't deserve that. I don't deserve to have your father's words put in my mouth. I love you with all I am and you will always be my choice. But I want to be more than your fuck buddy. And yeah, how horrible, I want a family, a house, to wake up in the same bed every morning. That was the deal. Remember? Ten years is up. Now you've got to decide if you're going to choose me, or let me go."

I tug her hand bringing her closer to me. "You have

never been just a fuck buddy and you damn well know it. As for letting you go…never…you will always be mine, Brynn."

I give her hand another tug, and capture her mouth. The second her soft lips mold to mine, I don't give a holly jolly fuck if the whole regiment catches us. Releasing her hand, I cup the back of her head, keeping her to me, and run the tip of my tongue over her bottom lip, sliding it inside the sweet, wet warmth of her mouth when she sighs. I slant my mouth over hers and guide her head so we fit like puzzle pieces. Home. Home tastes like Brynn, smells like Brynn, feels like Brynn. She is the only shelter I need.

I brush a kiss to one side of her mouth and then the other. "Mine."

"Yes."

"Maybe La Jolla, little bungalow, going at it whenever we want, and naked weekends."

"That works, but Christmas in Maine."

"Angel."

Heavy boots outside the door snap us apart and she breaks from me, standing. "Merry Christmas again, Staff Sergeant."

With a chuckle, I nod. "It sure was a second ago. Merry Christmas to you, too, Doc."

She pivots on her heels with a precision that would make any Marine proud and almost runs over Hanson.

"Good night, Staff Sergeant Hanson."

"Doc Reilly."

He barely gets the words out before the door closes behind her. She brought the light, love, and hope of Christmas in with her. With her gone, the room fades back into a dingy barrack. Even the small tree reverts to its former ratty, wiry self. I scrub a hand over my face and give my head a vigorous shake. Brynn. If anyone can have me imagining an inanimate object puffing up then slinking down, it's her. Hanson smiles. "You have a nice time?"

"Shut the fuck up."

"Well, it's just a marshmallow world in here."

"You know I don't allow that kind of bullshit innuendo about Brynn."

"Fuck me, man, I'd never talk about Doc with anything but respect. She's earned it. Just asking if you two had a nice time."

I grunt, not convinced, but I have more important thoughts running through my mind. Brynn's really transitioning. We'd made the deal when we were seventeen. Ten years, then we're out and settling down. We discussed it again a few months ago, but I didn't think she was already making plans. I wonder how long she's been processing out and how much time I have with her. Because when Brynn leaves she'll be leaving me.

"Brought you another piece of pie."

"Thanks, Hanson, but go ahead and chow down. I'm good for sweet things this Christmas."

"Sure thing." Hanson glances to where Brynn exited, but chooses the wise course of not commenting.

Brynn
December 26, Helmand Province

NOTHING BRINGS HOME the fact the holidays are over like patrolling with Afghan forces through a town in the Helmand Province. Helmand carries a reputation for being deadly and it has lived up to that reputation since U.S. troops first arrived over sixteen years ago. The economy here is driven by vast fields of opium poppies. The Taliban in this province acts like the mafia as it processes and smuggles drugs, funding its operations.

As our patrol moves past the buildings, a few concrete, most made of mud bricks, the occupants either stare as we walk by or duck into the doorways. It has the feel of an old Western; only here both the townsfolk and the bad guys hide in wait for attack, leaving us uncertain who is who as we patrol. All that's needed is some ominous music. Caleb holds up a hand for the squad to stop at a local shop. A man steps out of the building wearing the tradition khet, or top portion of the garment, and partug, the lower portion, along with a turban.

Caleb waves one of the Afghani troops over and begins a conversation. I pick up bits and pieces, mostly he keeps it small talk introducing the man to the new Afghani commander. We should be only advisors, but with the new commander Caleb was put in charge of the patrol.

The shop owner keeps glancing to Caleb's M-4 and then down the street. Caleb is, of course, in full combat gear, the carbine in one hand. I watch him for a second. He's a Marine's Marine, the kind who should be in recruiting ads. Oh, that's right, he *is* in recruiting ads. I shake my head, and allow a brief smile.

Children begin to edge toward us. This could be a good sign or bad, as they've been used as sacrifices; sent to get the candy or soccer balls we sometimes carry only to be blown up with Marines.

One little boy steps within Caleb's view, and Caleb reaches into a pocket, offering the child a few pieces of candy. I keep an eye on the children, but keep my gaze constantly moving. The scent of spices mixes with other, not so pleasant scents, and feral dogs roam the streets. A woman scurries across the street, her gaze over her burqa cutting from the patrol to the man speaking with Caleb. Even though the day is a decent sixty degrees, not the triple digits of summer, I feel sweat trickle down my neck. There is something off here today.

He asks the man again about any Taliban. The man

shakes his head no. Caleb waves us forward, and I can tell by the way he's walking he doesn't believe the intel he was given.

The man from the shop eyeballs me as I fall into step. Even the Afghanis with us tend to give me either hostile glares or a wide birth. As a woman I shouldn't be here. As full-fledged part of the Fleet Marine Forces, I've received a warmer welcome from my Marines. Some I've butted heads with and a few have been buttheads. I stay in my lane, and once we serve together, the majority welcome me as a sister-in-arms. When they started calling me the unofficial title, Devil Doc, I knew I'd made it. I am seen as a Marine; the only difference between me and them is the Navy rate chevrons on my Marine Corps utilities. Even earning my FMF device didn't mean quite as much.

I flip the Velcro on the holster for my Sig Saur, and bring my M-4 a little higher as I watch the Marines bring theirs to their shoulders.

Before I can lift my arm, I feel like a giant picks me up and slams me to the ground. I choke and struggle to stand. My ears ring and I hear people screaming, but it sounds miles away. "Doc!" My radio comes alive, and I can see shadows moving through the black smoke. As my ears clear a little, I recognize the staccato blast of M-4s responding to AK-47s.

"Doc!" The voice isn't over the radio, and close.

Snapping out of the shock of the blast, I call back, "Location, Marine!"

Instead of an answer, my sleeve is grabbed and Lance Corporal Garwin practically drags me to a wounded Private Christianson. Christianson's leg is bleeding; a piece of shrapnel protrudes from his knee. "How bad is it, Doc?"

I start administering Tactical Combat Casualty Care. The world seems to combust after the initial IED, and I hook my arms under his armpits and drag him behind rubble. Retrieving a tourniquet, I place it around his thigh and tighten. I hold his gaze and nod, hoping to reassure him as he groans in pain. "You'll keep it, Christianson. You'll be chasing that little girl of yours in no time."

Taking out my radio, I call in, "Bravo 2, this is Echo 1, 9 Line MEDEVAC!"

"Doc!"

I turn to Garwin. "Watch him!"

"Yes, ma'am."

I bend over keeping my head down as I run to the next casualty. I step behind the house used for cover, and I feel like another blast knocked me off my feet. The ringing returns to my ears, and even though I'm walking toward him, it's like quicksand keeps me rooted.

I crash to my knees by Caleb's side. Blood is spurting from his shoulder. I examine further and find a gaping hole and his blood loss is critical. There are other wounds, but I focus on his shoulder. My hands shake as I take out wads of gauze and padding. *Get it the fuck together, Reilly!* I chastise myself. Caleb needs his corpsman, not his girlfriend. I secure the padding around the wound and add pressure. Lifting my radio, I call again. "Bravo 2 this is Echo 1, cancel MEDEVAC, CASEVAC urgent need. Repeat, urgent-surgical. Request CASEVAC at new coordinates…" Caleb moans and I rattle off the coordinates.

"Caleb, hold on. You will not die on my watch. You will *not*, Marine, and that's a fucking order."

He blinks and then his ice-blue eyes collide with mine. "Angel. I love you."

The sand lifts next to us and I scan for the source. I can't move him like I did Christianson or he might lose more blood than the gallons it seems he's already losing. I put more pressure on the wound, his blood covering my hands.

I lift one hand for a second, and wave Corporal Myers over. "Put your hands on this and apply pressure, Marine."

"Yes, ma'am."

Pressing the button on my radio, I bellow, "Where is the fucking CASEVAC?" NATO requires those calling in MEDEVACS to always remain calm, but right now NATO can fuck me. He's going to lose his arm at the least, his life at most.

"Echo 1, Bravo 2, no safe LZ within coordinates…"

"Get me a fucking Marine aviator with balls!"

"Echo 1, Victor 5, Marine with balls inbound!"

"Roger, Marine."

"Doc!"

I could scream, and I do. "Myers!" The young Marine lifts his head. "You keep your hands on that and apply pressure, and don't you fucking move it!"

"Yes, ma'am!"

I hesitate, something a corpsman should never do, staring at Caleb's face.

"Doc!"

Shoring up every ounce of training I've had and leaving my heart with him, I bend at the waist and fire rounds to protect the wounded Afghani soldier. He shakes off my help continuing to fight until I tear open the pant leg of his trousers. I administer antiseptic and secure the wound. "We need to move you!" I shout over his rifle as he continues to stay in the fight.

I stand and wrap my arms around his waist, helping him up. He waves me away, and as much as it must hurt his pride, he follows a woman.

When we get back to the house, I fall to my knees next to Caleb and press two fingers to his pulse. It's dangerously faint. I lift my gaze to the sky, almost collapsing in relief when the silhouette of an MV-22 soars closer.

"Keep holding."

"Ma'am."

I take off once more, and with the help of Garwin, I get Christianson over to the LZ.

"Echo 1, Victor 5, It's too hot for landing."

"Victor 5, Echo 1, bring that bird in or I will shoot it down."

"Roger that, Echo 1."

I take over applying pressure to Caleb's wound and Myers takes over the squad, leading fire away from us.

The sand whirls and the other wounded men cover their faces as I cover Caleb's, taking the opportunity while hidden to brush a kiss on his forehead. The Marines who step off the Osprey aren't medics, they simply answered the call of a fellow Marine in trouble. They race from the Osprey and start loading the men. I keep one hand on his wound and lace our hands together with the other. I run alongside his stretcher to the door, hesitating to let him go. His hand squeezes mine, and then his fingers slip from my fingers.

"We've got 'em, Ma'am."

Nodding, I run back to the men who still might need me as the firefight continues, blaming the sand the Osprey kicks up for my tears.

TWO HOURS LATER, and what seems like an eternity,

what's left of our squad is evacuated. The Marines make a hole and let me hop out of the Blackhawk first. Without dropping any of my gear off or cleaning up, I barrel for the field hospital. Tugging off my helmet as I step inside, I scan the beds.

"You need something, Corpsman?"

"Staff Sergeant Caleb Quinlin, he came in two hours ago."

"Patched up as much as we could and shipped to Kabul," the surgeon tosses over his shoulder as he heads to the wounded he can help.

Gone. I can still feel his hand in mine and hear his declaration of love.

After stepping out of the hospital and out of the way, I walk to my barrack. I have three more days on this deployment…three days, that's all Caleb had too. We both have scars from previous deployments and I've dealt with bullets and shrapnel wounds as he's called for a corpsman—well, Caleb never called for a corpsman, one of his Marines would. But it's never been this serious, and I've always been with him during his recovery. And he will recover from this, or he'll deal with me.

Brynn
Bethesda Medical Center, Bethesda, Maryland

LONGEST WEEK OF my life, but I was able to secure permission to fly direct to Bethesda instead of back to

Lejeune. Now riding up this elevator feels like torture. After taking off my coat, I hook it over one arm. I tug down the red sweater I chose especially because Caleb thinks red is sexy on me.

When the elevator door opens, a case of butterflies hits my stomach. I frown and keep walking. I have never in my life been nervous to see Caleb. Then again, Caleb has never been as close to death as he was the last time I was with him.

Stepping into his room, I huff a laugh. No need for nerves, Staff Sergeant Quinlin is fast asleep. Laying my coat on the back of a chair, I lean over the railing to the bed and rest my palm on his forehead. He is alive.

I swipe at the fresh tears and step back so I don't bawl all over him. Once the tears start, the days of waiting and worrying catch up and I can't stop crying.

"Angel?"

I startle at his voice and lean over the rail again. "Caleb?"

"Angel! No!"

I scan his face. His scowl is deep and pained and he starts twisting. "Angel!"

Pressing the button for the nurse, I try to calm him. "Caleb, I'm here. I'm fine."

My voice doesn't seem to help, and I step aside when the nurse comes running in. She injects something into his IV, then smiles at me. "Sedative. He's been progressing well overall, but the nightmares are rough. Are you his wife?"

It's the question that always stings because I always want to say, yes. "Girlfriend. And corpsman." I shrug. "It's complicated."

She chuckles. "Sounds like it. So are you Angel?"

I feel the heat touch my cheek. "Affirmative."

She starts walking out of the room. "Unfortunately, he probably won't be awake today. But feel free to stay until visiting hours are over."

"Thank you."

After a few minutes, he's completely settled. I lace my fingers with his. "I love you, Caleb."

"Love, Brynn," he mumbles.

I STEP INTO his room and smile—he's awake like he was the day before. His blue eyes are bright and lucid, and when he sees me telltale sparks are there in the depths. My gaze drops to his arm and upper chest as I walk closer.

"I've got doctors for that, Brynn. Focus on me."

I lift my gaze to his. "You can at least tell me what they said."

"I'll keep my arm, thanks to your quick action. I'll have a hell of a scar, and my shoulder and chest will tell me when the weather is changing, but I'll be good to go."

"Outstanding." I sidle next to his bed and link my

hand with his. I lean forward and seal my mouth to his. With his other hand he cups my neck and deepens the kiss. He strokes my tongue with his and I swallow the low rumble of his groan.

When I break the kiss, I rest my forehead to his. After a few seconds, I press my lips to his again and fall into a sweet, slow caress. We're both breathing hard when I step back. "Have you heard from your parents?"

"Ouch, Angel, you were doing good up until then."

"Sorry."

He squeezes my hand. "I don't expect to hear anything from my father. Mom has called a couple times, but she just gives excuses on why she can't come, but it's because he won't let her. Mark and I video chatted a few times; the kids wanted to see me. He offered to come down, but he's got the bar exam."

I sit on the edge of the bed. "I'll stay as long as I can."

"But you need to finish your transitioning process."

"We'll finish together."

"Brynn, I'm not transitioning out yet. I've reupped."

I wait for the punchline. When it doesn't come, it's a feeling second only to seeing him bleeding out on a battlefield. "You promised. That was the deal. Ten years and then we start a life together. You promised."

"Brynn, I'm staying. I've got orders to the 3/7 onboard Twentynine Palms just as soon as I'm good to go. Maine is your dream. You need to go back and settle into life without me."

I narrow my gaze. "What do you mean without you?"

"Just that."

"I thought you were never letting me go."

"I'm not, Angel, I can't ever truly let you go. But who knows what the future holds. I might stay in until they kick me out. I found a family."

"We're family! We were supposed to be a family, have children."

"I can't leave. I don't know if I ever will."

"So, I'm supposed to just go on and start my life without you? You can just end us?"

"I hope this isn't the end, but for the first time in our lives we're headed in different directions and I'm not doing long distance with you."

I want to punch him, so I lobby a verbal blow. "What if I find someone else?"

"Then you'll know we weren't as meant to be as we thought."

"You're being an asshole." I don't want to cry, but the tears rebel and fall anyway. "Just because I'm transitioning you're turning into a dick."

He swipes at my tears with his thumb and I remember his hand cupping my neck, him telling me he'd never let me go. Before that, I remember us in a tent camping in Acadia National Park and promising we'd serve ten years, then marry and settle down. "Don't cry, Brynn, please. I'm not saying forever. I just think for now we try it on our own."

I stand and his hand falls from me. "I can't believe you're doing this to us. So, no phone calls, or texts, or anything?"

"You need me, you contact me however you want."

"But I do need you, Caleb, I need you to be mine like you promised. You *promised*."

"I can't do it now. I'm so fucking sorry, but I can't."

"Why are you doing this now when you're here alone and you know it will break me to leave you?"

"Because I didn't want you to care for me for days, or weeks, and take advantage. But you should go. I'll be fine."

I feel like my insides are being yanked from my body and my chest is empty. Looking up to the ceiling, I swipe at the torrid of tears. "I can't do this, Caleb. I can't let you go—you are a part of every memory I have, every beat of my heart. How can I just walk out that door and live?"

He grabs my hand and I try to focus on his face through the blur of moisture. My soul rips open anew at the tears on his face. "You are the strongest person I know, Brynn, not woman, but person, and you are my best friend, the woman I love. But we have been inseparable since birth and now we find ourselves at a crossroads. Whose path are we going to follow? We both need time without the other pushing. This hurts worse than any weapon man has created, but it's what we need to do."

I yank my hand from his and grab my coat. "It's what you want. I need you. Happy New Year, Caleb, I hope you find what you need on your own."

CHAPTER ONE

Brynn
Two Years Later

ASHIVER WALKS my spine as a gust of wind howls so loud I can feel the icy chill sweep through me even though I'm inside. The back door rattles with the force and I get another chill at how much it sounds like someone, or something trying to get in the house.

With a huffed laugh, I turn on my stove and set a kettle on for tea. Living in a lighthouse keeper's house on an island with no one else was supposed to be peaceful in its seclusion. Instead, I'm learning why some lighthouse keepers went insane.

"Aunt Brynn?" A voice reminds me I'm not alone.

Renewed warmth lights within me. Turning, I find Ella, four-year-old going on thirty, standing in nothing but her Disney princess nightgown and holding tight to her favorite stuffed bulldog. The one stuffed animal in her endless collection that reminds me of the day I thought I lost my heart, until I came home and spent time with Ella and her seven-year-old brother, Michael. Then my heart was wrenched open again.

After stepping forward, I sit on my heels in front of her. Her blue eyes, just like her father's and her uncle's, widen as a ferocious howl cuts by the window. Caressing her cheek with the back of a finger, I bring her attention back to me. "I think this night calls for hot chocolate before bed, don't you?"

Her tiny shoulders sag and her mouth curves in a big grin. "Yeah."

I drop a kiss on the top of her head and stand. "I'll start heating the milk, you go get your brother."

"He's in bed sleeping. He's not scared."

"He might not be scared, but I can almost guarantee he's not sleeping. Go get him."

Her forehead creases and she tips her head to the side as if she doesn't believe me. After a few seconds, she shrugs and walks to the bottom of the staircase just outside the kitchen. "Michael, Aunt Brynn says come down!"

I roll my eyes and exhale my exasperation. "Go *up* the stairs and get your brother, Ella. Don't yell for him."

She starts up the stairs, pounding her little feet on each stair to show her contempt. Turning, I know I shouldn't let her get away with the display of drama, but tonight I'm feeling a little defeated in the single parenthood category, so I let it go.

After setting the milk on to heat, I walk to the sink and lean forward to look out the window. I stretch to see the light from the tower shine over the choppy waves and high swells of the ocean. Until 1972, a guardian would tend to the light that now shines without aid. The lighthouse keepers on Curtis Island, being so near Camden, weren't quite as secluded as some, but their job was just as dangerous. Today, the Coast Guard, and specifically my brother, tends to the light.

The light from Curtis Island's lantern is a rare green. Staring at the beacon's light, I watch four seconds of green followed by a second of darkness. In the blink when the green occults again a boat appears in the tumultuous waters. Darkness. The light again, but no boat. This Nor'easter blasted into Penobscot Bay with no warning. I can't imagine the terror someone sailing on the previously calm waters would be experiencing.

I stretch and watch the light bounce off waves. Nothing appears but the snow and whitecaps cresting the tops of the wild waves.

"Ella said we were having hot chocolate."

I startle and pivot from the window. Once my heart returns to a normal rhythm, I smile. Michael pushes up his glasses on his nose. The black frames seem to almost swallow him, his face is so small, but nothing hides his familial ice-blue eyes. At seven, he's trying to be the man he thinks he needs to be while in his heart, thankfully, he remains a boy. He squares his shoulders and I see a weight still attached to him. He won't share anything about how he's feeling, or any memories of his parents, and I wish something in my medical kit could cure whatever plagues his young mind.

Ruffling his thick, dark hair, I wink. "She's right. I might even throw in marshmallows."

His eyes light up and he can't hide his enthusiasm. He and Ella speak in unison. "Yes, please."

Going back to the milk, I nod to the pantry. "Go grab them. They'll be better in hot chocolate than on your nana's sweet potatoes."

We both shudder and I laugh at Michael's aversion to my mother's determination to make sweet potatoes every Thanksgiving. No matter that my father's the only one who eats them and that's because he doesn't want to hurt her feelings—nothing dissuades her from tradition. Sometimes I wish something would so she wouldn't feel obligated to ask Audrey and Hal Quinlin to Thanksgiving and the New Year's party. Audrey is sweet, but Caleb's father is a toad. The ice touching my spine this time is remembering last year's New Year's Eve party.

I force my thoughts away from the jackass and back to the children. "Take a seat, Ella." The little girl crawls onto the chair, her pink tongue sticking out as she struggles with the height. Michael sits and drops the bag of marshmallows on the table. I pour the hot milk over the rich cocoa powder.

"Nana and Papa got home okay, right?"

The fear in his voice breaks my heart. Taking the bag of marshmallows, I tweak his nose. When he doesn't frown, I know how frightened he is, whether his sister thinks he never gets scared or not.

"They're fine. Remember, they called an hour ago, safe and snug. They already can't wait to see you again at Thanksgiving in a couple days."

"That's right," he mumbles. I put extra marshmallows in his chocolate and hand him the mug, then carry over my and Ella's mugs.

Setting her smaller mug in front of her, I cover her hands, "Just a minute, baby, let me add a little cold milk to cool yours down."

Her mouth opens in an O and she takes her hands back, nodding like she almost touched lava. Grabbing the milk, I study the two children at the table for a minute. For a year and almost four months they've been my wards, my charges, my children…mine. A family formed at the cost of my sister and brother-in-law. Just when it finally seemed they could settle into a new life in Bar Harbor and Mark could start spending more time with the children since his studies were over, one night on a curvy road snatched them from us all.

Joining them again, I pour a little milk in Ella's mug and we all start drinking our treat in quiet. The wind continues to push against the windows and doors, and I refuse to think about the amount of snow we'll wake up to if the large flakes continue to fall.

I know what will come later, and I know all the warnings against it, but they can add it to their therapy later in life. "Why don't you guys sleep with me tonight?"

"Yes," Ella confirms.

"If you want us to," Michael agrees, but he's fooling no one as his body deflates in relief. He jerks his head to the window when a scream pierces the night as if the storm resents our plan. "Aunt Brynn, there's a boat!" He shoves a finger at the lower frame of the window.

Pushing out of my chair, I snatch the handheld radio I keep on the counter. "Brian, this is Brynn, out. I swallow a curse. I should have radioed Brian the first time I thought I saw the boat. Brian, Brynn out!"

A million years seems to pass before the radio cracks to life. "Go for Brian."

"Boat approximately three kilometers off Curtis Light."

"Shit. We're on our way. You stay in, out."

"Hurry, out."

"You. Stay. Inside. Out."

Frowning at the radio, I don't respond. My brother wouldn't like the truth and I don't want to lie. Turning to the children, I point a finger between them. "You two stay right there until I come get you."

Michael's eyes widen. "But Uncle Brian told you to stay inside."

"You don't worry about me, you just worry about doing what you're told."

"But…"

"Michael, do as you're told." I use my corpsman voice and it must still work.

He sinks back in his chair watching me as I tug on my boots and rain slicker. I cut a look between Michael and Ella, both staring at me with big eyes and hot chocolate mustaches. "I'll be right back."

"Right back." Michael whispers.

"Right back, I promise."

They both nod and I grab the LED lantern, making my way over the grassy area now covered in snow, toward the rocks. The silhouette of the sailboat bobs closer. I can't see the condition of the boat itself, but from sailing and boating all my life I can say with certainty after this it will have to be scuttled.

A light in the sky draws my attention to the Coast Guard helicopter. I squint as the shadow of my brother repels down from a rope and to the boat just meters from the rocks.

With careful steps, I go from rock to rock. Brian brings the boat to a natural ramp and hops out. I make it to him in time to help him tug the boat farther onto shore. When he lifts his gaze, even in the driving snow and wind, his face is the scariest thing in Maine.

"Glad you stayed inside." The sarcasm is so thick someone who didn't know him as well would miss the hostility simmering below.

"Thought there might be injured."

"And we'd fly them to the hospital."

He walks around the bow and offers a hand to the person inside. The man emerging is tall and a bit broader than Brian. "Take him inside and get him warmed up. Got a cut on his forehead." Brian practically tosses the man at me.

"Brian, I can't take a stranger into the house."

"That's no stranger and you're both asses."

Brian waves down the rope and disappears back inside the helicopter before I can offer any more fight. The man is hunched over and it's clear his coat wasn't made for what he endured. I'm certainly not going to let anyone freeze on my watch.

Going to him, I inhale a sharp breath when he lifts his tired gaze to mine. Staff Sergeant Caleb Quinlin stares back at me.

Without a word, because my mind can't form a clear thought, I drape his arm over my shoulders and start walking toward the house. As we trudge along, the shudders from his body shake me in their violence. What he was thinking will have to wait. Any questions, and there will be many, will have to wait.

"Saving me again?" he says through chattering teeth.

"Seems like it!" I scream over the howling wind.

"How'd you get so lucky?"

"Patron Saint of Idiots."

I slide just a bit under him, so I can keep him propped up and open the door. Once the door is ajar, though, I practically shove him inside the kitchen. I slam the door and sit on my heels in front of him removing his boots when the shuffle of small feet catches our attention.

The moment they recognize the tall figure is clear by their scream of joy. "Uncle Caleb!"

They start running, but I hold up a hand. "Your uncle needs some attention first, then you can attack."

They step back and immediately their gazes shoot to the gash on his forehead and the blood on this face. He must notice their faces turn the color of parchment the same time I do and beats me to reassuring them. "I'm fine, guys. Just give me a couple minutes."

I nod to the living room. "Go watch some TV."

They keep their eyes on him as they walk away and until the archway conceals us. I tug off one of his boots and then the other and then his wet socks. Standing, I yank off my slicker. He rests his arm over my shoulders again, sinking against me.

When we get to the bottom of the stairs, I finally meet his gaze again. "There's not room for both of us like this. You climb up and use the rail, I'll be behind you if you need me."

"Brynn."

"Not now. Just do this."

He grabs the railing and his knuckles are white as he takes each step. With as cold as he is, his joints will be rejecting the motion, and I cringe with every step knowing he must be in pain.

At the top of the stairs we resume our previous position. I glance left, then right. The children's beds would be way too small. He gives me a half-smile. "Wherever."

I lead him to my room and use my shoulder to cut on the lights. Taking him to the bed, I ease him down slowly to sit on the edge. "You need to get out of those clothes. You need help?"

His gaze holds mine, and I move forward touching his forehead around the cut. "I'll get my kit."

He shivers under my touch and I don't know if it's the cold, pain, or my hand on him. I take his hands examining each finger and then, kneeling in front of him, I take his feet and examine his toes. "Can you feel my touch?"

"God, yes."

His voice is rough with a familiar tinge of desire. Pushing to stand, I turn and walk into the bathroom. Grabbing my kit, I take the opportunity to gather some brain cells and also come to terms with the fact Caleb Quinlin will once again be in my bed.

When I return to him, I step between his legs. He doesn't move or even flinch as I wash the wound and then start sewing the cut. "Sorry, I don't have any local."

"It's fine."

"Aw, I forgot Marines don't feel pain."

"We feel it, that's what Motrin is for."

His breath his warm on my neck and I want to ask if Motrin works for a broken heart. Instead, I force a chuckle, but it ends with a strangled sound as he rests his hands on my hips. "What are you doing?"

"You smell good." He slides his hands under my sweater and rests them on my belly. "And your skin is so warm."

"Caleb, stop."

"I thought this was the best way to warm up."

"Are you seriously trying to feel me up after I just dragged your ass out of a storm?"

One touch, just one, and already the fire for him was one thousand percent hot as hell, but I've got so much more going on in my life I can't think of adding another complication.

He drops his hands and stares at them like he wasn't

sure what he was doing. "Just wanted to touch you."

"Not happening, Marine." He'll never know how much I want his touch, but watching him put his life at risk, again, and patching him up, again, is twisting me up. I've needed him desperately for over a year, what he wants right now…I don't give a shit. At least that's what I'm telling myself.

"No bullshit or innuendos—can you undress?"

"Affirmative. But stay close."

All flirting is gone from his eyes and voice. He's asking for help in the only way he's going to, so I step back and lean against the dresser as he starts to strip. I try to think of anything and everything in an attempt to keep calm in the face of his body. But even thoughts of my mother's sweet potatoes don't diminish the broad chest uncovered as he tosses his sweater. I can almost feel the coarse dark hair smattered over his pecs, and my gaze drops to the happy trail tapering under the waistband of his jeans.—

My professionalism returns when he starts to weave taking off his jeans and I move forward. "Sit."

He complies and I yank off the wet denim and his skivvies. Tugging down the quilt and blankets, I point, "Get under the covers."

"I'd like a shower, Brynn."

"Not tonight, you're too unsteady."

His eyes narrow. "Would you wash me off then,

Angel?"

"Seriously?"

He raises his hand like taking an oath. "No bullshit, no flirting. Just hose me down."

Going back into the bathroom, I grab a packet of body wipes they use in the hospitals. He's sitting up, but by the way his eyes are fighting to close, he's not lasting long. Taking a wipe, I start washing over the chest I admired earlier and then his back and arms. With another wipe, I wash over the hard ridges of his belly and then down to his legs and feet.

My gaze locks on his thick cock for a second, before I hand him the wipe. "You can get there."

"There? Is that a medical term?"

"Just do what you need to do."

He does and I watch. My face burns when he catches me. It burns more when I walk to the dresser and tug out a pair of his old sweats and one of his T-shirts. I toss them to him. "You need help putting those on?"

"I can get it."

This time I remain with my back to him and stare out the window; watching the storm rage outside while fighting the battle inside me between anger and a love I've carried all my life. Thankfully he doesn't make a comment about me still holding onto his clothes. The Marine sweats and T-shirt were always my favorite cuddle clothes on lazy days. Over the last year, they've become my go-to comfy clothes for pretending he's holding me. There's no way I could explain away that and not sound desperate and pathetic.

"Have you eaten recently?"

"Not since lunch."

"I'll get some soup and grilled cheese."

"Sounds good. Better send the kids in."

"Oh, shit, that's right."

When I turn, he's under the covers. Leaning over him, I scan his face and he smiles. "This is familiar, only it was a lot hotter and you were in desert camo."

"Why the hell did you try sailing in a storm like this?"

"Shit, Brynn, that storm came out of nowhere. Thought I might as well try to make it here than stop in Camden."

I press the back of my hand to his cheek. "Jarhead."

"Squid."

I smile. "I'll get your food and send the kids in."

He holds onto my hand when I start to go. "If I shiver hard enough, will you strip and press close?"

"We have plenty of blankets and heating pads."

He lets my hand go and shrugs. "Worth a try."

When he closes his eyes, I watch him as if he'll disappear if I stop staring. *Stop looking and definitely do not touch.* Former lover or not, I've already been unprofessional enough tonight and Caleb doesn't need an ogling nurse in his life.

Curling my fingers into fists, I try to promise myself I won't let him in, but the truth is he has never been gone. Our history will always melt us together into one memory and one heart. I don't know what brought him here, but I know it's going to change the family I've been building forever.

"Either hit me, Brynn, or get my soup."

I want to scream at him for shredding us both two years ago. I want to rail louder than the wind. *You barely even talked to me at the funeral, you didn't hold me when I needed your arms so much.* But what does any of that matter now…and yet, it does.

He was supposed to be mine. I scan him from his dark brown hair cut high and tight, then down over the angles of his face and strong jaw. Dark stubble covers a scar he got at sixteen crawling out of my window one night and falling off the trellises.

His jaw flexes and my gaze moves back to meet the ice-blue of his eyes, and in his eyes I see that memory and so many more.

"Aunt Brynn?"

Ella's voice snaps my attention from Caleb to her. "Yes?" Her eyes, so much like his, cut to him then back to me. I sit on my heels in front of her. "You can go to your uncle Caleb, just be careful."

The little girl dashes to Caleb and I exhale a breath,

grateful for the interruption bringing me back to the present. I step from the room to find Michael standing in the shadows. He lifts his head, trying to smile at me. Ruffling his hair, I nod to the room. "I'm sorry I forgot to get you. Go in and see for yourself, he's fine. Cold, tired, and hungry, but fine."

His shoulders relax. "Do you need help?"

"No, but thank you."

"Do you think Uncle Caleb would mind if I stay with him tonight? Just to make sure, you know."

"I know, and no, I don't think he would mind, but ask him."

The boy, trying to be a man, walks into the guest room and I listen to the three of them chatter for a moment before walking down the stairs and into the kitchen. The second my feet hit the landing, my cell phone rings. Glancing at the screen, I sigh at Brian's name blinking at me.

I brace myself and answer. "Hi Brian."

"You two okay?"

"Yes. Caleb's a bit bruised up, but he's been worse—" I stop myself from thinking of those times. "I'm sorry I came out on the rocks."

"You're not Coast Guard, Brynn. And don't give me that you've been in combat shit—"

"I know," I interrupt. "And you're right, I could have caused more harm than help. I'm wicked sorry."

"Yeah, well."

I smile, realizing by agreeing with him I've ended the lecture he'd been planning. But my apology is sincere, it was stupid for me to go out there and I would have chewed his ass for doing the same.

The storm still rages and he has a long night ahead. Watching young Marines die on the battlefield was a devastating reminder of how uncertain life is. Losing Liz and Mark brought that devastation right to our front door. "Hey brother, be safe tonight."

"Roger that."

Hanging up, I get the grilled cheese and tomato soup started at last. Glancing at the clock, I'm surprised to see it's only nine o'clock; it feels like it should be two or three in the morning.

I dish up Caleb's food, setting the dishes on a tray. As I climb the stairs, giggles and chuckles echo from my bedroom. Yes, things are already changing in the small lighthouse keeper's house, and there's no beacon to guide me away from the rocks.

CHAPTER TWO

Caleb

WATCHING BRYNN DRINK her morning coffee is a study in how much a man can take before blowing his wad in his sweats. She swallows a drink and her eyes close. A small smile touches her lips and she exhales a sigh like she's tasted the finest thing ever.

I clear my throat, trying to clear my mind. Her hazel eyes open and all the colors of autumn dance in the orbs. Any sign of contentment disappears.

Not wanting to watch the flashes of gold disappear completely, when looking at me used to bring them to life, I scan the kitchen. The white of the walls, cabinets, and appliances is broken with the black-and-white design of the tile. On the walls, she's placed photographs of crates of blueberries and lobster boats against the various seasonal backgrounds.

There's no separate dining room, so she chose a table with a wooden booth bench set against the wall with the window and a chair on either end, and two on one side. I pretend to study the window above her, and the cloudy skies fit the mood in the room.

Lowering my gaze, I meet hers. She drops her stare to my plate of eggs and toast and then back to me. "Is your stomach upset?"

"No."

"Doesn't taste good?"

"It's fine, Brynn, just not hungry."

I cup my mug of coffee and check out the living room through the arch separating the two rooms. I can't see much but the fire crackling in the fireplace. When my gaze rests on the staircase, I tune my ears to the upstairs where the kids are still nestled in the bed they've shared with me for two nights, watching over me like little hawks. And then Brynn has come in each night resting her cools palms on my face and heating me up with reminders of all the times her touch brought comfort and healing.

"Is there something wrong with the house?"

Her question brings my full attention back to her. "Negative. I like the place. A little secluded."

She lifts her leg, resting her foot on the bench and her hands around her knee. "That's what I was looking for."

"You can have your bed back tonight."

She shakes her head. "I've slept fine in Ella's." With an exhaled breath, she pins me with eyes more brown than green, which is never a good sign. "So, you've been here two nights and a full day. Don't you think it's time you tell me why you risked your life to get here, and why you chose to land at my *secluded* lighthouse and not the sands of San Diego for your leave?"

My plan was to get to the lighthouse at least a week prior to Thanksgiving, giving us time to talk and work through things, or at least be closer to working it out. The United States Marine Corps' plan was to hold up my transitioning out by two weeks. Then, after my little brush with hypothermia, I chose not to try to get into a fight yesterday, and Brynn avoided me except for meals and to keep laying her hands on my face and checking my fingers and toes.

Could I feel her? Hell yes, all the way to my soul. I felt her when I was in the Middle East, and when I was in Japan, and Twentynine Palms. There's a part of her that never leaves me, the most precious cargo I carry. I'll feel her when I'm one hundred years in the grave.

I lower my gaze to where Brynn has covered my hand with hers. "You still with me, Caleb?"

"Got off course slightly." And I'm not just talking about spacing out now, or in the boat a couple nights before.

As if she understands the true meaning of my words, and I'm sure she does, she tries to take her hand back. I hold it for another second before letting her go. And letting her go is something I plan on never doing again. We'll face the families the next day for Thanksgiving. I need to get my head on straight and get focused, because we need everything settled, so no one can offer opinions.

"I'm a newly minted civilian as of a few days ago."

She combs her fingers through the brown waves of her hair, and I wish I could do the same. "Really? Why?"

After taking a well-worn and torn folded envelope from my back pocket, I slide her the letter I've carried for over a year. She turns the envelope in her hand, reading the lawyer's return address on top, my name in the middle. Lifting an eyebrow, she pulls the wrinkled letterhead out and unfolds it. Her eyes scan back and forth, and the lines in her forehead deepen the more she reads the words Mark wrote and stuck in his and Liz's will.

"This is bullshit!" She shoves it back at me.

"But that's why I'm here. I had a year and four months, and I made it…barely."

"I don't believe this. Why would Mark include a codicil? And Liz didn't have a say?"

Ignoring the fact she's pretty much calling me a liar, I turn the letter and point to the top. "If you'll notice, this was written after you returned to Maine. So, they didn't think we were still together—"

"We aren't."

I ignore that remark, as well. "Mark wanted me to have a place in his children's lives. And, with her signature at the bottom, it appears, Liz did, too."

"You expect just to come here and take my children?"

I hike my eyebrows at the use of the word *my*, but let it go. "No, the letter says they'd like us both to raise Michael and Ella."

"And you decided now would be the perfect time to separate from the Marines and come back to Maine and rescue us all."

"Don't be a shit. I decided I wanted to honor my brother's wish and be a part of his children's lives."

Her eyes narrow to a point so sharp it almost cuts. "So, co-guardian, what was the plan as you bounced over the waves? You'll move to Camden, which you hate? They stay with me one week, you the next?"

I shift in my chair. "I'm not moving just to Camden, Brynn."

"Well, we're not moving to San Diego. This is our home."

I flinch at the direct hit to my Achilles heel. "I'm moving here to the lighthouse. The letter states they hope we can raise the children as a couple. If we can't, we can decide custody arrangements. I'm suggesting we give the couple thing a try."

Her forehead wrinkles in confusion. "I don't under-stand."

"I think you and I should give us a try. Give it until New Year's. Be a couple."

"You are a complete asshole. Now you decide you want the dream and I'm just supposed to fall in line like this is some mission? You were the one who shredded our hearts, Caleb, and mine isn't ready for another round."

I link my fingers with hers, surprised she doesn't resist, but her hand is as cold as her gaze. "I know what I did, Brynn, and I know what I sound like coming to you now. You also know me better than anyone on this earth—do you honestly think this is all just something I'm pulling out of my ass? Sorry isn't enough, but please give me a chance to make the life with you we dreamed of."

"That dream has changed."

"Affirmative, so have we."

She snatches her hand away and stares at her palm before tucking her hands under her thighs. "How much of a couple?" Her voice is just above a whisper and I contemplate whether she's asking me or herself.

I decide to answer for my part. "If you're asking about fucking, yes." The frown returns to her forehead. "As much as we can."

"If this was what they wanted, why didn't the lawyer say so when we all met with him?"

I allow her to avoid the subject. "I met with him earlier, and asked him not to when I saw the letter. At the time I was still pretty messed up. If you're questioning if it's real, we can visit their attorney."

"I know it's real. I'm not calling you a liar. I'm just confused." She massages her forehead. "Why would you want to do this?"

If she needs to circle back a million times, we will. "Because I want to be a part of Michael and Ella's lives. And I want you."

"Me? Since when?"

"Oh, since about birth."

"You didn't even really speak to me at the funeral." Her cheeks turn red like the words came too fast for her to control.

"I was pretty raw that day."

"We were all raw. And we were supposed to be best friends, not just in-laws." Brynn pushes out of the booth before I can offer a defense. She separates herself from me by a few steps staring out the opposite window to the tower of the lighthouse and the forest beyond.

Standing, I step behind her and put my hands on her hips, studying our reflection in the glass. "Give me until January 1st. If it doesn't work, I'll go back to being Uncle Caleb just visiting here and there. No arguments."

Her gaze meets mine in our reflections. "What will we tell the families?"

"We're engaged. We won't let on it's a test, then if it ends you can tell them I blew it…again. I'll take all the heat. I deserve it."

She turns in my arms and tips her chin until our gazes collide. "This is more than sex, Caleb. It's more than us this time too. Michael and Ella are involved here. If they think we're together and then we're not, it will break their hearts. I've spent over a year trying to mend their tiny lives. You're their hero—what will they think if you walk away?"

"I know the stakes. I also know the prize when it works. But let's get one thing clear: unless you tell me to go, I'm here for the long haul."

"So, now it's on me and I'm the bad guy if—"

"Not even close. I'm the dick who shredded us, like you said."

"This is crazy."

I smile. "Not the craziest thing we've done."

It's not her brightest smile, but at least her mouth curves. The smile fades as quick as it appeared. "We were a team before; stronger together against anything. Now…I don't feel stronger. I feel off. Like I know you and you're my Caleb, my harbor, but at the same time you're the one who's hurt me more than anyone."

I'm thankful I didn't eat breakfast, or I'd throw up.

It twists my heart to hear the truth from her lips. Combing my fingers through her hair, I inhale the scent of lavender-mint shampoo and with it a lifetime of memories. "I won't hurt you or the children, Brynn. I'm asking for the opportunity to prove it to you all."

She barely nods. I lower my head, testing to see if she'll accept my kiss. Her gaze connects with mine and all the gold flecks are back in force. She opens for me and I run the tip of my tongue along her full lips before sinking my teeth into her bottom lip. An erotic whimper sounds deep in her throat. Capturing her mouth, I feed off the sound and her taste.

She's sweeter and softer than I remember, and I have given years of thoughts to the taste and feel of Brynn Reilly. She moans and I push my luck more by sliding my hands under her sweatshirt. I groan finding her breasts bare. I mold the full mounds and stroke my thumb over the hard nipples. Deepening the kiss, I stroke my tongue against hers, my hands rough on her body.

Kissing Brynn is all the warmth of the brightest fire in winter, and I push closer to see how burned I can be. She kisses me back with all her heart, shining a light in all corners of my darkness brighter than any star on any Christmas tree. A heart I broke, and a heart I'm going to heal like she's healed me a thousand times over. Smoothing my hand over her torso and ass, I grip her thigh and lift her leg high on mine.

"Aunt Brynn?"

The warm, pliable woman in my arms snaps to attention, her lips torn from mine, she pushes my hand off her thigh and lowers her leg. She angles to see around me. "Good morning, Ella, what do you want for breakfast, baby?"

She's got this mother thing down, because there is no way in hell my voice would sound so calm and normal. I slowly lower my hand from her breast, the shudder of her skin under my touch testing my willpower. I stay still, refusing to turn with a major hard-on pressing against my jeans. I can't see Ella's face, but I'd bet money she's wearing a frown that matches what Mark's used to be.

"Are you and Uncle Caleb married?" I smile at the tone of disapproval in her voice.

"No, baby."

"Are you going to be?"

It's the moment of truth. She agreed a few seconds ago, but this is Ella asking. The answer Brynn gives her seals all our fates.

Her chest rises and falls in deep breaths. "Yes."

She lifts her gaze, and I frown at the sheen of moisture in her eyes.

"We sure are," I confirm.

"Yay! Michael, Michael, Aunt Brynn is marrying Uncle Caleb!" She pounds up the stairs, repeating the news of the morning.

I cup Brynn's face between my hands.

"What have we done, Caleb?"

"We're going to work, Brynn. This will work."

"Is it true?"

Now that my body has stopped simmering, I turn and hook Brynn's waist with my arm as we face Michael. Brynn answers again. "Yes, it's true."

Michael's smile grows. "You're staying with us, Uncle Caleb?"

"Absolutely."

Brynn steps from my arm and combs her fingers through Michael's hair, straightening the bedhead. Her gaze cuts from Michael to Ella with all the tenderness a mother should have. "What do you two want for breakfast?"

"Oatmeal sounds good."

Ella wrinkles her nose at her brother's suggestion. "Cold cereal."

"Okay, one oatmeal and one cold cereal coming up." She turns her gaze to me. "Will you get the oatmeal going and I'll help Ella get dressed?"

At the moment, I'm so inspired I want to give a, *Yut!*, instead I give a short nod like I'm not celebrating inside. "Sure thing."

"Go get dressed, Michael."

"Yes, ma'am." He tosses another look over his shoulder like I might leave, as I start getting out the pot and oatmeal.

I keep my gaze on Brynn's back as she climbs the stairs with the children chattering about my staying and us getting married. She's a woman who always knows just what to do and always has it together—well, unless I'm inside her, then she's a storm uncontrolled and wild. But today I see a vulnerability with her day-to-day life, and guilt guts me she's had to go it alone so long; making all decisions for the children, and I'm guessing fighting both sets of grandparents with some. I'm sure my father has offered tons of advice, and a person should listen to him so they can do the exact opposite to be a good and loving parent.

Rolling my shoulders, I let go of those thoughts and get the hot cereal going. I open cupboards and find the cold cereal setting it on the table. Michael comes downstairs and into the kitchen dressed in jeans and a sweatshirt. "What do you like on your oatmeal?"

"Cinnamon and sugar. I'll get it." He sets the spice and sugar on the table. "The Marines are letting you go?"

I chuckle. "Yep. Time for a new mission." I nod to the table. "Take a seat and I'll dish up chow."

Watching him, I swallow around emotion. He reminds me of his father. Mark supported me no matter what and looked up to me with the same devotion. When Michael smiles at me, it hits the heart at how he looks exactly like Mark did when we were kids and I'd help him with something.

Dishing out the oatmeal, I almost stumble when a four-year-old with a death grip barrels into my leg and hugs it tight. I glance down at the chubby-cheeked face looking up at me. Brynn's braided Ella's hair into pigtails and dressed her in a pink sweatshirt and jeans. She's so cute she could wrap me around her finger if I'm not careful. Hell, I'm already wrapped.

Turning back to Michael, I finish dishing out his oatmeal until he snatches the bowl. "Uncle Caleb, I can only eat so much."

Brynn chuckles behind me. "He's not a Marine yet."

I have to admit I might have spooned out a Marine-sized portion. "I'll learn."

"Yeah, you'll learn," Michael confirms.

"Thanks, bud." I look down at the leech on my leg. "Come on, sweetheart, get in your chair. I'll get your cereal."

She frowns. "Aunt Brynn gets my cereal."

"I'm getting it today. Now get in your chair."

She glances at Brynn, and to her credit Brynn doesn't contradict what I've said. Seeing her aunt isn't going to take her side, Ella releases my leg and climbs on her chair with a few huff and puffs as her short legs work getting up on the adult-sized chair.

Watching how much I pour, I look to Brynn for

confirmation. She hides her nod behind her coffee mug. I set the bowl in front of Ella, pour the milk, and watch as she eyes the cereal like it might not be the same as what Aunt Brynn gives her. Stepping back, I accept the fresh mug of coffee from Brynn and lean back against the counter.

When she braided Ella's hair, she put her own back in a messy bun, a complete contrast to the tight regimented buns she wore as a corpsman. I give in to the urge to touch and run the tip of my finger along the line of her neck. She doesn't jerk away or frown, so I cup the back of her neck and then down and back up under her sweatshirt; a little disappointed to find a bra.

She turns those hazel eyes my way a dark forest green with desire. "Please stop."

I lift an eyebrow as I take my hand off her. "Problem?"

She lowers her voice. "We have two children here and being revved up with no outlet is painful."

"Roger." I hadn't thought of that. Like the cereal, there's a lot to learn about twenty-four/seven parenting. Things like Brynn and I can't just go at it whenever, wherever. Creativity and timing will be key and it's a good thing the Marines taught me both.

"These guys will make the Marines seem like sailing on a bluebird day with fair winds. There's no five-paragraph plan with them." She reads my mind. When

Michael smiles at us, she tosses a wink at him.

I lean forward and press my lips to hers in a quick kiss. "Yeah, well, I'm good at improvise, adapt, and overcome."

She actually returns my kiss with a quick kiss of her own. "We'll see."

"What the hell is going on?"

The kids cockblocking is one thing. Her brooding twin brother cockblocking isn't going to happen. Lifting my head, I glower at Brian despite his assist the other night. "What the hell are you doing just letting yourself in?"

Brian is a beast, but I straighten and fold my arms across my chest. He cuts a look from Brynn, to me, and then the kids, and back to Brynn. Before she can open her mouth, Ella dumps the news on her uncle. "It's okay, they're getting married."

His stare shifts from me to Brynn, where he holds. "What the hell, Brynn? Since when?"

She exhales a breath and rolls her eyes as if dealing with a room full of children instead of two. "Michael, Ella, go to my room and watch TV."

It must be the tone, because there's no fighting or complaining as they push off the chairs and start to shuffle out of the room.

"Don't you like Uncle Caleb?"

Brian smiles down at Michael. "Your uncle Caleb

and I have been friends for a long time. We're just going to talk about their wedding."

Michael shrugs, and the instant the kids are upstairs and we hear the muffled television, I snap. "First off, thanks for the rescue the other night."

"No problem. Now what the fuck?"

Brynn's scowl could bring an infantry regiment to attention. "Stop it, Brian. You know we're watching language around the kids. You're acting like seeing me with Caleb is some huge surprise."

"Seeing you with him, no. Marrying him after the wreck you were when you got home, yeah."

I cringe and Brynn's color fades, but she doesn't address any of the past. "Mark and Liz left the children to both of us." She raises a hand to stave off questions. "We're going to try to make it work. But I could sure use your help over Thanksgiving convincing the families this isn't a surprise and we're marrying out of love, not for the children."

Before Brian can answer, I grip her shoulders and turn her to look at me. "This isn't all about the children, thought I made that clear."

"Caleb, there has always been something between us, we both know that, but can you honestly say you'd be here offering marriage if not for the kids?"

Without hesitation I give the truth. "I'd be here."

"And we'd be in bed—"

"Halt!" Brian interrupts. "I'll act like this isn't a surprise and remind the families it's been you two forever, even before it was Mark and Liz. Just stop talking."

A flash of pain cuts through her gaze, and I step back. It was us before them. It was supposed to be us married before them.

Brynn turns to Brian. "I'm tired of talking. What brought you here in the first place?"

"I salvaged Caleb's ruck from the boat. It's by the door. I need to check the light, too, make sure there's no damage to the windows."

"You want some coffee first?"

"After."

"Okay."

It's Brian's turn to cross his arms over his chest. "Because we've been friends so long and I love my sister—" He turns his gaze to the ceiling as if trying not to throw up. "I'm off after I check the light. You want me to take the kids for a couple hours?"

I want to rush with a not only yes, but hell yes. Instead I defer to Brynn, not knowing any schedule she might have with the children. But deferring doesn't mean I'm not praying like a drowning man for land, for her to take the beast's offer.

Brynn smiles at her twin brother. "You sure? You've had tough duty with the storm."

"Don't make me say it again, Brynn. And I'll be taking you up on that cup of coffee after before I leave."

"Then yes."

Holding out my hand, I shake Brian's. "Thanks for the ruck and for the—"

"Don't even say it, Quinlin, or I'll kill you."

"Fair enough. Thanks."

CHAPTER THREE

Brynn

As I'm zipping up Ella's coat, I try to avoid her accusing look. "I want to stay with Uncle Caleb."

"You don't want to hang with me, Ella?"

Her tiny brow furrows more, and she pins Brian with a glare like he's missing the obvious. "Yes, but you could stay here with us."

I tie her scarf around her neck. "You'll get to spend a lot of time with Uncle Caleb."

She lifts hound dog eyes to Caleb, and I'm sure he's going to relent. "No go, Little Bit, you and Michael will have fun."

I nod and brush a kiss to her cheek. Cupping the back of his head, I press a kiss to Michael's forehead. "You have fun."

He shrugs, looking as disappointed as Ella, but too

well-behaved to say anything. Sometimes I wish he'd pitch a fit instead of being so good and grown up all the time.

Cupping his face, I meet those blue orbs that reminds me of his father's and Caleb's. "When you get back we'll play a game of chess, okay?"

"Okay, Aunt Brynn. Don't worry, we'll behave."

"I never worry about you behaving, Michael. *Have fun*," I stress again. When he only nods, I sigh and turn to Brian, who looks as concerned as I feel, and glance at Caleb, who's forehead is folded in a deep frown.

Brian gives Michael a playful shove. "Of course we'll have fun. It's Uncle Brian time. Come on, let's roll."

"Keep them tucked out of the wind on the boat."

"I will."

"And no scary movies, Brian." They were still getting over the fear fest with him on Halloween.

"I know, Brynn." His words are ground out through clenched teeth.

He picks up Ella and takes Michael's hand, grumbling as they leave. When the door closes behind them, Caleb's frown deepens. "Michael thinks he's the man of the house?"

"Has since day one. He's so good all the time, like if he says or does the wrong thing I'd let him go. I'd never let him go."

He cups my face. "I know, Angel. Maybe he'll let go

a bit once he realizes I'm staying and he can be a kid."

I frown, still not one hundred percent convinced this is going to work, but praying it does. "I hope so."

"If not, we'll find a way to get him through."

When he lowers his head, I step out of his touch. "Don't you think we should talk some more?"

He walks toward me with purpose. "Negative. I think a lot can be said with our bodies. Like your kiss earlier told me you've been wanting me as much as I want you."

I flatten my hands on his chest. "I've never not wanted you, Caleb." Lifting my head, I hold eye contact and lay out the truth. "But I don't want to feel used when the sex is over."

"Have you ever felt used after we fuck?"

"No, but you've never dumped me before and then returned in a whirlwind only for me to give in and have sex with you two days later."

"All right, then let's do this. We have two hours with no kids—what do you want to do?"

"I want to have sex."

"Then there it is, your choice of mid-morning activity. No guilt. All pleasure. A nice round of fucking we can both give thanks for tomorrow."

I chuckle and wrap my arms around his neck, bringing us closer. "I missed you, Caleb."

"God, I've missed you, Brynn."

He captures my mouth with his and the kiss turns white-hot in a blink. I tighten my hug around his neck, bringing his angles snug into my curves like a piece of the puzzle. He grips my ass and tugs me even closer, digging his fingers into the soft flesh. He tastes so good, like all the magic of the holidays wrapped in one treat and I'm the only one who gets to savor it. For a couple hours, I'm willing to let myself believe he's back—the boy I loved, who became the man I adored, who swore he would never let me go. I'm going to surrender to that man. I'm going to take the advice I gave Michael and toss consequences out the window and have fun.

I stroke my tongue along his and with a guttural moan he takes the kiss to a whole new level of heat. I rock my hips against him, in an unsubtle hint at where I want this to lead. "What—" My voice cracks when he breaks the kiss and tips his ear toward the door. "Are they back?"

"If they're going to come back it'll be now, so I wanted to make sure."

"Don't do that." I mold my mouth back to his, only breaking the kiss long enough for him to strip off my sweatshirt and bra. He molds my breasts like he did earlier that morning and strokes my hardened nipples until the ache building in my sex is unbearable and my neck arches back. With his lips and tongue, he trails hot kisses down my neck, nipping and sucking his brand on me as he goes. He slides one hand over my torso and inside my jeans.

"Oh god." My body jerks as he strokes my clit and then slides two fingers inside me. I grab hunks of his T-shirt and whimper. "Caleb, please, I need—"

His mouth curves in a wicked smile as he pumps his fingers in and out of my sex. "You need what, Angel? Say it."

"You. Always, you."

I let out a choked scream as he takes his fingers from me and unbuttons my jeans, tugging them and my panties down with them. I step out, and he stays kneeling before me. "Open."

I move my legs apart, and a primal sound erupts from me when his tongue and mouth connects to my sex. He doesn't leave a part of my sex untouched and I want it to last forever even as my body demands release. Scoring his neck and shoulders with my fingernails, I'm lost in feelings and memories only he can induce. The moment his two fingers slide back inside me, my body trembles and I come in a storm of calling his name.

Before I can recover, his mouth is back on mine and I gasp at my taste on his lips. He grips my thighs with his powerful hands and I hop, wrapping my legs around his waist. He holds me tight and carries me up the stairs. After laying me on the bed, he follows me down, settling between my legs. I rake my fingernails over his back, trying to find the hem of his T-shirt. With a grunt, he pushes away from me and strips before taking his place between my legs again.

With his hand on my ankle, he pushes one of my legs up until it's high on his back and, holding my gaze, guides his thick, heavy cock deep inside me. I arch my neck and back to take him deeper, even as my inner muscles work him, and my body fights to accommodate his thick length.

"Oh fuck, Brynn, that is fucking heaven."

"Mmmm…yes," is all I can manage as he begins slowly, methodically, easing out and then back inside.

"That feels good doesn't it, Angel?"

"Yes. Please. More."

He starts pumping harder and deeper. He pins my hands over my head and his strokes slow again as he slides up and down my body, so sensitized I feel every coarse hair on his chest as it rakes my breasts and as his legs brush mine. His cock stretches me wide and feels like hot steel branding me. Through it all, his gaze turns to winter fire and he never looks away, demanding I keep contact on all levels so he can watch every emotion I feel while he experiences my body's reactions to his touch and claim.

"Caleb." I rock my hips. "Caleb, it's too much."

"Never enough, Brynn. Never. Fuck me a bit."

He stops moving, and I rock my pelvis and work his

cock with my inner muscles until I feel sweat trickle down the side of my face along with tears of frustration as my body screams for orgasm. Grunting over me, he pumps so hard and deep the bed squeaks with the pounding.

The room is a sauna, and his flesh against mine is like flint against steel until I'm ready to combust. His voice reaches me. I can't compute the words, but the meaning is as clear as if he shouted orders. The lust, love, and everything we've ever meant to each other blends into every sound and every push of his body into mine. My only answer is to chant his name. He leans back and presses my leg wider. I hold the position he molds me into as he strokes my clit, and with a string of curses and praises I come so hard I break from reality and feel suspended.

He pushes balls-deep and comes hard inside me. I gasp and watch the shock in his eyes mirror my own, but he doesn't stop, he continues to pump into me, his orgasm too hard to do anything else. When his climax subsides, he crashes on me and releases my hands. We're so close, a snowflake would have to melt to get between us, and I wrap my arms and legs around him, holding him tight while I can.

"Holy—just fuck, Brynn, how have I lived without that?"

"I don't know."

He lifts his head and searches my face. There's no ice in his eyes now, only a clear, warm blue. "You okay?"

"I think you stole about five of my lives."

He chuckles. "I hear that." He traces my face with a fingertip. "But you know what I mean?"

"It just shocked me. It's only happened once before."

"Is there a chance we'll be adding a third kid in a few months?"

"There's always a chance, but ours is ninety-nine percent no. I have an IUD now."

"You mind then, or you want me to suit up?"

"I don't mind." I kiss his chin. "Would you have minded a third kid in a few months?"

"Not with you. Though, at only a few days in, I'm still trying to process what to do with the two we have."

"Don't process too much—about the time you figure it out, it all changes."

"Sounds like the Marine Corps."

I trail open-mouthed kisses on his neck. "You're the one who said we shouldn't talk. So, what position is next?"

"Don't care as long as it's me inside you. It's been a long two years."

"Didn't have to be; you were home a year ago."

He jerks from me and stands in all his naked glory. "Is this about the funeral again? My brother had just fucking died."

I lift to my knees and jab a finger at him. "So had my sister, and we might have been able to comfort each other, but all I got was a grunted *hello* and *sorry for your loss* like we were all but strangers. If you didn't want to be my lover, fine, but you were my best friend and you should have acted like it. Shit, you could have at least acted like we'd served together."

"It should have been me, Brynn. I was the one on deployment after deployment without a family. I should be in the ground, not Mark. The second I looked at that casket, I knew who should have been in it."

I drop my hand and inhale a gasp. "Never. Why would you say that?"

"It's the truth. He had it all, and on his way to more. So, yeah, to be fair you're not far off when you say I'm here for the children. I'm trying to do right by my brother. He counted on me and I wasn't there to protect him."

"You've always done right by everyone. Even when you sent me away, you thought you were doing right by me, asshole move that it was. But, you can be in the children's lives without marrying me and living in Camden. Don't continue this if it's not right for you."

His forehead creases like he doesn't even understand what I'm talking about, and my heart aches that he doesn't. I move a little closer. "If this isn't what you want, it won't work even if you're doing it for all the right reasons."

"This is what I want…Well, not this. I hoped we'd be doing something else while naked. But this…" He waves his hand to encompass the house and the bed. "And you…especially you, Brynn. If you knew how much I want you, you'd run."

He is chipping away fast at any resistance I have. Yes, he broke my heart, but it's my heart reminding me of the twenty-seven years when he was the harbor I sought in any storm. Those ice-blue eyes hold such longing, like I'm the Eagle, Globe, and Anchor at the end of the Crucible of Boot Camp.

With a sigh, I move forward, hoping I don't end up on a landmine. "I come with an old house constantly in need of repairs."

I watch his shoulders relax. "I'm handy with repairs, and expert level at cannibalizing."

"And a lighthouse the Coast Guard—read, my brother—is constantly visiting to care for the lens and operations."

"I like your brother when he's not barging in on us and being an asshole."

I smile and tip my head to the side. "And I kind of have two small children who are always under foot and are going to interrupt us every time we kiss and possibly during sex."

"I've had cold showers before and I'll get used to

being cockblocked."

I crawl forward and kneel before him skating my palms up his torso from the ridges of his abs to his broad chest, feeling the burn of his hair over the sensitive skin. Lifting my chin so I meet his gaze, I raise an eyebrow. "It shouldn't have been you, Caleb, anymore than it should have been me." I know the source of those thoughts and I wish I could cut him out of Caleb's mind like I cut the shrapnel from his body removing the poison. I return my focus to the man in front of me. "If I haven't said so, I'm glad you're here. I hope it will be home for you."

"But you don't completely believe me." He doesn't sound angry and he combs my hair back from my face with his fingers.

"I believe you. I believe you want me. I believe you love me and of course you love Michael and Ella. But, you're a man who has put others before yourself since we were children, as misled as some of those times have been, and after years of being that man for everyone, including the whole fucking nation, I'm not completely sold you even know how to do the right thing for yourself."

"So?"

The question comes with a little more bite than his last. "So—" I rise a bit and wrap my arms around his neck. "—you'll stay here, and we'll stay engaged, and we'll do all the crazy holiday hoopla with family, and we'll do some wicked wonderful things to each other naked that will put us at the top of Santa's naughty list with stars, and hopefully by New Year's we'll both know for sure this is right for everyone."

He grabs my thighs and flips me on my back as my startled laughter echoes through the room. Settling between my legs, he tugs me closer and locks his gaze with mine. "Let's continue the wild naked stuff. I think that's where we need to spend the most time if we're going to earn those stars."

Laughing, I lift up and brush my lips over his, willing to retreat back to enjoying the morning instead of hashing out the past and future in the hour we have left. I press my lips to his again. "I might start saying, I love you, again soon. Don't stomp on it with your big combat boot this time."

His smile remains in place, but his voice is deeper and huskier than normal. "I'll probably start saying, I love you, too. And I'll never take it for granted again."

I pinch his side to bring back some of the lightheartedness. "You better not."

He wags his eyebrows. "And if you're lucky I might say it first a couple times."

"Wow, it must be Christmas."

My laugh turns hysterical when he starts tickling my sides, but soon it dies when he stops and stares at me before sealing his lips to mine in a kiss that becomes a vow.

CHAPTER FOUR

Caleb

I TUG MY sweatshirt over my head and watch Brynn secure her hair back into a ponytail. The long dark brown strands of silk are restrained from the wild mass of minutes ago as she rode me to a blinding orgasm. She sits on the bed and pulls on her sweater, then glances up at me. The wild lover is gone and the put-together mother is back. I'm in love with both.

"What should we do about Michael?"

I sink next to her on the bed, turning my thoughts to Michael and Ella. "Any ideas?"

"I've tried all I know. I almost force him to play. He never complains, never asks for anything. Caleb, when I asked him what he wanted from Santa, he said he didn't need anything for Christmas except maybe some socks. Socks!"

"Ouch. Do you think he'd talk to me?"

"I don't know. He won't talk to Brian or Dad."

"And you've told them this?"

"Not Dad, and just a little to Brian. I just thought, he really loves you. The only time I've ever seen any true emotion is when your name is mentioned."

I give her a quick kiss and stand. Not having a real clue, I take a shot in the dark. "I heard you tell him you'd play chess; I'll take that game instead. Not that he'll crack in one night, but I'd like to hang out with him and maybe eventually he'll feel like talking."

She wraps her arms around my neck. "Thank you. He'll love it." When she tips her head back, I capture her mouth and instantly the kiss turns white hot and mimics what I want from her body. I grip her hips and tug her close so she can feel my body's response, and she moans and wraps her arms tighter around me, pressing herself closer. I reach under her sweater and unbutton her jeans, feeling the heat from her sex.

"We're back!"

We snap apart like teenagers when her parents caught us making out. Brynn smiles and buttons up her jeans. "We'll be right down, Brian."

I inhale deep breaths and think of my drill instructor from Boot to bring my body down. "At least he gave us fair warning."

She smooths back her hair. "True. I wish he'd given

us fifteen more minutes, though."

"Wouldn't have been enough." I caress her cheek with the back of my fingers. "Fifty years won't be enough."

Stepping from my touch, she shakes her head and tugs the plaid quilt over the bed as if hiding evidence. "Don't start again."

She pivots and starts walking down the stairs and I fall into step behind her. Once we step into the living room, I have a munchkin attached to my leg.

"Uncle Caleb!" The tone of her voice would lead people to believe we hadn't seen each other in years, not hours. She tips her head back and wins me over for the hundredth time with a big smile.

"Hey, Ella, what have you been up to?"

"Uncle Brian took us for cake and then to Nana's. She's making pies."

I narrow my gaze at Brian. "Cake, man? Thanks a lot."

He shrugs. "I'm the fun uncle."

Brynn's gaze is frightening. "You're the uncle who's pushing his luck. I suppose Mom gave them a treat, too?"

"We didn't get a treat at Nana's, Aunt Brynn."

Her face instantly softens as she tips her chin to meet Michael's gaze. "Good, it's almost time for lunch." She turns back to Brian. "Sorry, thanks for taking them."

I let the twins continue their conversation and help Michael hang his coat and scarf in the closet just inside the door. "I know you and your aunt were going to play some chess after lunch, but would you mind beating me instead?"

His eyes widen like I just pinned on a medal. "Really?"

"Absolutely."

"Definitely." His cuts a glance to Brynn, "Unless you'd be upset?"

She scrubs his hair. "Not at all. Now you and your sister go wash up."

When the kids are in the head, I turn back to Brian. "Seriously, thanks, man."

He nods and shifts his gaze between us. "I told Mom you were back and with Brynn. She wanted to know if your folks know."

"Mom knows I'm in Maine. She doesn't know I'm engaged to Brynn."

"Brian, you want to stay for lunch?"

He lifts an eyebrow at the change in subject. "Can't. Gotta be on shift soon. You two announcing tomorrow?"

I leave it for her to answer. She steps closer to me. "Yes."

"I'll back it up."

"Thank you." Her voice isn't much louder than a whisper.

"Doubt anyone will be surprised. We were all more surprised when it was Liz and Mark marrying and not you guys."

Hooking her waist, I pull her close to my side. "Well, it's happening now."

"So it seems. All right, I'm heading back to work. If you need me, use the radio."

Brynn steps toward Brian and rests her hand on his arm. "Be safe."

"You know it."

When Brian closes the door behind him, she turns to me and shrugs. "If you want to fall back, now's your chance."

"When have I ever fallen back?"

"Never. That's what got you a sucking chest wound in the desert. Listening to our mothers plan a full wedding over Thanksgiving dinner might hurt more."

With a huffed laugh, I take her hand and walk toward the kitchen. "True. But the rewards are going to be worth it." I look around the kitchen. "You need help with lunch?"

"Yeah, I'm heating up the chicken and noodles and potatoes from yesterday."

"Roger."

I start handing over dishes of leftovers to her. "Caleb?"

"Yep?"

"Are you going to want to stay at the lighthouse?"

I stand and shut the refrigerator door. "This is where you and the kids are, so yeah."

She doesn't look at me as she scrapes the chicken and noodles into a pot to reheat on the stove. "I mean, would you want us all to move off the island? It can get a little hairy when the boat is the only way to get to town."

"I know I didn't wow you with my sailing skills the other night, and I'm not on your seafaring level, but I can handle it."

She glares at me with a look like I'm dense. "Caleb Quinlin, you have always been Mr. Popular and then Staff Sergeant Popular. I'm asking if you'll go batshit crazy on an island where you can see the party but you just can't get to it."

"Negative. And I'm not sure Camden is party central."

"We'll see."

"You keep saying that fucking shit, Brynn—"

We both turn at the loud intake of breath. "Uncle Caleb you swore, you swore bad."

Ella's bright blue eyes condemn me on the spot. At the same time, I have to try not to laugh at the shock on her face. Brynn doesn't help by turning and unsuccessfully hiding her laughter as her shoulders shake.

"Sorry, Little Bit, I shouldn't have said a bad word."

"You said *two* bad words."

I hip check Brynn when the shaking increases. "I shouldn't have said two bad words." I scrub a hand over my face hoping to erase any humor. I'm going to have to reset from a lifestyle where "fuck" is a noun, verb, adjective, and adverb.

"Aunt Brynn says bad words, too."

It's my turn to smile as Brynn whips around to face the mini church lady. "That's enough, Ella, your uncle has apologized. Where's Michael?"

"Setting up the game."

"Go get him and tell him lunch is ready." Ella scampers through the archway into the living room. "She almost has me trained."

Adorable niece or not, I'm not letting her off the hook. "I'm serious, Brynn, enough with the 'we'll sees.' Either you're in or you're not, but I'm not walking around on eggshells while you're waiting for me to retreat. I'm going in one thousand percent. You need to be there, too."

"Fair enough. I just got engaged this morning—I'm still getting used to the idea this is real."

We both nod in mutual understanding as the kids join us. I set the table, while she sets the bowls of food out. I pick up Michael's plate while she picks up Ella's. She doesn't look at me, but out of the corner of my eye I watch her smile spread. "Remember, he's seven and isn't running ten miles after lunch."

Ella and Michael giggle—Michael at least having the good manners to try to cover his laughter.

"Oh, har, har, your aunt Brynn is funny."

"I'm hilarious." She winks and sets Ella's plate in front of the little girl.

I reach around her with Michael's plate and drop a kiss on her neck as I set his plate down. Being near her and listening to her laugh and then her intake of breath at my touch makes my heart ache at how much this is already feeling like home, and how all of this could have been mine years ago.

When she sits on the bench, I settle next to her instead of the chair opposite Michael's. She scoots closer during the blessing and I link our fingers together. My focus turns to the children as we start to eat, and I zero in on Michael choking down the peas as if he might gag. I turn to Ella, her plate vegetable-free.

"You forgot to give Ella peas."

"She doesn't like them. But she's good about eating other vegetables, so I let it go."

Frowning, I start shoveling in my food. Catching myself, I slow down realizing Michael's trying to keep pace with my Marine-at-mess tempo. He has the peas secured and is enjoying the rest of his meal. I don't want to question Brynn about showing favorites with Ella in front of the kids, but I toss her a glare. When she frowns at me in return, I start shoveling again.

When Michael looks at a missed pea like it's the enemy, I can't stand to watch him force it down. "Michael, don't you like peas either?"

The boy loses about five shades. "No, sir."

I shift to Brynn. "Why does he have to suck it up and Ella gets a pass?"

"Because Ella told me she doesn't like peas. He cleans his plate." Her no-nonsense corpsman voice has me turning back to Michael.

"Why didn't you tell your aunt or me? It's okay not to like things."

He shrugs and stares at the offending vegetable. "I didn't want to be rude. Daddy told us to eat what Mommy cooked."

"Your dad made you eat what you don't like?" Brynn rests a hand on my leg, I suppose to stop my interrogation, but the kid needs to open up.

"Some, but not always. Mom would sometimes make peas for them and broccoli for me."

"We can do that, too." Brynn's voice holds the heartache I'm feeling.

Michael shakes his head. "I don't want to be trouble."

I rest my hand over his, mine swallowing his small hand. "You are not trouble, Michael. We love you, buddy."

He swipes his other hand over his eyes to wipe at the

moisture. "I know, but we should be good."

I squeeze his hand. "You *are* good." I glance at Ella and back. "Both of you are the best. Telling us you don't like something doesn't make you bad. Sometimes you'll need to eat it or do what we tell you like it or not, and sometimes we can work on an alternative. Either way, you're good."

"Yes, sir." He lifts his gaze to Brynn's. "Yes, ma'am."

She shifts closer to me and lifts an eyebrow even as her voice is choked with emotion. "So, you do really like my pumpkin pie, right?"

His smile turns bright. "Yes, ma'am, very much."

"Good. 'Cause I'm making two this afternoon."

When she sits back, she brushes a kiss on my cheek and whispers, "Thank you."

I nod, but there's more to it that Michael's still keeping locked inside. I let it go for now, though; he's settled back into eating and has his color back. I wink at Ella, who's staring at me. "I suppose since you had cake today, you don't need pie tomorrow?"

"Yes, I do, a big piece."

I hold my hands close together. "This big?"

"Bigger." Her giggles start.

I move my hands just a tad. "Oh, this big?"

"No, Uncle Caleb, this big." She spreads her arms wide.

"You mean a Marine-sized piece of pie?"

She nods, her whole head bobbing. "Marine-sized."

"That's my girl."

Her nodding continues. "Yep."

Brynn nudges me with her elbow. "You two go ahead and start your chess tournament. I'll clean up and Miss Ella can help."

"Can I help with the pies? Nana let me help."

"I was counting on it."

Michael hops out of his chair. While standing I inspect the dishes on the table. "You sure?"

She nods to the archway. "Absolutely. Have fun."

"We will." Michael answers for us.

Resting a hand on his shoulder, I fall into step beside him keeping my stride short. He waves to the table. "It's all set up."

"Outstanding."

"I'm good at chess."

"I like the confidence."

"I'm not good at sports."

Feeling the tug of a frown on my forehead, I force a smile while trying to figure out where Michael is headed with the bombshell comment. "We can't be good at everything."

"But you're good at sports and Dad was, too."

Where he's going with this is a mystery, but my gut tells me I'm about to head down a path laden with IEDs. I settle across from him at a foldout table in the living room. He moves a pawn. "I could learn to be good at some sport."

I move my pawn opposite his. "If you want to take up a sport I'll help you out, if you don't want to play a sport, that's great too."

He moves the pawn again. "I was thinking, you know, it might be something we could do. If you're staying. And you want. Like—" He shrugs. This kid is ripping my heart out.

"Did you and your dad do that?"

He shakes his head and pushes his glasses up on his nose. "He was busy, and like I said, I wasn't any good at it."

Neither was Mark when he was Michael's age, and I can't believe I'm pissed at my deceased brother. I move my knight. "I'd love to toss a football with you; Lacrosse, baseball, hockey, whatever. If you want to learn how to sail, though, that's all on your aunt Brynn."

"Thanks, Uncle Caleb."

"Sure thing," I choke out with Michael acting like I'm doing some huge favor spending time with him. "Hey!" I glare as he laughs and takes my knight. I hear Mark in his laughter and I swallow around a lump in my throat.

CHAPTER FIVE

Caleb

"HOLY SH—" I step from the bathroom and drop the towel from my waist. I glance around the bedroom.

"What's wrong?"

"Just making sure the swear police isn't here."

She laughs, but it stops short when I drop on the bed. I feel her gaze sweep over my naked body. When our gazes connect, she clears her throat. "You were saying?"

Ignoring her question for a moment, I take my time studying her hair. The dark wavy locks, long and loose over her shoulders, and the outline of her breasts firm and full. I'm enjoying the trail my gaze is on, so I move lower to where the T-shirt darkens with the shadow of her sex. Then I inspect her toned legs, not missing the fact they're freshly shaved. This time I clear my throat before continuing. "Holy shit, am I tired. I've always known you were the ultimate badass Angel, but you taking care of them alone for a year…I salute you."

"They're really very good."

"I'm not disputing that. I just came in here thinking I'll just OoRah through it and things would fall into place like a well-oiled training. That crumbled fast. Michael put me through the ringer."

"It was amazing how you got him to open up. He's been a clam since the funeral. And you noticing his aversion to peas. That was outstanding."

"Him talking, I'm not sure I did anything but listen. As for the vegetable issue, you've been around them every day. Sometimes it's easier to see something when you're new. You know that from combat."

In a breath, she straddles my waist and her face hovers over mine. Her hazel eyes are on fire. I take a lock of her hair between two fingers and rub the silken strands shielding us. "That's just it, you listened. He needed that."

With a shrug, I continue to focus on the soft curl around my finger.

Her mouth curves in a smile more devil than angel. "You're not too tired, right?"

"Only when I'm dead."

When she doesn't answer, or move, I shift my attention from her hair to her face. Her gaze searches mine, and her eyes are fading to a cold brown. After combing my fingers through her hair, I frame her face. "It's just a saying, Angel."

"I know, but you've been too close too many times, and I wasn't there for your full recovery the last time."

"That was my fault."

"Yes, it was. But I don't want to talk about that right now. We have to face our families tomorrow and I want the memory of this morning, and how wonderful you were with Michael, and what we're about to do to be what gets me through it."

I let my fingers slip from the chestnut curls and rest on her hips. "We have twenty-seven years before all of this. Some of those memories should help."

She presses a kiss to one side of my mouth and then the other. "They do. Believe me, it's because of those years and the man I've seen with Ella and Michael that you're in my bed right now."

I want to argue that I've always been that man, but she'd know it was bullshit. That Marine would have never let her go. I can only show her over the next month, her Caleb is back. Her gaze drops. I grip her hair in a ponytail and tug her head, bringing those hazel eyes back to mine. "Then let's make another memory to get us through a family meal."

Her smile returns and she shakes my hand from her

hair. Securing eye contact, she presses a kiss to my lips and then shifts on top of me and sucks and kisses my neck. When she continues to slide down, my body tenses recognizing exactly where she's heading and anticipating every minute. Cupping her ass, I squeeze.

"This isn't a reward, right? For today with Michael?"

She sits back and tugs off her T-shirt. I lower my gaze to her breasts, and she lifts my chin with her finger, bringing my eyes back to hers. Her grin is pure sass. "Your reward was a piece of pie. This, is because I've been thinking of tasting you since this morning."

Before I can respond, she starts the sweet torture again, kissing and biting her way down my torso. I rock my hips under her in none-too-subtle hints, but she continues to feast on my abs. "So good," she mumbles.

My moan is ripped from my soul when she wraps her lips around my cock and sucks. Bending my neck, I watch her work my length using her mouth and hand. I arch my neck and rock my hips, adding to the building friction.

She replaces her mouth with her pussy, lining up my cock and sinking until I'm balls deep. When she bites down on her bottom lip, I watch her struggle not to scream. I almost will her to call out my name, but this time we have to be quiet, or wake the house. I stare entranced as she rides me while molding her breasts with her hands, all while keeping eye contact, pleasing every sense.

Sitting up, I capture her scream with my kiss. Wrapping my arms around her, I lower my head and suck and lick one breast and then the other as she grinds against me. She cups the back of my head and holds me close. She is so soft, so sweet, and her whispers of my name, combined with her whimpers of pleasure, are everything a man wants to hear when pleasuring his woman. So much has changed in our lives and, thanks to me, our relationship, but when I'm inside her nothing is altered. We're born for each other.

Her body tenses and I reach between us, circling her clit.

"Please, please, please," she pants.

I nod against her palms, not releasing her breast and increase the pressure on her nub.

"Caleb, Caleb, don't let go," she says even as she releases my head and cups my face, bringing my gaze to hers where fire and ice collide.

"Never." I capture her mouth again and kiss her deep. She is scorching from her lips to inside her sex. Her heat is melting us and molding us together. With a cry, she wraps her arms around me and holds tight as her inner muscles clamp down and her body trembles through her orgasm. Breaking the kiss, I flip her on her back and drive deep and hard into her until I clench my jaw against the ragged bellow ripping through me as my climax threatens to steal my life. I open my eyes and continue to rock inside her as we both struggle to come down from the adrenaline coursing through our veins.

Lowering, I press kisses to her face. "Outstanding, Angel." I sink lower and she cradles me with her body. "You good?"

"Yes, Caleb. I'm beyond good. I'm floating on wind touched waves. Don't move for a minute and we can do it again."

I chuckle and press into her curves. "Wind touched waves sound good to me. So does another round. If I remember right, you can go all night."

"Mmmm…I like you inside me."

"Like?"

"Okay, I'm crazy to have you inside me. It's been a long two years."

"No shit."

She nips my ear. "Are you saying you haven't been with another woman?"

"That's what I'm saying. You saying another man hasn't been here?"

"Never."

I lift my head to have eye contact. "Won't lie, I'm glad to hear it."

She smiles, and she presses a kiss to my chin. "I don't think I can go all night tonight."

Shifting behind her, I tug up the blankets before

enveloping her in my arms. It's been years since I've slept with Brynn and my body relaxes in a way it hasn't since the last time I held her close.

"We'll get you back in all-nighter shape in no time."

She chuckles and shifts her backside against my groin. "Are you going to put me through sex boot camp?"

"If you don't stop moving that fine ass, you'll have your first obstacle to climb in about three seconds."

She stops and drops a kiss on my bicep she uses it for a pillow. "It really was wonderful being with you again."

I squeeze her tighter. "It was every dream I've had for two years."

"Me, too."

Her voice is almost a whisper and I wonder if I'm losing her to sleep. The question is answered when her body grows heavy. I nestle close, and inhale her scent as it blends with mine as it always should. A storm threatens outside with the wind rattling the windows, but for once in twelve years, it's not a storm I have to fight. I don't have Marines to care for, or an enemy to prepare for, but the most important battle lies before me; caring for Brynn and the children, earning their trust, and becoming a member of their little family.

"Rest, Caleb."

I smile at her sleepy order. Still, maybe tonight I'll get more sleep than fifteen minutes at a time.

Brynn

"AUNT BRYNN?"

"Mmmm?" I scoot back into the solid wall of warm muscle holding me until my ass cradles his cock and he moans, tightening his arms around me. My body feels like lead sinking into the mattress, and I can't think of the last time I slept through the night and without dreams of hearing men scream for a doc, but not being able to get to them.

"Aunt Brynn?"

I come fully awake with a start when a small hand touches my cheek. A blue gaze collides with mine and I quickly take in the surroundings, making sure Caleb and I are still covered. "What do you need, Ella baby?"

"It's scary. I need to sleep with you."

Only then do I hear the wind howling and rattling the windows. Caleb presses his mouth to my shoulder and nuzzles his nose in the crook of my neck. He flexes his hip and presses his hardening cock closer as his hand moves down my stomach. I pinch his hand. "Caleb."

"Yeah, Angel, I know."

"Caleb!" I snap. His eyes open and adjust. I almost laugh as he comes fully awake and realizes he's face to face with Ella.

"Hi, Little Bit. What ya doing?"

"I need to sleep with you." She starts to move the blankets and I hold on for dear life.

"Ella." She's so determined, Caleb joins my side in the tug-o-war. "Ella!"

Her gaze jerks to mine. "Please, Aunt Brynn."

"Yes. But I need you to go into your room for just a minute. I'll come get you, I promise."

"Okay."

The minute she's out of the room, Caleb and I leap out of bed like we were caught oversleeping at boot camp. He yanks on his skivvies and I tug on the T-shirt earlier discarded and a pair of panties.

"She sleep with you often?"

"No, just when it's so windy. Something about the wind."

He nods. I don't have time to ask if he cares or not, I have to go get Ella since I promised. She practically tackles me heading out of her room and into mine...ours. When she sees Caleb in the bed, though, she slams on the brakes.

"Is he staying?"

"Yes." I climb in next to him and snuggle close. He wraps his arm around my waist and hugs me closer. "Come on, Ella."

She climbs on the bed and snuggles close to me. I cock my head when I hear footsteps outside the door. "Michael?"

A small form emerges from the shadows and he shuffles into the room. "I was just checking on Ella."

Before I can say anything, Caleb moves back, tugging me close again. "Come on, Michael. Might as well join the family."

The boy needs no other invitation before he crawls on the bed and shifts to his side. "Thank you."

"Go to sleep." Caleb grumbles and I hold onto my laughter at what a grizzly bear he sounds like, but it works. The children squeeze their eyes shut. This feels real and like it could last forever. I hear the earnestness in his voice when Caleb says he wants us and wants to stay always, and I feel it when he can't seem to get close enough to me and the way he interacts with Michael and Ella. He'll be tested tomorrow.

Turning in his arms, I smile when my gaze meets his. "You're awake," I whisper.

"You're tense. What's wrong?"

He just stares at me like he already knows the answer to his question. "Tomorrow, the family."

"You mean my father."

I've never heard him refer to Hal Quinlin as Dad, or anything but Father, and my heart cracks for what it must have been like growing up with him. He hid it well throughout our youth. "Yes."

He squeezes me, his large hand warm and strong on my thigh. "Don't worry, Brynn. This, the three people hogging the bed, are the only family I care about."

"Is it time to get up?" Ella mumbles.

"No, go back to sleep." Caleb grumps and I shake with laughter. He squeezes my hip again. "You, too."

"Yes, Staff Sergeant."

Burying my head in the crook of his arm, I absorb his warmth and strength and relax. No matter what past hurts, I have never not had his six. Tomorrow, whatever he faces with his father, this little family, hogging the bed, will have his back.

CHAPTER SIX

Caleb

THE SMALL HAND in mine is a dream forgotten suddenly coming true. I swallow the boulder of emotion in my throat and glance at Brynn. She's carrying a pie and resting a hand on Michael's back, but her eyes are fixed on Ella's hand in mine. Anyone would think we were a real family. My mission is to make the picture a reality just as soon as Brynn gives me the word.

Once I help her up the steps to the porch, I release Ella's hand so I can hold onto the second pie and open the door. Brynn steps into the foyer after the children and stops. "You ready?"

"Good to go."

"Sorry you woke up with the three of us on top of you."

I chuckle. "I'm good, Angel. I've woken up to

worse."

She steps across the threshold and I cut a look to the white SUV parked in front of the house. Luck was not on my side. It was my hope my folks wouldn't be here from the get, but here it is and we might as well face the battle head on.

With one less thing to be thankful for, I walk into Rose and Frank's house sweeping the living room with my gaze. Everyone is talking at once, welcoming Brynn and the children. Rose finds me and her smile spreads. "Welcome home, Caleb."

"Thank you, ma'am."

"Ma'am? No, no, Rose." She wraps me in a hug. Brian moves in for the save when the pie wobbles in my hand. Rose steps back and Brynn's father holds out his hand.

"Caleb, good to see you."

"You, too, sir." I accept his handshake and correct myself when his eyebrow lifts. "Frank."

The next welcome is my mother, and I give her a big hug. "Happy Thanksgiving."

"You, too, son. It's so good to have you home this year." When I release her, I search the room and find my father talking to an uncomfortable Brian. I drop my gaze back to my mother and she gives me a sad smile. "How are things going?"

For today, I'll allow her to ignore the fact her husband can't stand the sight of her son. "Good."

"Good is what you always say, then I hear things like you were in one of the worst firefights and critically wounded. Are you and the children getting along?"

Again, I remind myself it's Thanksgiving, and we're guests at the Reillys'. So I don't bring up the fact she heard I was critically wounded but never visited. Brynn and her parents are a few steps away visiting like a family who really cares about each other. The trust and loyalty is as clear as the trust and loyalty she had with the Marines. Mom tried to build that kind of family when we were little, but Mark and I only felt that with each other. After a few years apart, I turned more to my Marines and Mark to his friends at college. I envy the relationship the Reilly family shares even more than I did when I was a child.

"Affirmative." I mumble in a delayed response to my mother's question.

"And Brynn?"

"And Brynn what?" Brynn slides next to me and hugs my arm.

"Mom wants to know how we're doing."

"We're learning what it will take for us all to be a family."

"Now, *she* knows how to answer a question." My mother turns her attention to Brynn. "Are the children set with everything they need? You know you can always come to Hal and me."

"I do, Audrey, and thank you. They're all set for winter."

She holds tighter when I try to make a break as my father finally makes his way over. "Good to see you, Brynn."

Her hold turns to a death grip. She's never been a fan of my father's, but it almost feels like fear. "Happy Thanksgiving, Hal."

He barely glances at me. "Your mother says you're finally home for good."

"Yes, sir."

"About time."

"It's not like I was just out fu—" Brynn nudges me. "Fooling around."

"Well, you weren't here. You weren't helping out your family—"

"Dinner's ready!" Rose calls.

He mumbles and starts walking toward the dining room, and Mom touches my arm. "I'm sorry, Caleb, he—"

I hold up a hand. "Do not say Mark's death is the reason he's saying any of this. He's hated me since I was eight. Maybe earlier—that's just when I remember."

She nods, and Brynn and I follow her to the dining room. The joy of earlier that morning fades to a gray in the shadow of my father's animosity. Walking into the dining room, I almost want to about face and go back to the lighthouse. Even the abundant fall leaves, turkeys, and other fall decorations around the large room do nothing to hide the man sitting with a scowl directed at me.

"Uncle Caleb, sit by me."

Ella's voice is a sunbeam breaking through the clouds. I maneuver around the table to her, bringing Brynn along with me. "Michael, grab the seat on the other side of Ella, we'll sit together."

Not hesitating, Michael sits next to his sister. I take the chair Ella pats with her hand, almost dragging Brynn down beside me. I glance up, thinking everyone will be looking at us as if I'm crazy. Instead Rose, Frank, and my mother are smiling like their faces are frozen. Brian doesn't show a reaction. The only frown is on my father, but that will never change and has nothing to do with a seating arrangement.

We're all blessed with a reprieve as food is passed and Frank says grace. Following the blessing, I shift in my seat to help Ella cut her turkey. "Remember, Uncle Caleb, vegetables can't touch anything."

"I remember. The green beans are on the other side of the DMZ." Brynn rests a hand on my thigh under the table in a silent show of support. Despite my mood, I have to smile as the move also serves to remind me not to overload Ella's plate. "Okay, you're good to go."

"Thank you."

Since I forced Brynn into a seat farthest from the children, and therefore unable to reach their plates, I turn to Michael next. "Michael, did you need help?"

"No, I'm good."

"He's seven years old, he shouldn't need help with such simple things." My father grumbles, and I watch Michael push up his glasses and shift in his seat.

"He's seven years old, he needs all the help he can get to learn. You'll keep such opinions to yourself."

Brynn's hand grips my thigh harder. My father's face is a mixture of shock and rage. "Who are you?"

"I'm his guardian."

"Since when?"

"Since Mark and Liz made me co-guardian."

All gazes swing to Brynn. Her smile is forced. "It's true and legal."

"So, you just swoop in—"

"Hal, let's save all this for another day," Frank interrupts. "It's Thanksgiving and we don't want to ruin it. Looks like Brynn and Caleb have it under control."

"Fine."

I nod, embarrassed for bringing all this shit up at the dinner table. "Sorry."

I catch Brynn's gaze and her smile turns real as she mouths *thank you*. We both glance at the children. Chin deep in Thanksgiving dinner, they either don't care about the ridiculous adults or they're pretending not to understand. Michael lifts his head, pushes up his glasses and smiles at me, answering my question.

Just when I think the focus is off me, Frank turns to another hot topic. "So, Caleb, have you already had all the ceremonies and parties with your separation? Do you have to go back to California?"

"Yes, sir. My honorable discharge certificate is in hand and everything. No, I no need to go back."

Brynn tips her head as if she just thought of something. When she frowns, I cringe. Whatever she thought of isn't good for me. "You should have let us know so we could be there."

"It's no big deal."

"It *is* a big deal."

Why is she so concerned about being there for me? I was already in Japan and missed any parties she had—this is bringing me down to snail slime level. "Brynn, can we talk about transitioning later? Let's enjoy Thanksgiving dinner."

Her shoulders lift and fall and she starts digging into her stuffing. Thankfully, the others around the table start talking about their jobs, the weather, and football. Ella and Michael continue to ignore the crazy adults around them even through pie.

With the last bite of Brynn's pumpkin pie, I sit back. "That was an excellent meal. Thank you all."

"You're welcome. Do you want another piece of pie?"

"Oh no, Rose, two is plenty. Thank you, though."

Brynn stands and gathers her plates. "I hate to eat and run, but I don't think they got the weather right. I'll help with dishes and then we better go."

Frank smiles. "You could stay the night here."

"Please, Aunt Brynn." At the plea in harmony from Ella and Michael, I know we'll be staying, because I'm not leaving without them.

Brynn hikes a brow at me. "Do you mind?"

"Probably the smart thing to do." I ignore my father's mumbling about being smart and just absorb the feeling of Brynn checking with me and not just making the decision.

"Okay, we'll stay."

The children cheer. She and I share a look that says it's going to be the longest night ever. The only redemption will be if the, *you can't stay in the same room*, rule from when we'd visit on leave has been rescinded. No sex in my future in-laws' house, I can suck it up. A separate bed from Brynn is more suck up than I have left.

CHAPTER SEVEN

Brynn

TRACING HIS FACE with my finger, I smile when his forehead wrinkles. "Are you getting up this morning?"

"I'm up, believe me." He keeps his eyes closed.

I chuckle and press a kiss to his lips. "Mom said breakfast is almost ready."

He opens his eyes, but the frown remains. "How can you be so happy? Last night was torture."

"It was a little, but it was also amazing being held by you again."

"Yeah, that is pretty outstanding." He sweeps over me with his gaze. "What time did you get up?"

"Five-thirty. Ella was having issues in the different house."

"Sorry I slept through it."

"I'm not. You needed a good sleep." I rub my cheek against his, enjoying the burn of his whiskers before dropping a kiss on his cheek. "Now get dressed—Audrey is coming for breakfast."

The scowl returns tenfold. "My father?"

"No, just your mom."

He scrubs his hands over his face and flings the covers back, swinging his legs over the bed. "Thank God."

I've patched him up many times, but there are some wounds he carries I can't heal even if I want to with all my heart. "I'm sorry he's that way to you."

He angles his face over his shoulder and winks. "Don't worry, Angel, I've got what I need."

Climbing back on the bed, I kneel behind him and wrap my arms around his waist, resting my chin on his shoulder. For a minute I just let myself absorb being next to him like I did the night before, praying it wasn't a dream that he was there and really wanted a life with me and two children. "Caleb."

"Hmm?"

"I just like saying your name and have you answer."

"It's outstanding having your hands on me again, your voice in my ear, the scent of you around me. Everything, Brynn."

It's not so much the words, but the ache in his voice sharing all he's been through on a journey back to me that tears my heart. I press my lips to his shoulder. "And not sewing you up?"

His chuckle is low and rumbles like thunder. He'd make a good Santa Claus. "True. Though I can't say I minded your hands on me then either; I knew you'd save my ass and anything else bleeding."

He breaks from my embrace, standing, and I examine him from head to toe and then back up. He's beautiful in his ruggedness, like the rocks that break a storm's rampage. But he's so much more than a form to admire—he's been a fortress, protecting anyone who needed him, including me. And watching him with the children…

I've been warring with myself since the moment I agreed to the engagement. One voice screaming, I should hold onto the hurt and anger longer. I should make him crawl and beg. The other reminding me before there was the pain there was twenty-seven years of friendship and love; of shielding each other in the most dangerous areas of the world as the family the Marines made us. That's what makes the betrayal all the worse, I rail back. But what time does one put on forgiveness? On friendship? On love? On hope? How long does society require my righteous anger, before I can admit the wound is fresh, but the healing is coming being with him again, or that I'm not ready to say New Year's Eve is a hundred percent go, but I need his help with the children and I'm elated to have him home.

Releasing a deep breath, I lift my gaze to meet his; a melding of ice and fire he used to say. "I love you, Caleb. I love you, but I'm scared."

He cups my cheek with a hand and I lean into the calloused warm flesh. "I know. We have a few weeks; don't try to decide everything right now. Why don't you head on down? I'll be behind you in a few minutes."

Nodding, I slide forward and step off the bed. He starts gathering his clothes, deep lines forming on his forehead. "Caleb, what's—"

"Aunt Brynn! I need help!"

I cut a glance to the closed door and back to him. He lifts his chin, pointing to the voice behind the door. "Go take care of Ella. We can talk later."

"We *will* talk later," I promise before opening the door just enough to slide out, missing his mumbled response. "Ella, what did you do to your hair?"

"I braided it." Sighing at the rat's nest posing as a braid, I take her hand and lead her to the guest room she shares with Michael. "I want to see Uncle Caleb."

"He's getting dressed. You'll see him at breakfast."

"You got to see him."

I sink into a purple chair and turn her around, trying to comb through the knot as carefully as possible. "That's different."

"Why? Ow!"

"Sorry, but you made a real mess. And it's different

like with your mom and dad. Sometimes adults need to be alone in a room." I drop a kiss on her head. "Thank you for knocking on the door instead of just walking in."

"Welcome. Aunt Brynn?"

"Yes, baby?"

"Uncle Caleb, he's staying?"

"Yes, he's staying."

I finally get her hair untangled and start braiding. "Forever?"

"Yes, forever." I lift my gaze over her head to meet Caleb's as he leans against the doorframe.

"Uncle Caleb!" The squeal of joy cuts through the conversation we're having without words, and Ella breaks from my arms and flies into his.

"Good morning, Little Bit."

Swooping her up, he starts "eating her neck" as her peels of giggles must echo through the whole house. Michael peeks into the room. "Nana says you need to come to breakfast."

Pushing out of the chair, I comb my fingers through the boy's dark brown hair. "We better get down there then."

Resting my hands on his shoulders, I follow Michael down the hall with Caleb and Ella behind us. Family pictures line the wall from the three of us kids in Acadia, to Mark and Liz's wedding, and Mark, Liz, Michael, and Ella in Acadia; Ella so small she's in a carrier on her mother's back. Liz seems to smile at me through the images, and I pray I'm doing right by her children. A stone settles in my stomach thinking of them as hers, but I shake the feeling away.

"Can I tell you something and you won't get mad?"

I stop and turn the boy who seems much smaller than he did a few seconds ago, so I sit on my heels to meet him at his height. "You can tell me anything, Michael, anything."

He lifts his gaze to Caleb's. "Can I talk to Aunt Brynn alone?"

"Of course." He walks around us taking Ella with him.

When they're on the stairs, Michael turns back to me. "Gramma fixed the eggs with the sauce. I told her I didn't like them, but she said I had to try them. I told her I tried them before, but she said I needed to try them again."

"I'll fix you scrambled eggs, okay? I'll explain to Gramma."

"I don't want to embarrass Uncle Caleb—she's he's mom."

"Sweet boy, you never could. He's the one who told you to speak up."

"Dad didn't like it if we talked back to Gramma. He got mad like Granddad."

I take a couple breaths; no use getting mad at Mark

now. "I assure you, your uncle Caleb will not be angry. I am not angry."

"Okay."

"You just take your chair and I'll take care of everything."

"Yes, ma'am."

Opening my arms, I wrap him in a quick hug. Then, standing, I follow him down the stairs, unable to use the railing since Mom already started decorating for Christmas. Entering the dining room, I catch Caleb's look and his raised eyebrow. Michael takes his seat like I told him.

Audrey, dishing out the eggs benedict, glances up. "Good morning, Brynn."

"Good morning." She reaches for Michael's plate. "Oh, Audrey, Michael doesn't care for eggs benedict. I'll just scramble him an egg."

She pins Michael with a look before returning her attention to me. "I told Michael he needed to try it."

Straightening my shoulders, I take his plate from her hand. "He has tried it and he doesn't like it. It's no big deal."

"Brynn I—"

"Mom, he doesn't like it. No big deal, we'll get him a scrambled egg."

She nods in agreement with Caleb, and I smile and take Michael's plate into the kitchen.

My mom and dad are gathering up the waffles and bacon. Dad's gaze drops to the plate. "Something wrong?"

"I'm making scrambled eggs for Michael."

Dad shrugs. "Okay."

Mom's forehead wrinkles in disapproval. "Shouldn't he eat—"

I hold up my hand, stopping her. "He doesn't like them. He doesn't have to eat them."

"Well, okay." Mom and Dad share a look.

Ignoring them I quickly stir up an egg. Taking the plate with the egg to him, I set it in front of him and drop a kiss to the top of his head. "There you go, sweetheart."

"Thanks."

"You want bacon and a waffle?"

"Bacon, please."

Snagging a couple pieces, I put them on his plate, pour him a little more milk and then sit and fix my plate. Dad says the blessing and I roll my shoulders a couple times, relaxing when the grandmothers seem to let the whole egg thing go. I frown when I notice Michael won't look at Caleb, as if he still believes he'd find anger there.

Caleb seems to sense it too. For only being around the children for a few days, he doesn't miss a beat. "Good job speaking up, Michael."

"Really?"

"Absolutely. I'm proud of you. You were polite, but spoke up."

It was like he filled a balloon as puffed as Michael gets. He starts cutting Ella's waffle and once again this all feels real, like we're not playing a part and can really make this work…a family.

Breakfast passes without the tension of Hal's presence, or any questions about how I'm raising the children or Caleb's sudden return. Pushing my empty plate to the side, I pour another cup of coffee and topped Caleb's cup off. "Thanks, Brynn."

"Absolutely." I toss him a wink just because I can."

"Can we go play?"

He's almost out of his seat already, I wipe Michael's face with a napkin. "Yes, but don't make a mess; we'll be leaving soon."

"Okay."

He and Ella run back upstairs and the table falls quiet. The tick-tocks of the grandfather clock in the adjacent living room boom like artillery getting closer and closer. Audrey smiles at Caleb. "It's good to have you home, son."

Mom, Dad, and I turn to Caleb anticipating what? I'm not sure. The silence cut only by what seems to be louder ticks and tocks beats for fifty seconds, according to the clock. All of us continue to wait for Caleb to respond.

Caleb

"GOOD TO BE here."

"I'm sorry about your father yesterday."

"Not your responsibility to apologize for him."

She exhales a humorless laugh. "I'm not apologizing for him, I'm apologizing for me, for allowing him to hate his son. I probably shouldn't bring it up after a nice breakfast, but I shouldn't have waited this long."

My stomach roils hearing my mother voice the truth of what I've known since I was child and each of my choices, every interest clashed with my father's. I feel Brynn's hand on my thigh, and while offering support, comfort, whatever her words from earlier still sting. She's scared. Scared I'll leave? Scared I'll fail? Either fear, while understandable after what I did, stings. I thought we were on our way to building something together.

Still, I grab for her hand like it's my poncho liner on a cold night and feel her warmth seep into all the hollow places in my heart. "I appreciate you saying that, Mom, I really do. But if you mean it, then help Brynn and me change the course with Michael and Ella. Dad's rules don't apply to them."

When I hold her blue gaze, I see she understands I'm talking about more than eggs benedict versus scrambled. "Agreed."

"Then let's move forward and not get stuck in the past." I squeeze Brynn's hand, letting her know I'm talking to her too.

Mom nods. Brynn frowns. Both reactions are expected.

Brynn's father leans back in his chair. "I know we weren't part of the conversation, but Rose and I want to add our agreement. To be honest, when Brian told us you were back and engaged to Brynn, we had our doubts. And we can be a bit set in our ways about how children should be raised. On the first count, we were wrong. On the second, we're willing to step back and let you two raise the children how you see fit."

Frank's first count solidifies what I already knew when I sent Brynn away that day at Bethesda. I would be hurting her family, as well. As a teenager, I always puffed a bit when Frank or Rose would say I was "like another son." Today, I'm feeling more deflated.

"Thank you Dad, Mom."

Brynn's voice brings me out of my thoughts, and I clear my throat. "Yes, thank you both. Now, we better get cleaned up and back to the lighthouse, don't you think, Angel?"

We're halfway standing when Frank waves us back down. "Well, that's another thing, we wanted to ask if we could keep the kids today. Brian said he can bring them back home tomorrow late-morning after his shift."

I know my answer, but, like the day before, I hold back. "Did you have anything planned for today?"

Brynn nods to the ceiling where there are thumps from small feet moving around. "No, no plans, but what about Ella?"

I frown, not comprehending. "She's staying here."

Brynn's look says she's about ready to send me to the corner to color while the adults talk. "She won't want to stay if Uncle Caleb leaves."

The picture becomes clear without crayons. I can almost hear the toddler screams. "True, and she was forced from the house yesterday. Guess that's a negative, Frank." Rose stands. "Give me a minute."

She walks up the stairs, and my mom smiles. "Rose will have them begging to stay in seconds."

"Sorry we didn't ask you, Audrey."

Mom shakes her head. "I hate to say it, Frank, but I don't think the children should stay with Hal. He's too hard on them and it makes it stressful. But I'd love to stay longer today and join you all downtown."

"Of course."

I share a smile of understanding with Mom. It must break her heart to admit her husband shouldn't be around her grandchildren for long, especially as over the moon as she was when she found out she was going to be a grandmother.

"Okay, they want to stay," Rose announces and starts cleaning off the table.

The rest of us join in to help. Before the children can

recover from the mind-altering technique Rose used, Brynn and I double-time it. I hustle Brynn through goodbyes with the kids, instructions to the grandparents. We make it back to the lobster boat and out of the slip in record time.

CHAPTER EIGHT

Brynn

STEPPING ASIDE, ALLOWING Caleb to enter with the basket of leftovers my mom sent, I pull off my boots, coat, and hat. He sets the basket down and follows suit. I flip on the lights and stand still and listen. "It's *so* quiet."

He sidles up behind me and rests his hands on my hips. "True." A shiver walks my spine when he pulls back my hair and presses his mouth to my neck. "So, let's make some noise."

Turning in his arms, I wrap my arms around his neck and lean close. "We should put the leftovers away."

His mouth lifts in a grin hot enough to raise the temperature in the whole state of Maine. I definitely want to start stripping off some layers of clothing. He tugs me flush against him. "After round one."

I brush a kiss on his neck and smile at the warmth

radiating from his skin. He's not the only one who can bring the heat. "How many rounds were you planning on Staff Sergeant?"

"Brynn, I plan on being inside you all night and all morning. If you're lucky I'll let you up for water and chow a couple times."

Laughing, I nip his chin, then let out a yelp when he lifts my legs before pressing me against the wall. When he moves closer and pushes against me, nothing seems funny at the feel of his erection through his jeans. Our gazes collide and there isn't one thing amusing about the fire in his ice-blue eyes. Without a word, we share the memory of our last deployment together and how Thanksgiving Day ended like this, only in a barracks on a military base.

His smile returns to his full lips before he lowers his head, and I part my lips as he captures them in a kiss so tender I wrap my arms tighter around him and cup the back of his head. The gentle way he tastes me is full of love, but also an ache I can't understand, and I feel the sting of tears in my eyes. Trying to heal whatever brings him pain, I kiss him with all my heart and smooth my palms over the rough hair on his head from his high-and-tight cut. Both sensations add to the burn for him.

He brushes kisses over my cheeks. "What scares you so much, Angel, that you're crying?"

His words have the effect as if he dropped me in

Penobscot Bay in January. I startle and gulp in air. "Oh God, Caleb, you don't scare me. I know you're here for good."

He scowls. "Then what scares you?"

"All of it. Since the call after the accident, all my plans vanished, replaced with a vast unknown. I'm a mother of two and that frightens the hell out of me. I'm trying to get my nursing degree but don't want the children to feel like I'm ignoring them. I know I should move off the island so they can go to school proper instead of Michael going to school online. And I was most frightened of your father trying to take them away because he didn't like what I was doing. And I'm frightened that you'll hate living in Camden, but do it anyway and never be truly happy."

"That's quite a list."

I frown, but then cup his face. "It's been nice having you back. No, check that, it's been amazing having you back in my life. And to be honest, I still don't fully understand why you let me go. I'm trying to keep the children happy, and now keep you happy. Then reality hits and I can't heal everyone and there's no triage for what's bleeding. You know how much I hate that, and it scares me most of all because it's what I do. If I can't heal then why am I even here."

He jostles me until I wrap my arms back around his neck and lock my legs around his waist. The sparks in his eyes are back in full force. I don't know how the man could keep that spark after so many deployments, and being wounded so many times. But they were there the first time I patched him up and taped up shrapnel in his leg, and he winked at me. Or when I knelt over him, plugging the gaping hole in his chest. Or the other night when he came to me in a Nor'easter. But then again those sparks were there when he leaned his hip against my locker when we were fifteen and told me he'd come to the conclusion we needed to stop fucking around with friendship and start dating. I suppose the sparks remain through it all like my faith remains after being at war for ten years. We've had each other, so there's always been hope.

He shifts so I'm cradled in his arms. "We will talk about all your fears one by one and sort it out."

"Okay."

"I just want to be clear, I am listening, but right now I really need to be inside you."

"Yes." I smile.

"But before anything, let me address why you're here. You are the balm to all my wounds. And if you don't think you've been healing the hearts of Michael and Ella, you haven't been watching them. They come to you when the storms hit, because they know you will keep them safe. You're the warrior who fights their fears."

I rest my forehead on his chest. "So, I fight their fears, you fight mine?"

"We fight together, Angel, like always."

"Caleb." I breathe his name as if he's the one who gives me breath.

He jostles me again. "Now, we only have eighteen hours and that's just enough time for us to get started."

I meet his smile with one of my own. "And then we have to put away those leftovers."

His laughter is booming and glorious, and I always count it a win when I can make him lose all that Marine control and give an actual laugh. "We've got the whole house—where?"

I nod to the stairs. "I'm going to be boring and say bed. After years of wherever, whenever, it's nice to have a bed."

He starts climbing the stairs, and I hold tight. "Agreed. Bed gives me more access to all of you."

"Why does that sound like a warning?"

"A heads-up."

He sinks his knee into the mattress laying me on the bed, before capturing my mouth again, and the kiss is just as tender and masterful as the first, but this time joy replaces all the sorrow. The kiss lasts forever and I sink farther into the mattress as he presses his hard angles into my curves. I tighten my arms around him again, raking my fingernails over the rough edges of his hair. Completely drunk off his taste, I moan and hold him to me when he shifts.

He hovers over me, his gaze pure blue fire. "What do you want, Angel?"

I rake my fingernails down his chest watching the flames ignite. "I want you to fuck me to that sweet oblivion where I can't form a thought let alone worry about anything."

"Nice." He trails kisses down my neck and then nips my earlobe, and I rock under him. His breath is warm against my ear. "Let's find that oblivion."

I comply, raising my hips so he can tug my tights and panties over my hips. He pushes my legs open with his calloused palms and I grab fistfuls of bedding as my back bows with the first contact of his tongue on my sex. My torso twists, but he holds the bottom half of me stable as he circles my clit with his tongue and then sucks the swollen nub before turning his attention to every part of my pussy.

I try to grab for him, but he's under my skirt, which makes the experience more erotic, feeling him, hearing him devour me, but unable to see him. My mind shatters into a million stars. "Caleb!"

"Mmmm…" He brushes a kiss to one inner thigh, and then the other, even as my legs continue to tremble. "I missed those sounds you make. Now, lose the clothes, Brynn."

I nod and start stripping, too sex drunk to speak. When I blink and clear my vision, he's standing naked before me and I lift my gaze to his. He winks. "Looking at me like that will get you everything."

Before I can answer, he kisses me again and there is nothing tender in this kiss—it's raw, white hot and all-consuming, swiping everything but him from my mind and heart. When he breaks this kiss, he gently turns me on my stomach and nips my shoulder. "Open for me."

I spread my legs and bite my bottom lip as he guides his thick cock inside my sex. The stretch is almost unbearable in its pleasure, and I exhale a whimper when he pushes deeper then covers me, smoothing his palms over my arms until he links his fingers with mine. My inner muscles work his length as he moves just enough to build that magical friction but remains buried deep inside me.

Angling my head, I accept his kiss and moan into his mouth when he releases one hand to mold my breast and circles my nipple with his thumb. I start moving my hips to match his rhythm and break the kiss, resting my forehead on the bed as the sensations become over-whelming. Reality fades. Whether I'm in a little house in Maine, or the desert of Afghanistan, it all blends into moments of being a part of Caleb in the most base way.

I feel him surround me and inhale the clean scent of the soap he uses, mixed with his scent and the scent of sex heavy around us. I struggle to breathe with the humidity of the room, his thickness filling me, and rising tension pulling every tendon tight, even as my bones feel like rubber and my blood lava. Our bodies are slick with sweat, adding salt to his taste when I press a kiss to his bicep. He skates his hand over my torso and then pushes low on my belly where his cock stretches.

"Caleb!"

"Shhh, Angel, just let me consume you."

I tighten my grip on his hand. "Yeees…" I moan deep from my soul.

His strokes become harder and deeper, and added to our grunts is the thunderous sound of his flesh clapping against mine and his cock sliding in and out of my wet heat. I can feel him growing inside me as his climax starts, and then he strokes my clit and I go wild under him as the power of my orgasm robs me of sanity and all primitive instincts shout for what only he can give. Over and over he strokes me as he continues to ride me through his orgasm and demand my pleasure to continue until I hold onto life by the thread of the life he pours into me.

With one more deep push, he makes his claim complete. I cry his name into the bedding. Every nerve and tendon tensed to the maximum releases and I melt under him, and rest my forehead against the cool quilt. My breathing is harsh with the rise and fall of Caleb's ribs against my back and the throbbing of his cock still inside me.

He trails kisses over my shoulder and then on the back of my neck as he skates his palm back over my torso.

"Caleb."

"Shhh…I'm gonna let you rest a bit, Angel."

He eases his length from me and turns me on my back. I groan and every muscle revolts at being moved. Caleb hovers over me, his hair damp, his eyes still fire, an extremely satisfied grin curving his lips. He brushes his mouth over mine, then he runs the tip of his tongue over my lips. "Between your pie and you, it's a toss-up for what satisfies my sweet tooth more."

I stretch under him and smile, resting my hands on his biceps. "Once, in Afghanistan, you told me you'd be happy just holding my hand."

He presses his lips to mine for an all-to-quick kiss. "To be connected to you in any way is solace for my soul. There were times in my last deployment when I'd hold my hands out and think of them laced with yours, healing seeping into my veins. I would think of how these hands have had the surreal pleasure of touching you like I'm touching you now."

I'd been trying to keep it light, but his words solidify the depth of our connection. "There were times after the children went to bed, I'd do the same, examining the hands that have felt the strength of yours around them, that have touched you like I'm doing now."

"Then I'd pick up my M4 and head out on patrol, praying these hands would get one more chance to touch you."

"Then I'd pick up the toys left on the floor praying these hands would feel you again."

He presses his forehead to mine. "This is all I need, Brynn, to touch you and know you're mine."

"Me, too."

With one more quick kiss, he rolls from me and I shiver as the cold air hits the flesh he'd warmed with his. He pulls me to him and tucks me close, sheltering me from the chill.

His chuckle causes me to frown. "What's so funny?"

"Nothing really funny. I was just thinking how fucking lucky I am that I get to know all of you. None of those other Marines would think you had a soft side the way you barked orders. I will forever hear your voice as you called for CASEVAC."

"You're crazy."

"Really, I'm the crazy one? When all five foot four of you is yelling down the Devil Dogs from the sky and threatening holy hell if they didn't land for me."

"I don't like to think of that day, Caleb. It was too close, and I might have been tough on the aviators, but tears were also streaming down my face. And then when your hand left mine when they carried you off—"

His arms tighten around me. "Don't think about it. My hand will never be pulled from yours again." He squeezes me. "Why don't we put those leftovers away, maybe refuel?"

"Sounds good."

When I scoot away from him and grab my T-shirt and shorts, he takes my hand. "Sorry I fucked up the moment."

"You didn't fuck anything up. It was—It was how it always is with us, which I don't think there's a word…Yes, it was transcendent." Lifting his hand, I kiss the palm. "Let's go eat."

CHAPTER NINE

Caleb

I STUDY BRYNN as she chews a bite of stuffing. Her gaze shifts to me. "Stop staring."

"Can't. I've decided it's definitely you I prefer to your pie."

"You keep it up and you'll get lucky again today, Marine."

"I'm going to get lucky a few more times today and then a few more tonight."

She leans closer. "You think so, huh?"

I respond in kind, leaning forward. "You don't?"

Her nose wrinkles. "Yeah, you're going to get it a few more times."

"I'm going to give you a thousand more transcendent orgasms."

She tosses a napkin at him. "Don't make fun."

I frown, but smile at the same time. "I'm not, I love when I've given you such a hardcore orgasm you toss out the big words."

She winks and shoves a bite of turkey in her mouth, then proceeds to chew slowly and methodically. She holds my stare as she pokes the tip of her tongue between her pink lips.

I clear my throat and lean back on the bench. "I've been thinking about that list you gave me. Might be we can work it out."

"List?"

"Of fears."

"Caleb, it's on me." She raises and lowers one shoulder. "Don't worry about it. I'll figure it out."

I narrow my gaze. "Not worried. And it's *us* now. You said you'd started school for a nursing degree—how long do you have left?"

"Three semesters."

"That's outstanding, Angel."

Her cheeks turn pink. "Thank you."

"I've been working my internal whiteboard and figure you could finish school, then I'll complete my degree after. That way the kids only have one of us buried in books at a time."

She cocks her head to the side. "What's your degree?"

It's my turn to shrug. "Once I realized I was coming back here and the Marines weren't going to be a career I knew I had to decide what I could do as a civilian. I started getting an education degree, thought I might give teaching math a try—and don't laugh."

Her nose wrinkles, and she tosses another wadded-up napkin at me. "Wasn't going to, I think that's perfect for you."

"I was inspired by your parents."

"That's sweet."

"Better than taking after my father." With a quick breath I continue before we get sidetracked about parents. "In the meantime, I can talk to Mr. Sanders. He said I could get my construction job back anytime. It was thirteen years ago, but he's always been a man of his word."

She stares at me and I watch her features change as she works through all the possibilities. "I think it'll work, and I won't have to feel guilty. But you can wait?"

"One of us will have to, and you've been serving a year of single mom operations. My turn to step it up."

She holds her hand out to shake. "Deal. Thank you." When I accept her hand, I turn it and press my lips to her palm before releasing her hand.

"And about my father ever taking those kids, that will never happen, Angel, not on my watch."

"*Our* watch."

"Absolutely."

She raises an eyebrow. "How about school and living

in a lighthouse? You got a solution for that?"

I smile at the tinge of challenge in her voice. "I might. Right now, let's keep it status quo. But for spring semester, let's get Michael involved in some things in town. Whatever his interests are. Then this summer we'll reevaluate. Why didn't you keep Mark and Liz's place?"

"They already had it sold for the move. We had to double-time it to get their things in storage. I should have looked for a place, but we settled into life here and this little house became the home I wanted it to when I bought it."

"We'll monitor the situation."

She leans forward, a V forms between her eyebrows and her lips tighten. "You do realize Michael and Ella aren't Marines?"

I finish chewing a bite of turkey. "Yet, they're not Marines yet."

Her laugh is filled with pure joy and I wonder how with all the shit she's seen and been through. Taking her hand, I lace my fingers with hers and her laughter dies as she curls her fingers and squeezes my hand. "As for me just sticking around because hey, I'm Captain America and that's what I do? Negative. I'm staying because I love you, I love those kids, and I want a lifetime with you both. I'm sure you'll change my mind about Maine."

"I never called you Captain America."

I shrug. "It was implied."

She pushes her plate to the side. "So, you've got it all figured out?"

"Not even fucking close, but these are the plans I've come up with. If you've got something else lay it on the table, before I lay you on the table."

She shakes her head, but can't hide her smile. "They're outstanding." She strokes her thumb over my knuckles.

"But?"

"But now I don't want to talk about the serious things, or plan the future."

"I can get behind that."

She doesn't release my hand, but walks around the table and straddles my lap and cups my face. "I still can't believe you're really here."

I slide my hand over her thigh and then back up and under her shorts to the curve of her ass. "I thought I'd given some pretty convincing evidence."

"True, you've far surpassed the fantasies I've had."

"Why don't you tell me about one of those fantasies?"

Her gaze drops, and instead of the sexy smile I expect she frowns and covers the scar on my chest with her hand. I pinch her ass. Her frown remains, but her eyes now meets mine. "None of looking at the bad times. Fantasy?"

She sinks onto my lap and finally I get that sexy

smile. "My fantasy starts with us hand in hand—"

"Sounds good."

"Walking through a Christmas tree lot—"

I have a horrible suspicion this is not the fantasy I was hoping for. I squeeze her ass. "Brynn—"

"Shhh…you'll like this."

"Okay, we're walking through a Christmas tree lot."

"And we pick out the perfect tree and bring it here and you, me, and the children spend a cozy evening decorating the tree with cookies and hot chocolate after. Then the children go to bed and we snuggle on the couch enjoying the Christmas lights and a fire in the fireplace. Then you carry me to bed and then—"

I'm sold on her fantasy. "Then—"

A smile I don't recognize touches her lips. It's tender, sweet, and something I can't put my finger on. "The baby cries and—"

"Baby?"

"Our baby. Don't you want a baby with me?"

"Absolutely." I really hadn't thought of it before, but now it becomes a fantasy we share.

"Really?"

"Yes, ma'am. But—"

"But?"

"I think we should wait a bit, give Michael and Ella time to adjust to us as an us and all of us as a family."

"You're just the Marine with the plan for everything

today."

"If you don't agree, just say. We're partners."

She skates her fingertips up my torso and my belly flexes under her touch. "I don't know, it's only been a few days since you got here. So far, there are times I think we'll need to wait, other times I think we should all jump in, see what happens. We'll monitor that as well."

"Agreed."

She presses closer until her breath brushes against my cheek like a caress. "I'll let you in on a secret."

"Okay, Angel."

"This was a fantasy, too. For the last year I've sat out here after the children go to bed dreaming of you and me sitting like this talking everything through."

"Sorry it took me a couple years to get here."

"You're doing very well at making up for lost time." She tucks her head between my neck and shoulder and kisses my neck before nipping and sucking. These past few days have been my fantasies, just being with Brynn any way I can. She exhales a whimper when I move my hand under her shorts, moving closer and closer to her sex.

In a blink she pushes back. "When did that happen?"

"What the fuck, Brynn?"

She pushes the shell of my ear forward and starts inspecting. "This scar here, it's not that old. What happened over there?"

"War. You've been there."

"What happened? Who was the corpsman?"

"Piece of some shit ricocheted and cut me. Manelli. It wasn't that bad, didn't even have to slow me down."

"Manelli's good."

I pull her hand down from where she examines the old wound. "Kiss it again and make it all better."

She leans forward and resumes driving me wild with kisses, nips, and sucks.

"Fuck, that feels good."

I feel the curve of her smile against my skin along with the warmth of her breath. "You better start watching your language if you're going to live with Ella."

I chuckle and she lifts her head, but stays plastered to me. "I'll keep *fuck* for the bedroom."

Her gaze wanders the room. "We're in the kitchen."

"Okay, I'll keep *fuck* for when I'm actively fucking you or in the aftermath, no matter what room."

"And we'll have to remember skivvies after in case the kids need us."

"We can do that."

"Not quite how I pictured our first months of marriage."

Cupping her face, I bring her gaze to mine. "Not what I've pictured either."

"But they're good kids."

"Very."

"And they're cute."

I chuckle. "Very."

"We could probably talk Mom and Dad into babysitting for a week, so we can go away this spring."

"Angel, I've been away forever. Let's get Rose and Frank to watch the kids for a few days this summer, and stay right here in bed."

"I like that idea."

Gripping her hips, I stand and start walking into the living room. "For now, we have less than twenty-four hours before we're cockblocked again. No more talking, planning, or worrying. We still have rooms to conquer."

She nuzzles her nose against my neck. "Agreed."

"And no skivvies, all clothing is banned."

"Agreed."

Sinking onto the couch, she straddles my lap. Her smile is bright and her eyes have sparks of gold through the greens, blues, and browns. "And you will call me sir and worship me."

"Agr—" She pushes at my chest. "Hell no!" Her body shakes with her laughter and I shrug, unable to hide my smile.

"Worth a shot."

CHAPTER TEN

Brynn

A DEEP MOAN escapes between my teeth when I stretch. If there was any doubt Caleb's return was real, those were thoroughly pounded out of me and further erased by the marks from neck to inner thighs. Tugging down my sweater, I check the mirror one more time to make sure the marks are hidden and walk down the stairs to the living room. The source of my sore muscles and absolute euphoria is tugging up his turtleneck to cover one of the marks I left on him. Oh yes, I gave as good as I got.

He turns and gives me a "let's do it again" smile, and I shake my head. "We've got incoming, Marine."

His shoulders rise and fall. "Worth a try. Why are you acting nervous?"

I inhale a deep breath. "Does the house smell like

sex?"

His chuckle draws me to him. "No. You've sanitized the place to death and lit every scented candle. It smells like lemon cleanser and apples and cinnamon. There's no scent like we did what we did all night and this morning."

Resting a hand on his chest, I give a gentle push. "Come one, don't tease, this is my first sex fest with the kids coming back the next day."

"That's a relief, since I would have missed any other sex fest with the kids returning after. Seriously, I'm sure Mark and Liz had sex. Yes, I think the table needed a scrub-down after I had you for breakfast on it, but the house is good to go. Just don't act weird about it and the kids won't give it a thought."

"You're way too relaxed about this whole instant family dynamic. It's kind of pissing me off and at the same time turns me on like crazy."

"Let's focus on the part that revs you up."

I wink. "I focused on that part many times over the last hours. That part should be well satisfied."

He leans forward and brushes his lips over mine, a smile making the kiss sweeter. "Never."

When he angles to bury his head in the crook of my shoulder, I step back. "No way. It took me hours to find a sweater to cover the marks you already gave me. No more."

He steps back and lifts his hands. "Roger that. Since we can't touch and the house is stage four sanitized, fill me in on the plan for the day."

I slide past him and point out the window to the snow-covered ground. "Snowpeople. Last year we did very little for Christmas, so I want Michael and Ella to have the best Christmas we can give them starting today. I'd love to go crazy with all the cheesy and warmhearted traditions we missed."

"I'm onboard for snowpeople. Then what?"

Warming up to my subject since he didn't give me the raised eyebrow of *that belongs in a Christmas movie*, I continue. "Then I have some supplies for Christmas crafts I've been hoarding since September. I thought we could all make our own ornament."

He steps closer, but he doesn't look at me. He searches past the island to the harbor. "Not sure how crafty I am, but I've been known to patch a few things together."

"Ornaments, not ordnance."

He laughs. "Roger that, Angel. Sounds like you've got the day worked out, just let me know my place in the lineup."

"Oh, and then next weekend is Christmas by the Sea, we have to go to that."

"Nothing rings in the holiday season like Santa in a lobster boat, agreed."

I take his hand. "Absolutely."

His stare returns to the window and beyond to Penobscot Bay. It hits me square in the heart. He's searching for Brian's boat bringing the children home. "They'll be here soon. Brian said before lunch."

He ignores my statement. "You have an idea what Ella wants?"

"Ice skates and 'medicine'."

"Medicine?"

"A ruck like mine. That's what she calls it, simply medicine."

His smile is tender and he nods. "Cute, I like that. Those from us, Santa, grandparents?"

I slip my arms around his waist. "The first aid kit, and other things, are from us. Brian asked to get the skates. He wants to get them both hockey skates."

His eyebrow lifts. "Roger. The hug?"

"'Cause you ask the sweetest questions."

"Then I got another: how about Michael? He give you any clue other than socks?"

"He gave *you* clues. Pick a sport."

"Good point. But I'd like to get him something he's good at or doesn't have to work for right away. If Brian's getting him skates, I'm not sure we want to load him down with sports equipment."

"True, but I was thinking you could get him lacrosse equipment. He so wants to be like you."

"Let's give it some thought. Feel him out. I'm not sure I want him focusing on being like me."

"Caleb?"

He rests his hands on my shoulders. "No, I'm not putting my choices down. I just grew up in a house where being like your father was supposed to be the goal. I want Michael and Ella to be who they are instead of replicas of us. If she's interested in medicine and he wants to try lacrosse, by all means, I will back them up a thousand percent. But I don't want them to fear coming to us and telling us it's not for them."

He earns another hug. "Absolutely. I agree one thousand and ten percent with everything you said. We can watch next weekend, see if he gives any hints as we look or if he says something."

"Roger that. We can take them to see Santa."

"We'll give Santa a shot. We might have to settle for a view from Bay View and sending letters."

"Santa's not on their list?"

I roll my eyes but chuckle at the gag-worthy pun. "One year, Liz wrote Ella threw a fit to rival all fits when they tried to get a picture with her and Santa, and Michael just stood there shaking his head no. I know they're older, but I'm not into forcing a child to visit Santa."

"I forgot about that. And definitely, St. Nick is nixed if there's the slightest lip quiver."

I step away from him and shake my head. "What's with the lame puns?"

His shoulders rise and fall and he gives me a smile made to put someone on the naughty list. "Don't know. Woke up happy this morning and the day is getting better by the second. I mean you promised I get to make an ornament and everything."

"You're crazy."

His response is a wink. The sound of a boat engine sends him back to the window. "They're almost here, Brynn."

His voice is full of the same excitement and love Ella's and Michael's hold when he steps into a room. I push the emotion down refusing to cry at how happy I am in this moment, and force voice to be natural. "Come on help me with lunch."

Caleb

BRYNN LEANS OVER Ella to offer an assist with the little girl's ornament, which is an improvised glitter bomb. We'll be finding glitter in August, but I have to admit it's been the perfect start to the holidays, at least in my humble opinion. I continue to watch as Brynn helps Ella shape the ornament into a cat.

I turn my gaze to Michael, using popsicle sticks to create a Christmas tree-shaped ornament. Unlike his sister, his space is structure central. Every color he needs lined up next to any glitter or pom-pom he plans to use. His focus is zeroed in on the project and I'd bet his hot chocolate is now iced chocolate.

It was the same with the snowpeople. Ella started with no plan and created along the way and came up with a snowcat...with help from Brynn. I'm thinking the snowcat and ornament cat are also hints she wants a kitten, but she'll have to be satisfied with skates and medicine.

Michael almost analyzed every flake before bringing to life the image in his mind of a snowman. He preferred to work alone without input from his aunt or me. Both snow creations are perfect, although I'm a little biased.

I study Brynn, again, and the endless crafting supplies like the boxes of hats, mittens, and scarves she'd been collecting for snowmen. She knows what to say to each child and can spot when a naptime is needed from twenty klicks. If I told anyone she'd only been a mother for a year they'd call me a wicked liar. She's everything a mother should be.

She glances up from Ella and catches my stare. Her gaze cuts to the wreath ornament I'm trying to fumble through and back to my eyes. "You okay?"

"Outstanding." I lift the pipe cleaner wreath. "Better than this."

Her mouth curves in a smile at my attempt at a bow. "Looks great." She examines each project. "They all look fantastic."

Michael sits on his knees and stretches across the table to scrutinize my work. "Yeah, Dad…" His face turns a bright red and his voice drops to a choked whisper. "I mean Uncle Caleb. It looks good." He avoids eye contact and sinks back on his chair.

The floor opens under me and I'm tumbling in a storm a hundred times stronger than the one I fought days ago. All I can do is keep a firm hold on the rudder and focus on the boy across from me who needs reassurance.

"Hey, Michael, bud, look at me."

When he lifts his head and pushes up his glasses on his nose I inhale another deep breath. "You didn't do anything wrong. Thanks for the encouragement about my ornament."

His throat works as he swallows hard. "Okay, and you're welcome."

Still avoiding any eye contact with Brynn, I turn the circle of green pipe cleaner between my fingers. "Sure could use some help though, would you mind?"

He slides off his chair and starts walking around the table. "Yeah, sure. If you really need it."

"I really do."

Climbing onto the bench next to me, he takes the spot where Brynn was and turns to her. "Do you mind if I move your stuff, Aunt Brynn?"

I finally glance at her and her smile is so bright there's no need for the beacon next to the house. "Not at all."

After moving Brynn's intricate god's eye yarn ornament and supplies, he scoots right next to me. "Okay, now this is how a bow is made. We should use ribbon, not pipe cleaner."

My smile collides with Brynn's. Michael taps my arm with his finger. "See, this is how it's done."

"Aunt Brynn, my cat needs a tail."

We both turn our attentions back to the children. The day I arrived, I struggled picturing my life with a family. Now, I can't in a million years picture my life without Brynn, or Michael and Ella.

CHAPTER ELEVEN

Brynn

CALEB BACKS THE boat into one of the few available slips for the second time in as many days. Most personal boats have to be out of the harbor in October, but thankfully I was able to work it out with the city and harbor department. Having the old lobster boat of a respected lobsterman, my grandfather, didn't hurt when pleading my case. Every time I'm on the boat I feel his gentle strength and miss his wisdom. He would have approved of this family. I can almost sense it here on the boat. He would loathe the accident that brought us all here, but he would like Caleb and me together. He always had. My grandfather would also approve of attending as much of Christmas by the Sea as possible. It was his favorite time of year.

Yesterday, we bundled up and took our place along

the street for the Christmas Parade, then enjoyed a horse and carriage ride. We wrapped up the night with the Christmas tree lighting and carols at the harbor park. By the time we got back to the house, we were all popsicles, but smiling popsicles.

Michael and Ella lumber up the ladder from the cabin. "Are we here?"

Caleb chuckles at their heavy eyes and lack of enthusiasm. "Affirmative. Better get jolly, Christmas by the Sea is an all hands evolution."

Michael frowns. "What?"

"Your uncle is trying to be funny."

"Oh."

Ella simply shakes her head. Caleb shrugs and steps off the boat onto the pier turning and helping the rest of us off.

On the dock, I take Ella's hand, and Caleb hold's Michael's. "Like yesterday, stay close and keep hold of our hands."

"Yes, ma'am." The children harmonize, and I smile when Caleb's voice joins theirs. Before the mad dash from event to event starts, I take a minute to admire the town of Camden decked out in holiday style as we walk. Wreaths on the doors and LED candles in the window hail back to its history, as do the pineapples adorning some as a traditional welcome. Christmas trees twinkle from windows and more wreaths hang from streetlights.

A childlike excitement builds with each step.

"Dad texted—they'll be in or near the Owl and Turtle bookstore."

He shares a conspiratorial look with me. "Lead on."

After a few blocks on Bay View, and weaving through the waves of people enjoying an early start like we are, I wave to my parents standing in front of the bookstore. They meet us halfway.

"So, we meet again." My dad chuckles.

"Brynn had us up and squared away at O dark thirty. We're ready to get this holiday started."

Mom laughs and shakes her head. "It sounds like you need coffee." She drops her gaze to the children. "And Michael and Ella need to pick a book."

Both children are instantly awake. Michael's drops Caleb's hand. "Really?"

"Really." Mom winks.

Books are all it takes to turn loyalties and Caleb and I are dropped for grandparents. Dad nods to the bookstore. "Why don't you both grab a coffee or something at the café?"

I slip my hand in Caleb's. "Sounds like we've been dismissed."

He squeezes my hand. "Thoroughly."

We part ways with Mom and Dad once we step through the door. After we get our coffee, we settle into seats, grateful for the hot drink and warm atmosphere.

"Frank and Rose get the children books every year still?"

I lower the mug I'd just been raising to my mouth. "Sure do. They'll get one today and then Mom and Dad will pick out a couple more for Christmas presents."

"That's an outstanding tradition. Michael and Ella are lucky to have Rose and Frank. Hell, they're lucky to have Brian, too, not that I'd ever want it to get back to him that I said so."

"They're lucky to be a part of your family, too. Audrey is amazing, taking them aside and reading to them with hot chocolate by the fire every Christmas evening."

"Yeah, Mom is great, but my father—"

I wish I could ease his mind by defending Hal even a little, but he grills Michael about what activities he should be participating in and ignores Ella, so I can't find a defense, and after the last holiday I'm more likely to condemn.

"Michael has you now as an example.

His laugh is derisive. "Yeah."

His eyes turn glacial, and I angle my head to see what he's staring at outside. As if conjured by his name, Hal is walking past the store. A much younger woman walks next to him trying to catch his hand.

"His new paralegal, I take it?"

I shift in my chair, so I'm facing him again. "Yes. Alice."

"What a piece of—"

"Caleb, not today. No more talk about him, please."

He scrubs a hand over his face and then downs the rest of his coffee. "Absolutely, you're right."

I grasp for a topic to restore his good mood. "So, what are you asking Santa for?"

"You saying 'I do' January 1st." His answer was so quick and direct, I almost spit out my coffee and swallow hard to get it down. His mouth turns in a teasing smile. "You okay, Angel?"

"Yes, I—"

"Uncle Caleb." The familiar call of the four-year-old fills the space between the children and us.

I smile. "Our time is up."

He winks. "Our time is just beginning."

There's no time to respond. Michael beats Ella to Caleb and me. His eyes are bright as he takes a book from a bag. "Look what Nana and Gramps got me. It's called *Dog Tags*, about a Marine and his dog."

Caleb picks up the book. "Hey, that sounds like a great story."

Michael turns to me. "Can I read it to you, Aunt Brynn?"

"Absolutely. We'll start tonight." Surprising me, he climbs on my lap.

Ella pushes her way to Caleb and hands him her book. "*The Rabbit Listened.* This looks like an excellent choice, too."

She points to the cover where a child is hugging a rabbit. "Bunny."

Scooping her up, he sits her on his lap. "That's right."

I wrap my arms around Michael. Caleb chats with Ella and my parents are walking towards us, but the feel of the small boy on my lap is the focus of all my attention. It slams into me—Michael is mine. Somewhere in the last year, he became more than my nephew; he became my son. I hug him close.

When I meet my dad's smile, he nods as if I just spoke my heart out loud. He addresses all of us. "Do we want to watch Santa come in by boat, or get to the library so we're there right at the start of him reading?"

Michael stiffens against me. "Watch Santa!" Ella cheers.

Dad focuses on Michael. "We've got one vote. How about you, Michael?"

"We can watch him come in."

I share a look with Caleb at what almost sounds like fear in his voice. "You sure?"

He tips his head back to meet my gaze. "Yes, ma'am."

Dad claps his hands. "Okay, then let's head over."

Pushing out of the chairs, we gather the books and Mom puts them in her backpack. Caleb totes Ella, and I hold Michael's hand. Mom steps next to me as we walk out of the store. I lean closer, so I'm not yelling over all the chatter on the street. "Didn't Audrey want to come out again today?"

"She did, but her throat was scratchy this morning and she didn't want to risk giving the kids a cold."

I picture Hal and Alice walking down Bay View without a care about who sees their PDA. Poor Audrey, she's made her mistakes with her children, but I still feel for her.

My mom's voice brings me back to the present. "Michael and Ella told us all about the snowpeople and ornaments."

"Oh?" I give Michael's hand a squeeze.

"You're a good mother, Brynn."

"Thank you, that means everything coming from you."

She winks at Michael when he glances at her, then lifts her chin using it to point to Caleb. "Looks and sounds like he's fitting in, too."

"He is." I hold her gaze asking without words what she thinks about Caleb and me.

"That's your choice, sweetheart, but make it quick." She gives an almost invisible nod to Michael.

Dad and Caleb are deep in conversation, as well, but I can't hear them even when we stop. I hope it's about sports and not Hal.

When I tap Caleb's arm, he turns. "Sorry to interrupt, but Michael can't see. Can you lift him and I'll lift Ella?"

"Absolutely."

He passes the lighter Ella to me and lifts Michael onto his shoulders. The talk stops and all eyes turn to watch the small lobster boat approach, then applause. Santa and Mrs. Claus usher in the season with them. The couple waves as the lobster boat sails by. I'm not familiar with the couple playing the jolly Clauses this year, but they're excellent choices as they look like they stepped from a Rockwell painting.

"Wave, guys!" I encourage the children. Ella's little hand waves frantically, but Michael barely holds his up.

When Santa passes us, Caleb turns. "Let's start towards the library."

I hook Ella to my hip and start walking, my parents leading the way like bodyguards clearing the crowd before us.

I look to Caleb, who has Michael riding on his shoulders so we can move fast. "I'm thinking we should eat lunch after Santa reads *The Night Before Christmas*, then wait in line to see him. What do you think?"

"Yeah, we can backtrack if they want to see him."

"Mom."

"Yes," she hollers back over the cheering and chatter.

"We'll need to eat after the reading. We had a big

breakfast, but it's going to wear off with all the moving and excitement."

"Got it." She slows for a second. "Just remember we have to be to the auditorium by three for *The Nutcracker*."

I jostle Ella and join her joy when she squeals at the announcement. "We won't."

CHAPTER TWELVE

Caleb

WITH LUNCH WINDING down, I decide to brooch the Jolly Old Elf subject. "You two want to get a picture with Santa?" I try to put as much ho, ho, ho in my voice to encourage a positive response. Ella's eyes grow big and a sheen of moisture gathers. Michael drops his gaze and gives his head a quick shake.

I shrug at Brynn. "Looks like a no, Angel."

Her brow furrows and she replaces the spoon in her broccoli and cheese soup without taking a bite. "Ella, you love Santa. Why don't you want a picture with him?"

The little pixie doesn't blink. "I like him leaving presents and reading."

"Michael?"

The boy doesn't lift his head, just gives it another

shake. Frank opens his mouth then shuts it, remembering his promise to let us parent the children.

Brynn mirrors my earlier shrug. "You're right, looks like a negative."

I shove in the last bite of my Italian sandwich and stare out the window to Camden Harbor while I think. Decision made, I turn from the cold water and gray sky to the warmth and fall colors in Brynn's eyes. "Well, if we're not going to see Santa, Michael and I have a stop to make."

Michael's head snaps up and he slides from his seat. "I'm ready."

I smile at how eager he is for a mission he knows nothing about. He reminds me of the young Marines.

Brynn lifts an eyebrow and I return the gesture and then wink. "We'll meet you at the ballet."

She stops staring me down trying to read my mind regarding where I'm going and smiles. "Never thought I'd hear, 'meet you at the ballet', out of that Alpha mouth."

I chuckle and shift my gaze between Michael and Ella. "I have a feeling you're going to hear and see a lot you never thought you would in the next few years."

"Oh, can't wait—"

Before she can continue, Ella tugs on her sweater. "Aunt Brynn, do we have a stop?"

The smile she gives Ella could bring a man back to

life. "Yes, we do with Nana and Gramps."

The little girl claps and starts to sing a made-up Christmas song about stopping with her aunt. It's adorable and hits me right in the heart.

I lift a hand saying goodbye to Frank and Rose, then drop a kiss on Ella's head and then Brynn's. "See you in a bit."

"Okay," Ella answers before Brynn can.

Tucking Michael's hand in mine, I lead him from the Camden Deli. "What's our stop, Uncle Caleb?"

"We're heading back over to Bay View to Camden Jewelry Company to get your aunt an engagement ring."

"Good, she needs one of those." I hear Liz speaking through her son.

I hold back my laugh. "I thought so."

Spending the past couple days in downtown Camden is leaving me torn. It's feeling more like home with every shared look with Brynn and stroll holding the tiny hand of Michael, or Ella. But then I see Hal and his paralegal and recalling similar images throughout our childhood strips the day of some of its merriment.

Michael's hand squeezing mine brings me back to the moment and the trust and love in the small movement erases the last dark shadow from the scene earlier. "You want to go to the toy store later?"

He shakes his head. "No thank you."

What child doesn't want to go to a toy store near

Christmas? My new mission of the day is to forget my shit and focus full force on what's going on with Michael.

Walking into the jewelry store, I guide him over to the rings and sit on my heels beside him. He angles his head toward me. "What do you think?"

"I think Brynn likes color, so we'll steer clear of the solo diamond."

He nods and turns back to the rings. "Her eyes turn almost green when she's happy. You make her happy, so green?"

I squeeze his shoulder. "Good call, that's why I brought you."

"May I help you?"

I stand when the clerk stares over the counter at us. "We'd like to see these two rings with emeralds."

"Yes, sir."

She sets them on the counter, and smiles when I lift Michael to show him the rings. I point to the ring with the white gold setting.

"I'm thinking this one, bud, what about you?"

He studies each as if he's the one proposing. "Yeah, I like that one best, too."

I set Michael back down on his feet, before straightening and handing the clerk the ring. "This in a six, please."

"This is a six, sir. Should I box it up?"

"Please."

"Uncle Caleb?"

I hold up my finger to stop her. "Yeah?"

"Gramps gave me a little money to get you and Aunt Brynn something. Is there anything here I can afford?" He hands me a ten-dollar bill.

"Absolutely. How about some earrings?"

His mouth curves into a 100-watt smile. I turn back to the clerk. "Would you mind showing the young man some earrings? Silver."

"Yes, of course."

God bless her, she brings a selection of silver earrings that don't cost hundreds of dollars. Michael gasps and points to a pair of snowflakes. "Those. Do I have enough for those?"

"Just enough, bud. Perfect choice."

He frowns. "But then I don't have anything for you."

"No worries."

"You sure? Is there a cheaper pair?"

"Michael, your aunt Brynn deserves a nice gift. Get the snowflakes. I'll enjoy looking at her wearing them."

His forehead tugs into a frown and he runs a small finger over the fifty-dollar pair of earrings. "Okay. I'll get these."

I push the ten dollars and my card at the cashier. After she rings us up and wraps the earrings, I tuck the bag into my coat. "As far as Brynn knows, we struck out at our stop."

He smiles and nods. "Yes, sir."

"You and your son have a Merry Christmas."

Taking Michael's hand, I smile at the clerk. "Thank you, Merry Christmas to you."

Walking to the Camden Opera House, I keep my strides as small as possible so he doesn't feel like a chihuahua keeping up with a Great Dane. With a few warm days after the storm, the snow is melted from the sidewalks, but the piles from being shoveled bear witness to it. I check the sky, and while overcast, it doesn't look like anything is brewing.

After a few minutes of silence I ask, "Why didn't you want to see Santa?"

"I'm too old for Santa."

"I hope not. I'm older than you and I'm not too old for Santa. Now the truth."

"Only good kids should see Santa. He'll know I'm bad."

Holy shit. My mind races with what to say and how to get my heart dislodged from my throat. "Why are you bad?"

"I don't want to talk about that, please."

"I'll let it go, for now."

"Thank you."

Brynn and Ella are waiting for us outside the opera house. Ella's smile grows. Brynn's drops when she sees us and I realize I look as much like shit as I feel. "Didn't you have fun?"

Michael seems to recover. "We sure did. But we struck out at our stop."

"Oh, that's too bad."

He glances back at me. "But I liked being with Uncle Caleb, just us."

"Well, then you didn't strike out." He takes her hand and she lifts her gaze to me and raises an eyebrow, which seems to be our mode of conversation these days. I shake my head and she nods toward the door. We're getting the silent chats down to an art. "Mom and Dad are guarding our seats; we better go inside."

"Absolutely."

She keeps hold of both Ella and Michael's hands, and I follow the little family into the theater. There's been a shift from aunt to mom with Brynn, and even though the kids still call her Aunt Brynn, a person would have to be obtuse not to hear it in their voices; they're addressing their mother.

How do I fit in the family? I'm not "Dad" yet even if Michael did call me that the other day. There are times I feel like I'm there, and then I'm Uncle Caleb again. So far, I've been playing the part of Staff Sergeant with all the answers but feeling like first-day recruit who doesn't know which way the mess hall is. Meanwhile I'm batting at hand grenades like the one Michael just tossed and hoping I say and do the right thing. Fun Uncle Caleb is running out of fun, and reality is biting me in the ass.

Brynn angles her head over her shoulder and smiles at me. I try to smile back, but by the way hers fades, I know I missed. When we settle into our seats, she laces her fingers with mine. "You okay?"

"Yeah, we'll talk later."

"Ella, what are you doing?"

The little girl stops her low crawl over Brynn's lap. "I want to sit on Caleb."

"Did you ask him?"

Ella, clearly spending too much time around Brynn and me, lifts an eyebrow with a look that says she never even considered I'd say no, and I don't. "Come on over."

She continues over and then nestles in my lap. More shifting occurs as Michael moves from his seat to sit next to Brynn. As the curtain opens to the Christmas scene, the ballet fades, and in front of me plays out the scene of Brynn bringing a ragged-looking Christmas tree over while I sat in a plywood barrack and held her hand just like I'm doing now.

The scene changes on the stage and the Nutcracker is doing battle with the Mouse King. In my mind, the scene changes and I'm opening the letter from Mark's lawyer in a barrack in Afghanistan. Reading it for the millionth time, I battled with tossing the letter and letting Brynn raise the children alone, or coming back to

Maine hoping it wasn't too late for us.

Days on deployment give ample time for thought as one blends into the next with a *Groundhog Day* experience. That's what I did: think. The more I thought about Michael and Ella, the more I wanted to be their guardian. The more I thought about Brynn, the more I realized how much I've always wanted her and what an asshole I was for doing the one thing I promised her I never would, letting her go.

Ella leans back and rests her head on my chest, snapping me out of my inner musings just as the Mouse King falls and the Nutcracker becomes a prince. Ella, Michael, and the Reillys are transfixed as the Snow King and Queen appear. Brynn is staring at me. I hold her gaze sharing without words where my thoughts were. She shifts in her seat and directs her attention back to the ballet.

Staying in the present, I split my attention between dancers and Ella squirming this way and that on my lap, humming along to the music from the orchestra. Who needs sugar plum fairies when there's Ella in the world? When the curtain closes for the last time, we join in the standing ovation even as Brynn starts herding the children out. We switch children outside the theater and continue shepherding the kids to the heads.

Meeting back in the lobby, I hold up a finger for her to give us a second and take Michael aside, sitting on my heels so we're forced to make eye contact. "Michael, did you want a picture with Santa? No lies."

"I would, but…"

Resting a hand on his shoulder, I give a slight squeeze. "I'm not going to push you for an answer today about why you think you're not a good kid, but the big elf and I, we know different. If you want a picture, we'll take you and you'll see—he won't even blink."

He glances at the family and back. "He's gone, though. I'm too late."

"He's in Lincolnville. We'll have to triple-time, but we'll make it."

He kicks at the ground and pushes his glasses up. "You sure, Uncle Caleb? I don't want to—"

"You're not putting us out. You're not bad. What's the choice?"

"Please."

"Good."

I give his shoulder an encouraging squeeze and then lead him back to where everyone is waiting. Brynn zips Ella's puffy pink coat, and her gaze cuts from me, to him, and then back. Her mouth curves in a questioning smile. "Everything all right?"

"Yeah, we've gotta hustle, Angel. Michael wants a picture with Santa."

"Oh!" She glances down to Michael and then to her parents. "Can you drive us to Lincolnville?"

Frank jingles his car keys. "Sure thing. Let's go."

Like an operation where every Marine knows their part, we manage to get to Lincolnville and in line for photos with Santa. Brynn has Ella on her hip as I stand behind Michael with my hands on his shoulders. He steps from one foot to the other.

"You still good to go?"

"Yes, sir."

With all the people waiting, the room feels like my last training in the jungle. Brynn unzips Ella's coats and manages to wrangle the girl out of it while still holding her. "You want a picture with Santa?"

The little girl shakes her head. Michael hands me his coat and looks around me to Ella. "You could go with me. That way you're not alone." The kid isn't fooling me—he doesn't want to go alone. Whatever works.

Ella's brow furrows and she stares at the jolly old elf laughing with another child. While not looking completely convinced, she nods. "Okay."

Michael's shoulders relax, and it's our turn. He nervously smoothes the front of his red sweater. Brynn and I walk the kids up, and Santa opens his arms. "Ho, Ho, Ho."

Mrs. Claus bends closer, and she looks like she stepped out of the North Pole for real. "What are your names?"

The children mumble a response. I lift Michael onto

one knee and Brynn sits Ella on the other. We step back and I have to hold back my laughter. Neither child looks altogether sold on the experience until the Santa starts talking to them. I thank God he's a good Santa: real beard, real gut, and Santa personality all the way.

He asks each what they want for Christmas and Ella rattles off a list. Michael shrugs and then says something only Santa can hear.

"Okay, look over here."

The three look at the photographer taking the pictures and, finally relaxed, their smiles are real. With a reminder to go to bed early Christmas Eve, Santa helps them down and they scurry over to us.

Brynn catches Ella and I catch Michael. We're getting good at this partnership. "How'd it go?"

"You were right. He was nice. He didn't even ask me."

"Ask you what?" Brynn glances back as we make our way to pick up the picture.

"If I was a good boy."

She chuckles. "Because he already knew you were. He could tell that just by looking you're wicked good."

Again, she proves she knows the perfect thing to say as his chest puffs up a little. This was a step, but it's not over. Whatever happened to make this kid think he's so bad Santa would reject him can't be solved with one visit and a picture.

This all comes down to one person. I could almost hear the voice when Michael told me why he couldn't see Santa. That Mark either fell so far he started spouting the same bile, or let his son be around it, disappoints me on two fronts. I could kick Mark's ass for allowing it. Hell, I could kick mine for avoiding home as much as I did and allowing the darkness too close to my little brother and his family, and to Brynn for the last year. I thought I could ignore my father, avoid him like always, but to do so lets him continue on as if he's right.

"Oh, these turned out great!"

I snap to attention at Brynn's voice and focus on the photograph, though the image would stay with me forever physical photo or not. "Yeah, those are outstanding."

She shows the kids, who don't see what we do, and if I had to guess aren't as thrilled about memorializing the moment.

Brynn nudges my arm. "Caleb, let's get a big print, okay?"

Her excitement at having a picture with the children and Santa makes the trip doubly worth the rush to get here. "Yeah, sure."

She ruffles Michael's hair and jostles Ella on her hip. "Thanks for doing this, guys."

Michael steps back against me. "You're welcome, Aunt Brynn."

"Welcome," Ella echoes.

Taking the sample image, I turn to order the large print with Michael still almost wrapped around my leg. Brynn is chattering with her folks about how adorable the kids look in the picture and what a great Santa they have this year. It would be a perfect moment if Michael's little hands didn't tighten on my jeans when Frank asks him what he asked Santa for.

"Socks and something else."

"What else?"

"Something I can't say."

Frank leans back and nods like an all-knowing sphinx. "Ayuh, a secret between you and Santa? I understand."

His grip tightens and it's like he's squeezing my heart. I can guess what his other wish is and I'm praying for the same. We're both wishing for home. If I thought Santa could help, I'd go sit on the big man's lap myself.

CHAPTER THIRTEEN

Brynn

ELLA AND MICHAEL dump their paper plates in the trash. "Thanks for the pizza, Aunt Brynn, Uncle Caleb."

"Thank you." Ella echoes her brother.

"You're welcome." I glance between the two. They look almost ready to crash after the busy day of Christmas activities. "You want to watch some television?"

Michael shakes his head. "Can I read to you?"

"Yeah!" Ella chants, always up for anyone to read, even her brother.

"Sure. Let me finish up here."

Caleb pushes off the bench. "You guys go ahead. I'll clean up."

Michael's gaze drops and I can see he wanted to read to Caleb, too, but I sense Caleb needs some alone time.

"Sounds good. Let's get ready for bed and then you can read to Ella and me."

Padding downstairs and to the living room fifteen minutes later, I drop next to Caleb on the sofa and snuggle close to his side. He drapes an arm over my shoulders, and for a few minutes we sit in silence listening to the fire crackle. "How long did they last?"

"About five minutes before even the adventures of a Marine and his dog couldn't keep them focused. Then it took me another ten minutes to move just right to pry myself loose without waking them up. Michael wants to be a Marine."

He huffs a laugh. "We'll see how long it lasts."

"You don't think he could make it?"

"At seven years old, no. I'll reserve judgement until he's at least ten."

I shove at his side and chuckle. "Good point." We sit in silence for a little longer. "Caleb, what's wrong? You've seemed sad all day even though you hid it well from the others."

"Not sad. Thinking things through." He scrubs a hand over his face. "Scratch that—one revelation was a bullet to the heart."

"I'll ask first, what were you thinking through? Doubts?"

"Not about us. Finding my footing."

"That's a little vague." He shrugs. Exhaling a deep

breath, I try another question. "Okay, you don't want to talk about it. I get it. So what hurt your heart?"

"I asked Michael why he didn't want to see Santa and he told me it's because only good kids should see him. He was afraid Santa…fucking Santa would turn him away. I could hear the voice of Hal Quinlin telling Mark and me the same thing."

I can feel the tears cut down my cheeks, but I can't stop them. "Oh shit, it's so much worse than I thought." My stomach churns. "You don't think he's been telling Michael that at family get-togethers?" It would rip me open to think I let Michael near such toxin.

He shakes his head. "I think it's been going on before the accident. I don't know if Mark started spreading that bullshit. But for all I know my father spread it while neither Mark or Liz knew it. I intend to find out."

"I'm so sorry, Caleb."

"Don't be. It's not about Hal and me anymore, it's about the boy. I won't let Michael down like I did Mark."

I caress his cheek with my fingertips. "When did you ever let your brother down?"

"Just when I announced at thirteen I had no intention of being a lawyer, turning all Hal's attention to Mark. Or leaving when I was seventeen and only coming back when I wanted to be with you on leave. And let's face it by the time I was done with Boot, training for my

MOS, and first deployment, we couldn't get our earlier closeness back."

"You were young. You were living your life."

"I was focused on me and the Marines and little else. But I can do something now, for Michael and Ella."

"Yes, you can. You can be their father."

He breaks from my touch and paces to the window, looking out at the sea and to land where the Christmas lights bring the coast to life in the dead of winter. "Mark is their father."

Pushing off the couch, I stand in front of him. "He is, but he's gone. They need a father who's alive, Caleb, not just an uncle who cares for them. I realized today I'm no longer Aunt Brynn; I'm their mother. Correct that, I realized it months ago, today I decided to stop acting like I'm not."

"I recognized that, too. I'm not there yet, Brynn."

"I know. I've had longer to merge into the role."

"What if I never merge into the role of dad?"

His voice reminds me of Michael when he doesn't think he'll ever understand an assignment. I allow a smile and slip in front of him, resting my palms on his chest. "I think you already have. You have to allow yourself to see it and it might take some time, but don't close yourself off to the children or to me." The last three words come out as a choked whisper as old hurts creep into a tender a moment.

He cups my cheek with his large calloused hand. "You should have made me pay a lot longer for the pain I caused you."

I rub my cheek against his warm flesh. "I probably should have, but I've loved you too much for too long. I let twenty-seven years of friendship override two years of pain." I smile against his hand. "And I think we both paid long enough."

He drops his hand. "I didn't plan this op very well."

"You thought you'd come here and we'd fuck and take care of the kids as aunt and uncle, which means endless fun and none of the problems."

"Exactly. Familiar to you."

"Very. Although I didn't think I'd have you, so the whole fucking part wasn't even in the scenario."

"Well, it's a huge part of the current picture."

My hands are still on his chest, and I curl my fingers around hunks of his plaid shirt and give it a tug. "Seriously, Caleb, give us some time and don't let Hal's voice into your head."

"I'll give it one hundred and twenty percent, Angel."

"You're really doing an outstanding job."

"Glad you think so. I feel like I'm treading water. You're a pro."

I try not to, but I burst out laughing. "Glad you think so."

My laughter dies when his lips connect to my neck.

"You're amazing. Don't ever doubt it."

"Mmmm…" is all I can manage.

His breath is warm when he moves his mouth to my ear. "What's on the plan for tomorrow?"

"Tomorrow?"

His laugh rolls through me. "Day after today?"

"Oh, Christmas tree."

He leans back and raises an eyebrow. "Really?"

"Yeah."

"So soon?"

"We didn't have a tree last year; I want to make up for that."

He shrugs. "Roger that."

Lacing the fingers of both of our hands together, I side nod to the stairs and wag my eyebrows. "You ready for bed? We can make some waves."

"Yeah."

Before I can start walking, he closes his fingers and gives me a tug. "Are you going to ask the kids to start calling you Mom?"

"No, I want that to be their choice, not mine. I've crossed that line, but I don't know if they have." He doesn't say anything, just gives a sharp nod. "Why?" I lift on the balls of my feet and nip his chin trying to bring a little light to what turned into a bleak night.

"I wasn't ready to face their questions, or know what I'd say if they turned to me next. Michael calling me Dad the other day shook my foundation."

"I noticed. But I have full faith you will know when they look to you and ask, or if they simply start calling you Dad. Just like you always knew what to do no matter what surprise came our way in combat."

He smiles and I feel like I won a small battle. "Glad you thought I knew what I was doing. I was just fucking tossing whatever I could out there."

"Good, then you're already halfway to parenthood."

He opens his mouth and I squeeze his hands and shamelessly toss all Devil Doc out the window and whine, "Come on, love, no more talk tonight. I really want you and we're taking a risk of a storm moving in."

"Say no more."

"Wha—" is all I get out as he tosses me over his shoulder and starts running up the stairs.

CHAPTER FOURTEEN

Brynn

THE MIRROR FOGS with steam from the shower, and I wipe it off with my towel. I turn back to rubbing my moisturizer into my face when I cut a glance to the shower curtain opening. As much as I try to keep my focus on the moisturizer, it keeps straying to the mountain of chiseled muscle stepping out of the tub and scrubbing a towel over each hard, yummy ridge.

"You're staring, Brynn."

I shrug. "You're worth staring at."

He drops the towel on the white tile floor and pads over, standing behind me. I catch his gaze in the glass. We're getting our rhythm with sharing a bathroom every morning. He reaches around me and opens the medicine cabinet. I chuckle when he presses unnecessarily close. "Hey, Marine, that's a big gun your carrying. Back up."

I smile at his image in the mirror as he winks and wags his eyebrows. "What? I'm just getting my toothbrush."

"Yeah, well you were close to giving me something, too."

"I would again, Angel, but three times last night and once before the kids were up—you're wearing me out."

"I'll believe that when I'm dead. If Michael and Ella weren't downstairs watching cartoons—"

"You'd be up against the wall getting the pounding you deserve."

Our conversation is making the bathroom a hundred times steamier than it is already. I twist at the waist and give his chest a gentle shove. "I give. Stop talking and back up."

The low rumble of his chuckle only makes me burn more. After putting toothpaste on his toothbrush, he steps back, but I can still connect to those ice-blue eyes in the mirror. Thinking of Christmas carols and anything else to cool me down, I return to the task of getting ready. I start rubbing lotion on my arms and legs.

His baritone voice is rough, but there's a hint of teasing. "You need help with that?"

I refuse to meet his gaze and see just how serious he is. "Negative. You're dismissed."

"Dismissed?"

With a sigh, I point to the door. "You are way too

distracting this morning, and I need to get ready. Please, get out."

"Yes, ma'am."

Grabbing the towel on the floor, he tosses it in the hamper. As he starts to walk past me he stops and lowers his head. I don't hesitate to meet him in a quick kiss.

I also don't hesitate to watch every move he makes, and how sexy he is even tossing laundry or how mouthwatering he looks walking away.

There's something odd but comforting about hearing him move around in the next room getting dressed. I wonder if when we're eighty he'll still step out of the shower and we'll flirt until it gets too hot. The lightest tap on our door captures my attention.

"I've got it, Brynn."

"Thanks."

When I hear Ella's voice, I lean closer to the half-open bathroom door to listen to the conversation. I peek through the slit between the door and the wall and—my heart. Caleb is sitting on his heels as Ella, still in her footsie pajamas, swings the bulldog he got her a few Christmases ago, and he nods. "Can you come feed me, Uncle Caleb?"

"Absolutely. What do you want?"

"Waffles, please."

He stretches to his full height, towering over Ella, and takes her tiny hand in his before they walk out of my sight. I finish braiding my hair and go into the bedroom to dress. After tugging on my jeans and favorite blue sweater, I sink onto the bed. Taking a minute alone, I swallow a few breaths and simply listen to the clatter of dishes and chatter of little voices downstairs along with the occasional "uh-huh" from Caleb.

Standing, I walk to the window and look across the inlet to the town of Camden. Rooftops are covered in snow against the blue of the sky and water. Since 1835, keepers have lived in this house, and I wonder how many looked to the town just like I'm doing now. Did they crave the isolation, or in their desire to save the lives of those at sea, ignore the loneliness?

I lean my head on the window frame. Since Caleb arrived, I haven't had those moments of feeling alone. Even with the children, I found myself wishing for the adventure, comradery, and terror of being a corpsman. But this house, for whatever reason, seems to hold me. I release a laugh with my breath at the fanciful thought that the beacon and I shared the duty of rescuing brave souls tossed about in a storm, whether on sea or sand.

I turn my attention to the sound of small feet padding into the room and smile down at Ella, holding her bulldog close. "Aunt Brynn you gotta help Uncle Caleb."

"Why?"

"He's putting ham *in* the waffles."

With a chuckle, I push off the window frame. "It's

something he learned from another Marine named Hanson. It's good."

Her nose wrinkles and her forehead tugs together in a distrustful frown. "Like peas are good?"

My chuckle turns to laughter, and I sweep her into my arms. "No, like ice cream is good. You can at least try it?"

"Okay. Are you?"

"Absolutely. I love your uncle's waffles." *Among other things.*

"Is Michael eating them?"

"Yes, he'll try them, too." Her head bobs in a silent agreement and I give her a squeeze. "Let's head down."

After setting Ella on her feet, I follow one step at a time as she holds onto the railing with one hand and her dog with another. As our feet touch the floor, Caleb steps from the kitchen. "Bringing reinforcements, Little Bit." Taking my hand, she nods and Caleb tosses her a wink. "It's ready."

Walking into the kitchen, I help Ella into her chair and then step behind Michael's chair and cup his cheeks. Tipping his head up, I drop a kiss to his forehead. "How are you, kiddo?"

"Good."

I pat his cheeks and glance around the table. "Wow, you set the table and everything."

Caleb points his chin at Michael. "I had help."

Sitting down, I smile at the small boy, and my heart and smile grows when he pushes his glasses up on his nose. As usual, Caleb slides behind me and wraps an arm around me while placing the waffles on the table. I tip my head to meet his gaze. "Looks good."

"Sure does."

"Caleb." I try to say his name like I do to the kids as a warning, but it comes out as an invitation. He brushes his lips against mine for the briefest taste that holds so many promises, and I know he'll see each promise kept.

He sits next to me, and I return to the moment, almost laughing at the wide eyes and opened mouths of the children. Caleb starts serving up the waffles. "Didn't your parents kiss?" I ask, and Caleb chuckles and shakes his head.

Michael shrugs. "You guys kiss different."

"How?"

"Longer."

I try, but my lungs will explode if I don't laugh. Caleb joins me with his full, deep rumble of thunderous laughter. He manages to get a waffle on each child's plate and ruffles Michael's hair. Both children look at us like we've lost it. I continue to shake with laughter even as I get Ella's waffle buttered and pour syrup on top. Caleb helps Michael.

Caleb manages to say a quick blessing and we dig into breakfast. Glancing over to Ella shoveling in the waffles, I don't even have to ask if her uncle's breakfast suits her just fine.

"When do we go get the tree?"

I swallow hard and take a sip of coffee to keep from choking on Caleb's question. "Brian's bringing the tree after church."

"Brian? And do you guys go to church?"

I take another gulp. "Not as regular as we probably should, and I'd arranged for Brian to bring our tree since he's getting Mom and Dad's at the Christmas Market."

"When was that decision made?" He shrugs and shoves another bite of waffle in his mouth.

"What?"

"Maybe I wanted to get our tree together. I'd have appreciated a heads-up."

Unable to stay sitting, I push up and point a finger in his face. "I do not have to get your approval on anything I do in this house or with these children. I have been handling everything for over a year and you come in here with your answers for everything and outstanding waffles and…well, other things that are outstanding and think I need your permission? Negative. I arranged this with Brian in October when he mentioned doing it and we'll wait for him."

"You finished?"

My blood pressure shoots to unhealthy proportions. "I'm about done with a lot of things."

His gaze cuts to the side, and that's when I groan and sink back down at the fearful faces of Michael and Ella glancing between us. When he starts speaking again, I'm impressed and want to slap him for his even, calm tone. "I was in no way suggesting you needed my go-ahead to do anything. Not knowing the plans were made long before my return, I just wanted a heads-up so I could have said I'd like to take the kids for a Christmas tree. We can do that next year. Whatever else is bugging you that caused that, I think it's best if we discuss later."

"Right." I resume eating, but the first bite goes down like a brick when I look up and the kids are still staring. "It's fine."

Michael nods and takes a bite, and my stomach flips when I watch him struggle swallowing as much as I did.

"I'm so sorry, to each of you. But really, it's fine."

I get a mumbled okay from each and I stare at the few bites, left sick that I ruined Caleb's breakfast. When Caleb finishes, he pushes off the bench and takes his dish and silverware to the sink, and the children follow like little ducklings.

"You want more coffee?" Caleb holds up the pot.

"No, thank you. Would you all want to help me get the decoration boxes?"

"Sure thing." Caleb's voice holds no hesitancy.

The children nod, still staying as close to Caleb as possible, waiting, I'm sure, for me to kick him out and crush their dreams. Sitting on my heels, I force a smile. "You both know people sometimes disagree, or say things they don't mean, right?"

"Yes, ma'am."

"Well, your uncle and I are human and that means there are times we're going to drive each other crazy. But it doesn't mean he'll leave, or I'll leave. Do you understand?"

"Yes, ma'am."

"Then you both can let go of his jeans so he can move."

Caleb shifts a bit to loosen their grip. "Come on, guys, let go. Your aunt and I had a blow-up, it's over. We're both sorry we lost it in front of you."

Their gazes drop to where their hands are secured around the legs of his jeans. They open their hands and return their eye contact to me.

Standing, I meet Caleb's raised eyebrow. "All good?"

"Good to go. Lead the way."

Pivoting on my heels, I start walking toward the guest bedroom upstairs with the plodding of feet behind me. It's been six days since Caleb arrived, six days, and it feels like he's always been a part of our little family except for this morning when he asked about the tree. Then it felt like six days and yet another person questioning my parenting. I'll have to make it right, but it's time we have a talk we should have had before I said yes to his plan.

CHAPTER FIFTEEN

Caleb

"OKAY, TELL ME if it's straight." I look through the balsam branches and smile at the furrowed brows on Brynn's, Michael's, and Ella's faces.

"Come on, Caleb, straight or not?" Brian grumps above me. I don't know what the rush is for him, he's standing and holding the trunk. I'm the guy under the stupid thing, tightening it into the tree stand and getting major rug burn.

Brynn inspects the tree from stern to bow. "Looks straight to me. You guys?"

"Yeah, to me too." Michael nods.

Ella steps closer and squats on her heels in front of me. "Is it pretty under there?"

"Come under and see."

In a blink I'm joined by Little Bit staring up through

the branches as I tighten the screws into the trunk. "It'll be prettier when we get the lights on."

"Oooh." She crawls closer with her bulldog being dragged by the ear. She scoots under my arm, bulldog and all. Her eyes close and it's the sweetest picture of contentment I've ever seen when she inhales the scent of balsam fir. "Nice."

Dropping a kiss on the top of her head, I try to absorb some of her light. "Very nice."

She turns on her side and in her four-year-old stage whisper leans close. "I love you, Uncle Caleb."

"Love you, too, Little Bit."

She kisses my cheek before crawling out butt first. "It's beautiful under there, Uncle Brian." I shake my head at her *booti-full*.

"Sure is."

My smile drops at the catch in the big man's throat. Sliding out from under the tree, only Michael and Ella are still looking at the tree, Brynn and Brian are avoiding eye contact at any cost.

"All right, Angel, you got the lights?"

Brynn snaps to attention. "Yeah." She grabs a coil of lights from the couch where she spread out the decorations. There's not a knot to be found in the wires. The lights are so squared away a drill sergeant would be proud.

"I'll head out then."

She rests a hand on her brother's arm, stopping him. "Stay. We're having hot chocolate after."

Brian leans down and brushes a kiss on her head. "Tempting, but I have a better offer at Mom and Dad's. It's taco night."

"Oh."

He holds out his hand, and I accept. With a firm shake, he tips his head to where Brynn stands. "Sorry, Caleb. I misjudged you. I should have known you'd do right by them all."

"I've messed up enough to give you doubt. Thanks for the tree."

"Absolutely." He sits on his heels. "Can this uncle get a hug?" The kids don't hesitate, but give a joint hug to the bear. "Okay, have fun." He turns to Brynn before stepping out. "I'll be out to check the light later this week. If you notice anything…"

"I'll let you know."

Michael and Ella start picking up each ornament and discussing which should go on first. I wave to the tree when Brynn's gaze snags mine. She takes one side and I take the other as we start winding the lights around the tree.

"This is a nice tree."

"Sure is, but not as nice as the one you gave me in Afghanistan."

She peeks around the tree. "It was the best I could

do."

"It was perfect." I wink and enjoy her cheeks turning pink. A woman who served alongside Marines and heard and saw more than anyone should, and she still blushes when I wink at her. Damn, I love this woman. She hands me the coil of lights and I hold her hand for a second before sending them around the tree.

"Looks good, Brynn." I conduct one more inspection, knowing each white fairy light will be in perfect order if it's in her house.

She sidles next to me. "You know what was perfect about that Christmas in Afghanistan?"

"What?"

She twines her fingers with mine. "We were together. Thank you for coming home."

"Thank you for always being home for me."

Michael steps next to us with an ornament. "Can we start decorating?"

I squeeze her hand. "Yep, get busy, buddy."

Michael hangs an ornament with his baby picture in it and *Baby's First Christmas* across the top of the frame. He lifts his face. "Mom always hung that one first. Then Ella's. She said those were her best Christmases, when we made her a mom." As he says it, Ella hooks hers a few branches down.

"Outstanding. Liz knew how to do Christmas."

"She did." His smile is pure pride.

Brynn releases my hand and I can feel she's trying to hold it together as much as I am, but I keep my focus on Michael. "Anything else she did you'd like to do?"

"She let Ella, or me, put the angel on top. We switched off years. Dad would lift us up to reach."

"Whose year is it?" Brynn asks as she hooks a little mouse ornament.

"Ella's. Mine was last year."

"We didn't have a tree last year. So, if you want…"

He shakes his head. "No, she can do it."

I pat his back. "You're a good man, Michael Quinlin."

"I want to be."

I don't respond, not sure that I could. I join in hanging ornaments. After a few, I switch jobs, and wait for Ella to hang hers. I then rehang hers since she's determined to cluster a hundred in one spot. The decorations belonging to Liz and Mark are clear as they are all figurines of *First Home, First Christmas Together,* and those belonging to the children such as Disney princesses and Transformers.

Michael passes me with two ornaments which halts my reaching for the last decoration Ella put on the tree. One is a Marine dress cover and the other a Navy dress cover. The only Navy uniform she wore were dress whites, the rest were Marine regs. I love her in dress whites, and she knows it. "What are those, Michael?"

"Those are mine," Brynn states, and then turns to hang a couple red bulbs.

I examine the ornaments. On the Marine cover there's writing: *Her Marine*. On the Navy is *His Doc*. "Where'd you find these?"

"Had them made at one of those custom ornament shops."

"Did you want to hang those, Uncle Caleb?"

"No, that's fine, bud. I was just looking." Tipping my head to the side, I continue to stare until I force Brynn's gaze to mine. "When did you have those made?"

"Before that last deployment. I thought…" Her shoulders lift, then drop.

"Yeah," I mumble. She thought we were getting ready to get out, take the next step.

The song on her phone changes to *Up on the House Top* and she and the children start singing along. "Caleb, you know the song, too…no shirking and no lip syncing."

Joining in, the air becomes lighter and I force past failures down. Laughing, I watch Ella shake her tiny toosh to the song as she and Michael belt it out with all the delight of children thinking of Santa. The picture of the two of them on Santa's lap setting on the mantle draws my attention. Their smiles appear real and their joy in this moment is tangible. Brynn's eyes sparkle a pure gold and her laughter is brighter than any Christmas star.

Inhaling the balsam like Ella did under the tree, I close my eyes and let the moment seep into my bloodstream and the marrow of my bones. But it isn't the tree, or the music, or the lights infusing my soul and filling the dark spaces. It's the three people around me. It's a tiny voice telling me she loves me, and a much huskier one telling me the same, and Michael working beside me this morning and squeezing my hand for a second before acting like he hadn't. There is no paper, or box, or even season that could contain the love each gifted me with.

I open my eyes when Brynn slides her arms around my waist and hugs me close, and each of the children hug one of my legs. No words are said. No words are needed. I don't know what song is playing; the music in my ears is much sweeter. As I hold tight to my anchors, the joy of the moment builds and I start laughing. Brynn and the children break from the hug and join in until we're all standing there laughing like we've lost our minds.

"Let's have chocolate!" Ella yells.

Laughing, I swing her up on my shoulders. "You've got one more job."

Brynn hands her the angel and Ella gasps. "Oh, she's pretty."

Sharing a smile with Brynn, I position the little girl to put the angel on the top. Michael stands at my side.

"You've got this, Ella. Just don't mess it up."

I chuckle at the typical brotherly encouragement. Ella places the angel on the limbs and spends a few moments primping her dress. Swinging the little girl down, I smile through her giggles. She lifts her arms. "That was fun! Again!"

"Let's get chocolate."

"Carry me, please." She stands with her arms up.

Lifting her back into my arms, I nod to the bulldog. "You want Chesty?"

Shaking her head, she curls her tiny fingers around my shirt. "I got you."

Yeah, you've all got me right by the heartstrings. I pray as I follow Brynn and Michael to the kitchen that she's ready to make this permanent, because there's no force strong enough to keep me from this family. My family.

Setting Ella in her seat, I grab the mugs for hot chocolate when my phone buzzes. After grabbing it out of my back pocket, I frown at the name on the screen then swipe to answer. "Hey Lisa."

Brynn narrows her gaze, but starts fixing the hot chocolate.

"Hi, Caleb, sorry to call you on a Sunday, but the owners of that bungalow in La Jolla are willing to meet you halfway on your bid."

"Oh shit…" I cringe at Ella's side-eye. "Sorry, Lisa, I meant to call you. I'm no longer planning to settle in La

Jolla."

"Oh, that's too bad." I know Brynn can hear Lisa, who's a bit loud, plus she's putting a lot more effort into fixing the children's chocolate and loading up the marshmallows than necessary.

"Yeah, sorry. But thanks for all your help."

"Anytime. You've got my number."

"Absolutely. Thanks again."

I swipe the off button and relax when Brynn turns to me and lifts a mug. "You want marshmallows?"

"I'll just take it straight today."

She sets the mug down with hers, almost overflowing with marshmallows. Michael and Ella are already sporting chocolate mustaches.

"For tonight only we can have dessert first. I got these yesterday." Brynn slides a plate of pastries on the table.

Ella eagerly snags a chocolate donut. I push the plate to Michael and I can see the war across his face. Once when Brynn and I were home on leave, we got dressed down for ice cream before supper. I shake my head; kind of like Brynn and I brought the hammer down on Brian for cake before lunch. I can't imagine the rules changed. What does a boy trying not to disappoint anyone do?

"Come on, bud. I'm having one." Nodding, he grabs an apple fritter. I grab the other fritter. "Good choice."

When Brynn finally settles next to me, she takes the

Boston crème. "You were looking at La Jolla?"

There's no anger or sarcasm in her tone, and her eyes are still bright and filled with joy. "For a bit when I first started to transition. We'd talked about it before."

Before we were guardians to our niece and nephew and the plan was a house by the beach with nights of skinny-dipping and days of fucking in every room. When I thought there was nothing on this planet that could bring me back to Maine and close to my father.

"Is it still something you want?"

I can't read the question, if she's testing me or thinking it might be a possibility. "I wouldn't say never, but we're happy here now." I decide to turn things around. "You?"

"If you ask me in January I'll be ready to pack, but I'm happy snug in our house here on Curtis Island."

"Me, too." Michael says around a bite of donut.

"Me, too." Ella agrees.

I wave a hand to the children. "Then it's unanimous."

Brynn leans closer. "So, who's Lisa?" She nudges my arm and winks.

"Hanson's cousin. He told me she was a good Realtor, and he's right."

Her eyes widen. "Hanson's cousin?"

Hanson lives the reputation Marines have for banging. I hold up a hand. "Don't even. She was my Realtor, that's it."

She frowns and licks my palm, which causes the kids to laugh and me to wish she was licking something else. "Don't be an a-hole, I know. I just can't imagine Hanson having family."

There's giggling from Michael and Ella even though they have no idea who Hanson is. Bending, I take a huge bite of her donut.

"Hey, Marine." She pushes me even as she laughs. "What was that for?"

I hike a brow, saying everything as I slowly chew the donut and try not to puke since I can't stand Boston crème.

Knowing that, she smiles and takes an equally big bite. "Mmmm-mmm."

"You guys are weird." Michael's face is the image of Mark when disgusted, from wrinkled nose to curled upper lip.

We both struggle to swallow and not yark the donut as we laugh…made even harder when Ella wrinkles her nose and shakes her head. "Gross."

After another day of holiday shenanigans, I sink onto the sofa and scrub my hand over my face. "No more waffle, donut, hot chocolate days," Brynn decrees as she flops next to me.

"Agreed. Sugar monsters replaced our kids."

"Holy shit, you're not kidding. And Ella's end-of-day

meltdown sealed the deal."

"Lessons learned."

Sharing a smile, we fist bump, but she opens her hand and I lace my fingers through hers. Her smile fades. "Sorry about this morning, I just..." She shrugs. "...lost it."

"Something tells me you deserved to lose it. And I could have phrased my question in a less accusatory manner. You want to share?"

"Until you imposed the no-questioning-our-parenting rule, everything I did was questioned. Guess I flipped out on you instead of them. And..."

"And?"

"Sometimes I think about our plans for sunshine and beaches and making love wherever, whenever we want, and naked weekends. And I wondered if you did, too."

"And now?"

"I know you do. I saw it on your face when you turned down the house in La Jolla, but I also saw how much you meant this is your home, and I heard your heart when you told Ella you loved her under the tree."

After leaning forward until she lies back and opens her legs, I settle between them and brush my lips over hers. "I'm really going to miss naked weekends."

Her laughter holds her heart and brings mine to life just like her hands did on the battlefield. "We never actually had them."

"Oh, I did, at least in my dreams. I dreamed of naked weekends every night."

Rubbing my nose against hers, I moan when her knuckles skates against my abs. My stomach muscles flex as she works the opening of my jeans. "I'm so sorry your dreams can't come true."

"I'm a man of many dreams, and you are very close to another one."

"Today was a dream for me."

"Except for breakfast."

She chuckles. "Affirmative."

"And Ella's meltdown."

"Affirmative. Now stop and sit up—let me give you a dream that's always top on your list." As I start to shift off of her, she nips my chin. "I want you to come in my mouth this time."

There is one part of sex with me Brynn never got into, and that was swallowing. "You don't have to, Angel, I like…"

She nips my chin again. "I want to."

Sitting up, I watch, entranced as Brynn steps between my legs and tugs off her sweater, then unhooks her bra. In the shimmer of the fire and Christmas tree, her skin glows. Her mouth curves in the smile only I get to see as she raises her arms and unhooks the messy bun, letting the chestnut waves tumble. The soft lights pick up the hints of red and gold in the thick locks.

She sinks to her knees and my erection strains against my jeans. I lift my hips as she tugs down my jeans and skivvies. I cannot take my eyes from her mouth as she edges closer and her pink tongue peeks between her lips.

"Holy shit!" My hip jerks when she touches her tongue to my cockhead and licks.

Her gaze shoots to the stairs. "Shhh, love, we don't want interruptions."

Cupping the back of her head, I bring her lips back to my cock. "I'll be good."

Locking her stare with mine, she opens her mouth and sucks my cockhead between her lips with gentle tugs and plenty of tongue right where it's needed. I lift my hips and she accepts more and then a little more as she pumps the root with her hand. I rock my hips and she closes her mouth tighter around my length.

Her response is a feast for all the senses. The soft moans and whimpers mix with the erotic sucks and deep draws. The way her eyes glaze over in lust and shift to a deep green with sparks of light. In those depths is what I want to see most—pleasure. As she provides out-of-this-world pleasure to me, she's contributing to her own bliss. Getting sucked off is always a fantasy. Getting sucked off and watching your woman's skin flush, nostrils flair, and eyes turn to fire is nirvana.

Brynn takes me deeper and I clench my jaw against the raw primal bellow. "You sure? 'Cause if I need to pull out, it needs to be now."

She frowns and anchors her fingernails into my thighs to keep me down. I dig my fingers in the soft silk of her hair and hold her steady as I flex my hips, driving deep and releasing as she keeps her lips sealed tight. Her throat works my cockhead as she swallows. It is by far one of the most sensual moments in all my experiences with Brynn. I push just a little deeper as I shudder through my climax and final stream of release. She pinches my thigh. Pulling her slowly off my cock, I unlock my fingers from her hair and flop back.

I open my eyelids with the sound of rustling clothes. Brynn, naked, straddles my lap. Her lips are swollen and red and her hair is a mess. She reminds me of an archangel, all fire and redemption. Her eyes are so hot the gold flecks consume the orbs. "Caleb, please."

I slide a finger between her pussy lips; she is soaking wet and trembles in pre-orgasm with just that touch. Massaging her clit with my thumb, I ease three fingers inside her. Her head falls back as her sex clenches around my fingers and her leg muscles shudder. Watching her orgasm, makes me hard.

"Shit, Angel, let me make you fly again."

She lowers her head and her fiery gaze collides with mine, and she runs the tip of her tongue over her lips. "Mmmm…Yes, please."

After a quick, hard kiss, I take my fingers from her

and guide my cock inside her. Gripping her hips, I slide her down until I am buried fully inside her.

Her eyelids flutter and then open, and she presses her lips to mine. Her lips part and I slide my fingers inside, and she licks her essence from them. I smile, and ease them from her mouth, before stroking my tongue with hers so we both savor just how perfect we are together.

She grinds against me as we deepen the kiss, never loosing either connection. I cup and mold her breasts as she explores my back, chest, and abs when her hands. Her kiss turns hard and desperate and her skin turns to fire under my hands as she whimpers into my mouth while she edges closer and closer to her orgasm. When she screams into my mouth, I flip her on her back and stroke deep as her sex grows even tighter while her inner muscles work my cock. With a jolt, I bury my head in the space between her shoulder and neck, roaring her name.

Her body vibrates under mine and I lift my head, expecting tears, but she's smiling and…laughing.

I'm helpless not to smile. She wraps her arms around my neck. "That was fun! Again!"

My smile turns to full-blown laughter at her echo of Ella's words earlier that day. "Oh, you're gonna get it again." Hiding my face between her shoulder and neck, I blow raspberries and nip her while tickling her sides.

"Caleb! Caaa-leb!" My name is shrieked on hysterical

laughter. My stomach burns with laughter as she struggles under me.

Her head falls back and her joy explodes in a loud burst of laughter. She slaps my shoulders. "Shhhh…shhhh…"

I drop a kiss on her neck. "You're the one being loud, sweetheart." I tickle her again and she pushes against me, still busting a gut and telling me to be quiet.

"Uncle Caleb!"

Brynn's arms are ramrod straight, pushing me, her eyes round.

"She's such a little cockblock." I press my lips to Brynn's, then holler back to Ella, "Yes, Little Bit?"

"Can I come downstairs with you?"

"No, it's past your bedtime. You need to go back to bed."

"Okay."

Brynn lifts to kiss me, but I shake my head. "She's not done."

"Uncle Caleb!"

"Yeah?"

"Will you come up here and sleep with me?"

"No, but I'll come up and tuck you in."

"Hmmm…okay."

I capture Brynn's mouth in a hard, hot kiss. "Do not get dressed, we're not done. I'll be right back." Rolling from her, I yank on my jeans and glance back. "No dressing."

"Roger. Will Comply."

Taking the stairs two at a time, I head to Ella's room. Walking by Michael's room, I glance in to find him still conked out, but I step inside and tug the blanket up over his shoulders.

"Thank you," he mumbles.

"You got it, bud." I drop a kiss to the top of his head before turning toward Ella's room.

CHAPTER SIXTEEN

Brynn

BENDING MY KNEES, I wrap my arms around them and rest my chin on the blanket. The only sounds in the house are the occasional floorboard creaking above me, and the crackle of the fire across the room. The Christmas tree lights cast a soft white glow. I second Ella's thoughts, *Oh, that's bootiful.*

I angle my head over my shoulder at the padding of feet jogging down the stairs. When Caleb stands next to the couch, I smile at his frown.

"What happened to you staying naked?"

"I *am* naked." He lifts a brow. I roll my eyes. "It's a blanket, Caleb. You ditched me for another girl for a long time. I got cold."

Once he has his jeans off, I open the blanket and he settles between my legs. Closing the wrap over both of us, I nuzzle my nose with his.

"Sorry about that."

For his sweetness, I pepper kisses over his face. "I love that you did that."

He grips my hips and tugs me more securely under him. "What's the plan for tomorrow?"

Lifting my hips, I rub against him. "You really want to work the whiteboard right now, Staff Sergeant?"

His grip tightens. "Brynn, come on, you know I like a plan."

With an exaggerated sigh, I stop. "Michael has class starting at eight thirty. I'll get him started and Elle usually works on her 'school' which is learning letters and some basic 'Matt the Rat' type reading." I curl my arms around his neck and drag my fingernails over the back of his head. "Do you want to keep your Little Bit occupied from two to three when I help Michael with his spelling, or do you want to work with spelling and I'll have tea?"

"If we want him to pass spelling, you better work with him. I'll help with math. Is the tea good?"

"Oh, it's the finest invisible British blend."

When he lowers his head, I meet him halfway for a kiss. "Do you still think this is a test, Angel?"

"I think this is more real than anything we've ever done before." With a sigh, I rest my forehead against his. "We should go to bed."

"I think we're doing damn fine on the couch."

I trace his lips with a fingertip. "Better than fine. But eventually you're going to let me sleep and I don't want Michael and Ella finding us tangled up under your poncho liner in the living room."

"My poncho—" He tugs the liner I'd been using as a blanket. "You stole my poncho liner?"

The betrayal in his voice makes me chuckle. That the outrage isn't all a joke, makes me laugh more. A Marine and their poncho liner, like a child and their woobie. I hold tight to the cover, there is a reason the bond with a liner is strong. They're the best in all weather and used as a bed, pillow, shelter—a lifeline in desert or jungle. "Yes. You should have known I would. It's not hurt, don't worry." I close the distance until my lips brush his when I talk. "There just might be some stains we'll have to get out."

He tugs my hair bringing my gaze to his. "God, Brynn, you are by far the most beautiful fucking thing I've seen in this world."

Stunned at the vehemence in his tone, my throat aches with emotion. Instead of drowning in it, I smile. "So you forgive me for the poncho liner?"

He frowns, not liking my avoiding his words, but then returns the smile. "Maybe not that beautiful."

I punch his arm and shake my head. "Come on. Tuck me into bed."

In a swift move, he gathers me and the liner in his arms and starts up the stairs. "Our clothes."

"We'll get them tomorrow. The kids know we wear clothes."

I give up, but smooth my palm over his cheek. "Wipe off that victory smile."

"Yes, ma'am."

He tosses me on the bed, but grabs his poncho liner and shoves it near his gear. I laugh until it hits me… "Caleb, why haven't you unpacked?"

"Am I staying forever?" He spoons behind me and tugs me flush against him.

"I thought you said you were."

"I am as long as you say."

"Then I say forever."

"I'll unpack tomorrow."

"And the rest of your things?"

"In storage."

Twisting in his arms, I tuck my head under his chin. "Bring it all."

"This place won't fit all my things on top of what's here, but I'll get what I can."

"Bring it all. We'll make room. I don't want a single button of yours out there where I can't touch it if I want." I place my hand over the scar on his chest. "I should have been on that last deployment with you, too."

"Negative."

"Why?" I whisper.

"Manelli thought I was trying to kill myself. Maybe I was."

My heart stops beating for what feels like eternity as the world around me moves in slow motion. When I can breathe again, I don't make eye contact for fear of seeing the truth. "Why would he think that? Why would you?"

"I'd lost my brother. I'd lost too many brothers in arms. I'd lost you."

"Don't say that, you never lost me."

"For a bit there, after the funeral, I did. You've always been a candle guiding me over rough waters. I couldn't find your light. When you were gone. I was gone."

I brush at the tears, so he won't feel the moisture on his chest. "And you tried to—" I can't even say it.

"I don't know. I took a lot of what was thought to be suicide missions. Threw myself into some positions I probably shouldn't have, but that was to keep Marines alive. Manelli believed I was either after a Medal of Honor, or a body bag." He drops a kiss on the top of my head. "Sorry, I brought up that shit, Brynn, let's forget it."

"I can't. I was furious with you, Caleb, but my love for you never dimmed. If you couldn't see the light or feel my warmth it was because the storm inside you was too dark."

"It was. And whatever I did brought me through it and I found you again."

"It's a good thing Manelli's the top corpsman he is, or he'd have answered to me."

"Believe me, he knew it."

"Do you still feel that way?"

"Never. Haven't since those first months after the funeral. Don't worry about me, Angel."

"I will always worry about you. And don't hesitate to call 'Doc' if you need me."

He exhales a ragged breath. "Roger that."

Snuggling closer I keep my hand over his heart, my cheek close to where his pulse throbs under his neck. It picks up when the window seems to shake with the force of a gust of wind. Joining him in a moan, we roll from each other and I tug on a T-shirt and panties and he yanks on a pair of skivvies. We come together again in the same position, each knowing we don't have long before our bed is invaded. At least nature was generous and held the storm at bay until we'd enjoyed each other a few times. After his confession, I admit I won't mind the distraction I can hear padding down the hall.

"Aunt Brynn."

I turn as Caleb flips back the covers and Ella snuggles against me. My smile returns when he doesn't drop the covers as a greater gust shakes the house. "Aunt Brynn?"

I wave Michael under and he joins the family. Caleb

drops the blanket and then a kiss on the top of my head. "Go to sleep." He grumps his command. He presses his mouth close to my ear. "Thank you for tonight, Angel."

I angle my head and accept his kiss. "Repeat tomorrow."

"You're on." He winks and squeezes me closer.

"ONLY ONE MISSPELLED. Great job, Michael!"

He doesn't look up from the math he was just assigned by his online teacher. "Thank you."

"Do you need help?"

"No, math is my best subject."

Like someone else I know, who's upstairs keeping Ella from bothering her brother. "I'm going to go let Ella and Caleb know snacks in fifteen minutes."

"Okay." The little man ducks his head and works through the figures. He works so hard to make sure he's good and does what's right. In him I see another boy doing everything he could to be accepted.

"I love you, Michael."

He lifts his head and red tinges his cheeks, but he smiles. "I love you, too, Aunt Brynn."

When he drops his head back down, I leave him to his work and jog up the stairs and stop short just outside Ella's room.

"More tea?"

"Please. It's divine."

I slap my hand over my mouth to silence the guffaw at Caleb's falsetto voice.

"Thank you."

"No, thank *you, dear.*"

Biting my lip, I take a step and peek into the room where Ella and Caleb are sitting at her tiny pink table. His knees are practically to his chin. I take him in, stopping at the pink fascinator hooked to the very little hair he has. I press my lips together and pray I don't explode with laughter. I dig in my back pocket for my phone.

"Don't do it, dear, or I will have to seek vengeance and it will be terrible and swift."

My gaze snaps to his and his furrowed brow confirms he was talking to me. Despite the ridiculous pink hat on his head and falsetto voice, it's Staff Sergeant Quinlin in all his lethal Marine role issuing an order. "Sorry, I had to try. Caleb…"

"Uh-uh-uh, sweetie, the name's Eugenie Phillapot…Mrs. Eugenie Phillapot."

My ability not to dissolve into hysterics has never faced such a test. I tip my head to the side, as a different emotion pushes away the humor and starts in the heart.

"Aunt Brynn, to play you have to have a hat."

Ella's irritated tone interrupts my thoughts. I don't break eye contact with Caleb, but respond to Ella. "Sorry, I just came to tell you snacks in fifteen minutes."

"Yay."

"Yes, very good." Then he tests me again lifting a tiny china teacup and sipping at invisible tea, pinky out.

I take the three steps necessary to put me in his space. "Marry me, Caleb."

"*Wh-at?*" His voice remains high until he coughs and clears his throat. "What?"

"Marry me, please."

Slipping off the fascinator, he pushes to his full six foot three and I lift on the balls of my feet and wrap my arms around his neck. He rests his hands on my hips, but still doesn't answer. "Why don't you take Ella down for snacks and I'll be down in a minute?"

"Caleb, I just asked you to—"

"Affirmative, I heard. Give me a minute."

I drop my arms and step back. Did I misread this whole situation? I hold out my hand for Ella and when her hand slips into mine I start downstairs. He'd asked me to marry him by New Year's. Is he having second thoughts? I'm sinking into a portal of déjà vu.

I help Ella into her seat and help Michael clean up. Neither of them say anything but thank you when I give them apple slices. I need to pull myself out of my funk, but my mind is clouded with the pain of rejection.

When Caleb steps into the kitchen, he bypasses the children and takes my left hand. "Yes, Brynn, I've wanted you all my life. I can't wait to marry you."

Still shell-shocked, I frown at my hand in his. "You had to think about it?"

"No, I had to get this." He releases my hand and pulls a box from his pocket.

"Uncle Caleb, that was for Christmas."

I glance at Michael and then meet Caleb's gaze at last.

"Your aunt can have it early."

I frown, irritated with the coded conversation. "What?"

"Michael helped me pick it out."

He lifts the lid and the emerald set in white gold blurs, but not before I notice tiny anchors on either side of the dark green stone. I reach for it, but pull my hand back. "Can I?"

"I was hoping you would." Caleb takes the ring out of the box and lifts my left hand again slipping it on my ring finger. When I lift my face, he brushes a kiss on each cheek. "I have loved you since your mom put you in my playpen when we were one. You have been the anchor in my life and the healer of all my wounds. I have and will always be yours."

"You always take the best lines."

"And you still never need to say anything, Angel, it's all in your eyes."

Pressing my lips to his, the world fades. Caleb Quinlin is mine, he said it himself. His mouth slants against mine as he takes control of the kiss, my mind, and my heart. I've known he would be mine one day. He gave me what he could for years, but there was always that part of him he never trusted anyone with, even me. As he tastes me, his arms wrap around me and he holds me tight. I feel our life together begin. We don't need a preacher or judge to pronounce us each other's, we just are.

I rub my cheek against his and his ragged breaths matches mine. Resting a hand on his chest, I curl my fingers and let the pulse of his heart guide mine. "This is really happening."

"It's all real, Brynn." He squeezes me closer. "Including the two children looking at us with wrinkled noses, a little like they might puke."

"When they puke, you can let me go."

He leans back until my feet come off the ground, and I laugh while his gives me a Caleb bear hug. He growls and rubs his five o'clock whiskers over my cheek and neck. I arch my neck, laughing and also giving him better access. When he sets me down, the smile on his face in one I haven't seen in forever.

"Me next," a small voice calls up, and we both tip our heads down to find ice-blue eyes staring up at Caleb with adoration as Ella stretches her arms. Shaking his head like he's fooling anyone into thinking this is a hardship, he gives Ella the Caleb bear hug experience, eliciting piercing squeals so loud I wouldn't be surprised if dolphins gathered around the island.

Turning to Michael, my smile falters. His gaze is fixed on Caleb and he's smiling at his sister's howls, but he seems distant. I go over to him to bring him closer.

I ruffle his hair. "You did a great job helping your uncle with the ring."

"It's pretty, but I didn't do much."

"Didn't do much? Don't be modest!" Caleb sets Ella down, and before Michael knows what's happening, Caleb sweeps him up and it's his turn for a big bear hug. At first it's a squeak of surprise, then he dissolves into the same riotous laughter Ella and I did.

When Caleb sets him down, I have to draw on every hard ass moment to keep from crying at the joy shining from the small boy who is looking at his uncle like the sun rises and sets with him.

"Okay, Devil Pups, you are dismissed for an hour of TV. Get moving."

"Yes, sir," they shout behind them as they pivot on their heels and head into the living room.

With a sigh, I turn back to him and then drop my gaze to the ring. "It's kind of sad, though."

"What?"

His tone has turned gruff, but I shrug it off. "Everyone already thinks we're engaged, so it's not like we can announce it for real."

"It was real when we announced it, Brynn."

Crossing my arms, I lean a hip against the door-frame. "It didn't feel real then."

"Did to me."

"Well, I was still in shock. Anyway, it doesn't matter. It's real now. So, when are you going to make an honest woman of me?"

"Tomorrow sound good?"

"It does. But I kind of like the idea of New Year's Eve like you first suggested."

He frowns. "That date was a deadline, Brynn. You can't for second believe I'm leaving now?"

I press my palms to his wide chest. "Of course not. It just sounds romantic." My cheeks heat even saying the sappy line.

"I like that. New Year's Eve it is."

"And small, like just immediate family, me, you, and a preacher or judge or whoever can say 'man and wife.'"

"Sounds outstanding."

"Then we'll be a family." Caleb and I both share a look before turning our attention to Michael, who slipped in while we were lost in a dream.

I sit on my heels. "Then we'll be a family."

"And you and Uncle Caleb can adopt us."

I tip my head to see Caleb's expression. He nods. "You want that, bud?"

"I'd like it a lot."

I smile. "I'd like that, too."

Holding my breath, I wait for Caleb's answer. He'd just admitted a few nights before he wasn't sure if he'd be ready to be "Dad." Now Michael is looking up at him with eyes so full of faith, I refuse to turn and add my hope-filled gaze, as well. He's made so many wishes come true, it's unfair to want more, but inside I scream for him to make this one come true as well.

"Well, then I guess your aunt and I better see about getting that done, too."

"Really?" Michael and I harmonize.

His mouth flickers in a smile before he takes on a stern look. "Like you said, we're family. Better make it all legal."

Relief wars with unease. He sounds more resigned to his fate than excited to have a ready-made family, until he sits on his heels next to me. He waves Michael closer and the boy complies. "I'll tell you a secret, I'm kind of crazy about all three of you and can't wait to make you all mine."

I'm expecting Michael to fly into either Caleb or my arms, but instead he flies from the room. "Ella, we're going to have a mom and dad!"

"Who?"

I huff a laugh and meet Caleb's gaze. He smiles, but there's a pain in his eyes I haven't seen since the funeral. He takes my hand and brings me up with him.

I lower my voice and step closer. "You sure?"

"Absolutely. Just fighting the side of me feeling like shit for how much I really want those kids and how much I feel like I'm stealing my brother's family."

I cup his face and press my forehead to his. "I know, I've felt the same and fought the battle for over a year. But they are ours now."

He lifts his head breaking contact but renews the touch by cupping the back of my head and dropping a kiss on my forehead sweeter than any sugar cookie. We grasp the few seconds of shared joy and pain before the scamper of little feet is followed by small hands grabbing my jeans and tugging. "Michael says you're my momma?"

Breaking from Caleb, I bend and lift Ella up, sitting her on my hip. "Do you want me to be?"

Her brow furrows. "Will my other mommy care?"

I inhale a deep breath and release the pain. When I give my answer, I know in my heart it's the right one. "No, this is what your mommy and daddy would want since they can't be here."

"Then yeah. Is Uncle Caleb my daddy?"

He chucks her chin. "Affirmative."

Ella tucks her chin and giggles. "Good."

I cut my gaze between Michael and Ella. "Now, you two go watch a little TV while I get supper."

I set Ella down and my heart almost melts when they

both call back, "Okay, Mom."

I lift my shoulders and let them fall. "So, there's that now."

"There is that."

"So…"

"So you just told our kids you were making dinner. We better decide what we're making." His shoulders are relaxed and then he winks, assuring me he's good to go. I'm not fooling myself: all guilt is gone. This is right. Our family is right.

CHAPTER SEVENTEEN

Caleb

"IS IT STRAIGHT?"

"Perfect."

I slide out from under my second Christmas tree this season. "All right. You want some help decorating?"

"At least getting the lights on." Mom digs in a plastic tub for her strings of lights, the complete opposite of Brynn's squared-away Christmas decorations. "Thank you for helping me. I thought your father would help, but I should have known."

"Not a problem. We needed to come inland and get some supplies. I'm sure Brynn and the kids are enjoying a trip into Augusta to load up."

A small smile touches her lips. "You seem to have taken to the family life."

"You mind the kids calling me Dad?"

"Not at all. I think it's wonderful for all of you. Mark worshiped you. I can't think of anything that would make him happier since he can't be here for Michael and Ella."

"Brynn and I are going to start the adoption process after we marry."

She rests a hand on my arm. "I'm so glad. And the children, I bet they're ecstatic?"

I can't help but chuckle at the number of times they call us Mom and Dad, sometimes five or six times in a sentence. "You could say that."

"And you, you're…"

"Just stepping right into the family your brother built."

Both our smiles falter. If there was ever a man who could darken a room with his presence, it's my father. Like in a bad horror flick, I almost expect somber music to play when he's around. I drop my gaze to Mom, who's the exact opposite, like the mothers in Christmas movies, or she tried to be when we were young.

I take the lights from Mom and meet the dark slits of my father's cold eyes. "I'm stepping into my life and doing what Mark asked me to do, and that's be a dad to his children. So fu—"

Mom's hand on my forearm stops me. She smiles at me and then turns to her husband. "Hal, don't. The children adore Brynn and Caleb; I'm thankful they love the little ones back."

For a second, I think she got to him, but I should have known—he's spent decades being an asshole, so he can't stop now. "So, what, Michael joins the Marines instead of what Mark wanted?"

I step around the tree and jut a finger in his face as we stand nose to nose. "Better than some bastard like you. I know you've been putting bullshit into that kid's mind." I didn't know the truth, and even believed Mark might have turned into a sonofabitch. Watching my father's eyes widen, the truth is revealed. Mark just left his kids with their grandfather thinking the man couldn't really be as big a fucking asshole as we thought. He was wrong. I ache to ram my fist in his face, and it sickens me. No son should feel that way about his father, but he stopped being anything to me years ago. "You let that boy believe he was bad. That's over. You're over."

"Hal? What did you say to Michael?"

My father steps into my space until I narrow my gaze and he backs off. "I just helped him see his weaknesses before he never amounted to anything. And him believing he's bad, that's true. I heard Mark telling Liz. Mark disciplined him for using Mark's phone without permission. He yelled at Mark and Mark told him he was grounded. He told Mark he wished Mark would never talk to him again. Well, he didn't—that night was the accident. I merely pointed it out to Michael that words have consequences."

"Holy shit! You are a wicked sick, evil twist, and you are out of those children's lives." I pivot to Mom. "You can see them anytime—without him."

"Please stop, both of you."

The low almost maniacal chuckle brings our attention back to Hal. "I'm not out of anything…son." It's said with such disgust I almost puke. "I'm filing for joint custody…might go for full custody if you keep talking."

"The fuck you are!"

"Hal, no!"

"Yes. I'm going to raise those kids right, especially Michael. Mark was finally starting to understand how it should be done. He was on the fast track in his firm and well respected in Maine." He pins me with eyes of pure hate. "He didn't deserve to die. It should have been you. I wish you'd never come back."

The words hit like mortar rounds into the gut, and I stumble back. A buzz fills my ears and then a loud crack snaps me back to the living room. My mother is lowering her hand as my father stands stunned, her handprint on his cheek.

"I told myself over and over you loved Caleb, that you were just disappointed he wanted to be a Marine and was better building things than in some office. You'd come to realize it one day. But now I see how wrong I was about that and a lot of things. You hate our son.

Maybe because he's a man you only wished you could be. You sue for custody and I'll fight on the side of the kids." She walks over to me and cups my face. "My poor boy. Give me a minute to get a few things."

She doesn't even stop as she walks by Hal, but her voice is ironclad. "I'm leaving you. I only wished I had when the boys were little."

"Audrey." He reaches for her, but she shakes him off.

"Caleb, come help me."

I follow her upstairs, neither of us looking back. His words haunt my steps. Not because of who said them, but how many times I've said the same thing over the last year.

When we step into her room, I force myself out of my shit thoughts and to my mom. "You sure about this?"

She points to the closet. "Get the big suitcase for me. Yes, I'm sure. Oh, the tree."

"Did you want to stay?"

"No." Her glower is harsher than I've ever seen it. "Stop asking that. I'll ask Brian to come get it tomorrow."

I flop the suitcase on the bed. "I can come get it."

"I don't want you around him." She pins me with ice-blue eyes, and once again in my life I'm thankful Mark and I took after her side of the family. "Promise me."

"Roger that."

"What does that mean?"

I can't believe I can find a smile, but I feel the tug of my mouth curve in a brief flex. "Promise."

"Okay."

As she starts packing, we fall into silence until she packs the framed pictures of me in my dress blues, Mark and Liz's wedding, and Michael and Ella. "We'll move the children in together, and you can have Ella's room as long as you—"

"I'm not going to the lighthouse, Caleb. You and Brynn need to build your family and don't need me around."

"Don't be ridiculous."

"I'm not going to fight you. I'm tired and I don't want to be stuck out on an island either if there's bad weather. Take me to the Camden Harbor Inn. I'm going to stay in one of their finest rooms and spend all your father's money.

"Mom—"

"Caleb Michael Quinlin, take me to the Harbor Inn."

"Yes, ma'am."

Taking her suitcase, I follow her out of the room and down the stairs. If my father is still here, he's decided to stay out of her way. I search the house with my gaze and a sense of sadness weighs down on me. I roll my shoulders in an attempt to shake it off.

I can see the good times with Mark and I up by six on Saturdays for cartoons and Mom decorating every space for Christmas and baking so many goodies the house smelled like the holidays into March. But then the image morphs into me standing in front of my father at eight, then thirteen, telling him I was going to be a Marine and the hate that flashed in his eyes. Then showing him the signed papers I'd just brought home from the recruiters office and having him lift his hand with every intention of striking me, until I held my ground without flinching. And Mom telling me how proud she was. And Brynn waiting outside for me, her Navy recruit papers in hand.

"Caleb?"

I turn my attention to my mother. "I shouldn't have left you and Mark with him."

"Yes, you should have. It wasn't your responsibility, although you've always thought the world was your responsibility."

"I should have at least come home when I could."

"Maybe, but we all did what we could. Mark idolized you, Caleb, and no matter what your father thinks, he wasn't on any fast track to work with the firm—he was going to leave and start his own partnership with a friend. They were going to work to help people. He said it was as much like you as he could get." She nods to the door. "Come on, let's go."

My chest aches when she glances back at the tree, now dark and cold. With long strides, she walks out of the door. After shoving the suitcase in the back of her SUV, I climb in the driver's side and start the vehicle. "Maybe it would have been best if I hadn't come back."

"I'll slap you, too, if you ever say that again."

Putting the SUV in drive, I pull away from the house. I hadn't meant to say that out loud. "Sorry, ma'am. Would you mind if I borrowed the car after getting you settled?"

"No. Where are you going?"

"Just need to think."

NOT TAKING MY eyes off the stone in front of me, I hold out my hand and Brynn laces her fingers with mine as she settles into the passenger seat. For a few minutes we sit in silence; the only sound the SUV's engine. Even outside the windows nothing moves, no birds sing. Clouds have moved in leaving the scene gray and white with splotches of green provided by the pines. When I turn to her, gold flashes in the browns and greens in her eyes. Focusing on those eyes, kept me breathing and fighting for life many times.

"I'm not leaving."

"I know you're not." She brushes a kiss over my knuckles.

"Mom called you."

It wasn't a question, but she answers. "Yes, she wanted to let me know not to go to the house and—"

"That my father wishes I was dead."

"I'm so sorry, Caleb. But she was more concerned that you said you should have never come home."

We both cut a quick glance at the gravestone bearing the names of our siblings. "If I wouldn't have come home, he never would have made a move for custody."

Her hand turns cold. "I'm not sure about that. He wasn't happy with me. But, we won't let him win even if he's stupid enough to try. We'll fight him together."

"Absolutely."

"And Michael and Ella are thrilled you came back. And I think I've made it clear how I feel."

I hold her hand to my chest where she can feel my heartbeat. "It was said coming out of the blow he delivered, but it was a stupid thing to say. I think I was just pissed he could still get to me; that I had any reaction to anything he said or did."

"What he said to you was monstrous. I can't imagine anyone who wouldn't react."

"Just wish I could have kept from giving him the pleasure of knowing it." I shrug. "And if I'm a hundred percent with you, I'm floundering a bit outside the Corps. I knew how to lead there. I have no idea what I'm doing ninety percent of the time here."

"I know, love, I struggled for months, I still do, and

then with Michael and Ella…Marines are definitely easier to control."

"And you did it alone. At least I have you." I hug her hand. "I am sorry I didn't talk to you at the funeral. It was chicken shit, and you never deserve to be treated that way. On top of feeling like I belonged in the dirt, I'd promised my Marines one more year and I knew if I talked to you, I'd be staying. But I should have told you. I should have held you. Brynn, I never should have let you go to begin with."

"It *was* chicken shit, but I'm understanding a bit more why now. Why didn't you ever tell me how bad it was between you and your father? I knew it was bad, but not like this."

"Who wants to tell his girlfriend his father hates him and home can be hell? I just wanted to get out of there."

"Yeah, but I wish you could have told me."

"It's over now. And we know the source of Michael's insecurities, which thank God wasn't Mark and Liz."

"My hap-hap-happiest Christmas is unwrapping fast."

"Let's go get the kids and get it back on track. Mark would try to kick my ass sitting up here giving Hal a second thought."

"Caleb, before we go, we need to talk."

Those words rarely mean anything good, so I brace myself for the next punch. "I thought that's what we've been doing."

"Yeah, but this couldn't have come on a worse day— Michael wanted us to take you out to dinner for a welcome home party."

"Are you kidding me?"

Her gaze drops and she starts drawing hearts on the palm of my hand with her fingertip. Even through the coat and Henley T-shirt, I feel her touch to my soul. "He doesn't know. He remembers me mentioning something about it at Thanksgiving and how you didn't have anyone with you, and he wants to welcome you home."

I let me head fall back. "Tonight?"

"Well, no, he asked if we could include the family and dress up."

"Dress up?" I know I'm a step away from whining, and the humor in Brynn's voice confirms it.

"Don't sound like Ella. Yes, dress up. If you don't want—"

I snag her hand and press a kiss to her palm. "Plan it with him. I'll dress up."

"He will be thrilled."

I tip my head forward. "Will you wear that red dress?"

The curve of her grin is trouble and her voice lowers to a husky whisper. "Yes."

"Then I will be thrilled."

"I love you."

"Love you right back." I brush a quick kiss to her lips. "We better get back before Mom sends someone else to find both of us."

She shifts in the passenger seat and opens the door. After stepping out, she turns back. "If you need more alone time, I can tell Audrey and the kids you're okay."

"Negative. I'll follow you back. We better get back to the island."

I catch her hand before she can close the door. "Thanks for coming for me."

"Always."

CHAPTER EIGHTEEN

Brynn

THE SIDE ZIPPER closes without issue and I smile at my reflection in the mirror. It fits. It's a miracle. I haven't worn the red dress since before our last deployment together, and the past couple years haven't left much time for obsessing about keeping my recruit weight.

The front of the dress is quite subtle. Red lace overlay, form fitting to mid-hip, with cap sleeves. But it's backless, not daringly so, but low enough it made Caleb's nostrils flare when I wore it to an engagement party for mutual friends. His rough hands had driven me crazy all night as he made a point of touching me whenever he could until it ended in a quickie in the bathroom.

Caleb's image joins mine in the mirror, and then he skates his hands over my sides and the curves of my hips and then lower to the hemline. His fingers curl and I slap my hands over his, meeting his frown in the glass. "No, Caleb. We don't have time and the children are waiting."

His ice-blue eyes melt to the rough waves of a freshwater bay. "Tonight."

"Absolutely. All night."

He steps back, still keeping me surrounded with his size, and traces the line of the dress around my back. My skin rises in tiny bumps, eager to reach for his touch. His gaze lifts to my face and then shifts to my hair, fashioned in a pile of curls. He doesn't have to say how much I please him; his eyes tell the tale.

I smile when he chuckles, as I walk around him inspecting him in a navy suit with a simple white button-down shirt and matching blue tie. His laughs ends on a groan when I skate my palm over his ass. Turning back to the mirror, I give him a wink. "You look yummy."

"You can have a bite whenever." His breath is warm on my neck as he bends and presses his lips there.

"I prefer the dress blues, though."

"I know you do, Angel. You proved that a number of times."

Pivoting, I'm pressed up against his muscled form and I could melt into his warmth. "We better go."

He steps back farther and straightens his tie. "A man should get to celebrate coming home how he wants."

I laugh and give him a slight shove. "You've been

celebrating for a few weeks now, Marine. No acting all denied."

"Not denied, just insatiable. You are the ultimate Christmas treat."

"Treats after dinner," I caution, and step around him while I can.

He stays behind me as we make our way downstairs and I feel the heat of his gaze as if he's touching me. "Do you think we should get rooms for tonight? Looks like there might be a storm with high winds later."

"It's off season; we'll be fine if we need something."

When we walk into the living room, Michael and Ella are sitting on the sofa like little mannequins, taking their father's words to stay clean and pressed to heart. They look adorable; Michael in a dark brown suit and Ella in a forest-green dress with velvet top and full taffeta bottom.

Michael's eyes grow wide. "You look so pretty, Mom."

The word still hits me square in the heart. "You both look amazing."

Michael's gaze sweeps over Caleb. "You're not wearing your uniform?"

"That's not really done, son."

"Oh."

Ella slides off the couch and flounces to Caleb, lifting her arms. "Please."

Without missing a beat, the big softie picks up his favorite girl. Michael stands next to me, and it feels like four puzzle pieces found their place.

Caleb sets Ella down. "Okay, get your coats. Let's roll."

He gets her into her coat, then opens my full-length wool coat and helps me. Michael follows his steps as they put on their winter gear. I pick up my red pumps by the door, wearing flat shoes to the dock, and take Michael's hand while Caleb carries Ella.

As we walk to the boat, I take in the lights from Camden dancing on the water and the green light from the lighthouse stretching out, showing sailors the way into port. After years of war and noise, this island and the keeper's house was a refuge of peace. It was like a sign when the town of Camden let me buy the house. But for the millionth time since the children came to live with me, I'm questioning if I need to give it up and move my family to the mainland.

I glance over my shoulder at the house. Even without the Christmas lights on this evening, there's a peace I find looking at the old house. It will be harder to move now with so many more memories filling each room.

Caleb steps onto the boat and then lifts Michael and Ella, setting them both down. "Get below, so you're warm." No fights tonight, they scurry below deck. He holds his hand out for me and finds no arguments here either as he helps me aboard. "What are you thinking, Brynn?"

"It might be time to let the lighthouse go."

He drops a kiss on my forehead. "Not just yet."

Nodding, I silently agree not to think about things we can't change tonight and follow him.

After a ride on the boat, and a brisk walk to the restaurant, I settle into my chair at Fresh & Co. I help Michael, while watching Caleb settle Ella in a booster seat. My parents' gazes are focused on us. Mom opens her mouth to speak, but shuts it when Ella calls Caleb Daddy. I can only imagine the fresh pain of watching us become a family after being there from the first as Liz and Mark started their family.

Caleb sinks into the chair across from me, only to stand when Audrey arrives. "Sorry I'm late."

Caleb raises an eyebrow. "Everything all right?"

"Of course, you know me—I like to make an entrance." Audrey scans the table, and as she sits her mouth curves into a knowing smile. "It's a bit of a shock how well they all fit together, right?

Dad finds his silverware interesting. "A little."

She turns her focus to me. "That's some dress, Brynn. You're stunning."

Heat touches my cheeks, and I refuse to meet Caleb's gaze and the fire I know I'd find there. "Thank you. You look beautiful tonight, too." And she does, with her silver hair cut in stylish bob and the blue dress that makes her eyes pop just as Caleb's suit does for his.

"Thank you. Rose and Frank, you're looking wonderful tonight. We all should fancy up more often. Michael, you're so handsome. And Ella, adorable as always."

My dad finally snaps out of his funk. "Agreed, Audrey. Do you need any help from us?"

"Not at all. Caleb has me well settled. I'll find a permanent place after Christmas."

I glance around the restaurant. "Where's Brian?"

"Oh, he was called in last minute." Mom smiles at Caleb. "But he says welcome home and then a few other words I won't repeat."

Caleb chuckles. My dad clears his throat and nods to Michael. "Okay, this is your show, young man."

Bless him, when Michael speaks he holds eye contact and doesn't fidget. "I want to welcome my dad home from the Marines. Me and Ella are glad you came for us." He stops and flashes his gaze to me. "Not that we weren't happy with you."

I wave my hands like I'm pushing him on. "I know. Go ahead." I choke the words through a closing throat. Caleb's chest rises and falls as he struggles to keep it together as well.

Michael shrugs. "Well, I don't know what grown-ups do now, but that's it. Welcome home, glad you're not hurt, and we love you."

"Here, here!" Dad lifts his glass of beer.

We all join, until Caleb waves us to stop. "Thank you, Michael. It's my honor to be a part of your life and Ella's." He tips his head to the little girl looking at him like he controls the tides.

Before he can say more, people from other tables stop by to welcome him home. We've known these individuals all our lives, but Caleb's shoulders are so tense I can almost feel the pain, guilt, and all-around awkwardness flowing through him. He plasters on a smile and shakes each hand as they remind him who they are, like he doesn't know, and slaps his back.

When the last one departs his haunted gaze collides with mine and all air leaves my lungs. The fire is still there, but more, he's reaching for a lifeline, a Marine calling for his doc, but I can't reach him.

Audrey comes to our rescue. "Caleb, take Brynn to get a little air and check the specials board."

"Yes, ma'am." He stands so fast I'm surprised he doesn't sprint from the restaurant.

I push my chair back and address Michael and Ella. "You two be good and order what you want." I pin Michael with my gaze. "What you want, not what you think you should have." I give Mom, Dad, and Audrey a look, and they nod in agreement.

Caleb's hand spreads over my naked back the second

I'm next to him, and we grab our coats and step out on the patio. He inhales, filling his lungs with the crisp air and the sea. I expect him to ravage my mouth the second we step outside, but instead he cups my face and gently presses his mouth to mine. My lips part on a sigh with the sweetness of the touch and as I inhale his scent. He still doesn't deepen the kiss, but nips on my lower lip, and then with just the tip of his tongue he enters me. I open my eyes and gasp and attempt to step back from the intensity of his gaze, but he presses his hand over my back and brings me back into his orbit.

I caress his cheek with the backs of my fingers. "What hurts?"

"It was too much. Michael's pride in me, not as a Marine, but as his father."

"He should be proud to have you as his dad. You're really more dad than father."

He rests his forehead against mine. "And you are one hell of a mom."

"Thank you. And then all the people?"

"That took me over the edge. There's so many of my Marines heading for conflict, I don't want a slap on the back for coming home."

"I felt the same, Caleb, but so many are truly grateful allow them to show it."

"I'll get there."

"I'll help."

When his mouth covers mine again, the gentle caress turns controlling and claiming. I slant my head, accepting the demanding touch. Leaning into him, I stroke my tongue against his, letting him lead the way. Whatever he needs, I'll give it.

He shifts, dragging kisses up my neck and then presses his mouth to my ear. "You are home, and Christmas, and love, and joy to me, Brynn."

"You're everything to me, Caleb."

He brushes his lips behind my ear, then steps back. I study his strong profile. He's looking beyond me to the inlet and then the ocean beyond.

"We better get back inside." I smooth my palms over his chest, wishing layers of clothes didn't keep me from his flesh.

His ice blue eyes lock on me like heat-seeking missiles. "Go ahead. I'll be right behind you."

I frown. "I can stay."

"Seriously, Brynn, I'll be just a second."

"Okay." I lift and drop a kiss to his chin, then turn and walk back into the restaurant and to the table.

Michael touches my hand. "Is Dad okay?"

"He is. He'll be right back." I meet everyone's gaze, answering them while answering Michael. Squeezing his hand, I smile. "What did you order?"

"Pasta."

"Pasta?"

He glances to my mom for help. "He wanted chicken alfredo. Ella wanted spaghetti."

"Yum." I look back to her. "And me?"

"Sirloin steak with garlic mash like your father."

"Thanks, that's perfect."

"And I ordered Caleb the porter house with the garlic mash."

"Sounds good, Mom, thank you."

Caleb nods to Audrey, then slides into his chair and winks at Ella. "I'm getting ghetti."

"That sounds yummy." When he lifts his head, he smiles at Michael. "Alfredo?"

"How'd you know?"

"I'm psychic, and I heard your grandma tell your mom that."

Michael's chuckle lightens the table even more. I meet Caleb's gaze for a second, and he winks at me, the spark is back.

The conversation around the table turns to plans for the upcoming week and the most recent forecast for a snowstorm. When the food arrives, I cut Michael's noodles and Caleb helps Ella. He has always been a sexy man, whether in full dress blues at the Marine Corps Ball or in utilities out on the battlefield calling out orders. But nothing prepared me for the ultimate hotness that is Caleb Quinlin cutting spaghetti noodles and tucking a napkin over the dress of a four-year-old while answering her questions and responding to her endless chatter. It isn't just that he responds, but he sounds as if he was talking to a private under his command instead of a little girl in a fluffy green dress.

I finish cutting Michael's food and slide the bowl back in front of him. "There you go."

"Thanks, Mom."

"You're welcome."

Audrey clears her throat, and I have a feeling it's something that might disrupt my meal, so I rush a bite of steak and potatoes. "Not to interfere, but the manager at the Camden Harbor Inn told me they had a Christmas Eve wedding cancel. They're stuck with all the decorations and of course most parties are over by then so, no one else is looking for a venue for Christmas Eve. They're willing to rent the room and provide decorations for cheap. That is, if there's a couple planning a holiday wedding."

"Oh, that sounds nice. The Harbor Inn is a beautiful venue." My mom sounds like she might explode from excitement.

"Brynn and I will discuss later and get back to you."

My nerves unravel one by one at Caleb's response. But why? Why, when I have wanted to marry Caleb since…well, since forever, would I tense up at the thought of pushing the wedding up a week?

"Brynn?"

I startle, but snap out of my thoughts. "Yes?"

He raises an eyebrow. "I asked if you wanted more wine?"

"Oh, no thank you."

"Momma?"

"Yeah, baby?"

"I need to potty."

I start to push my chair back, but my mom waves me down. "I'll take her."

She has Ella up and moving before either of us can respond. I glance at Michael and his forehead is scrunched. I hope he's pleased with how the party he wanted for Caleb is going.

"Gramps, did you bring it?"

"Sure did."

Michael slides from his chair and takes something from my dad. He walks around to Caleb and pushes his glasses up on his nose. "This isn't a great present, but…" He shrugs his small shoulders.

"Thank you, Michael."

Caleb tears open the wrapping and frowns at the box with a picture of a MV-22, Osprey on the front. "This is the model your mom gave you years ago."

"My other dad didn't have time to put it together with me. I was hoping you would."

Caleb hugs Michael close. "Absolutely, bud, absolutely."

"Sorry it's not a new present."

"It's the best." He bends to Michael's level.

Michael's blue eyes shift left than right in time with his feet. "I love you."

"Love you, too."

Despite a couple awkward moments, this has been the welcome home Caleb needed. Helping Ella with her ghetti, as she calls it, and receiving a gift straight from a seven-year-old boy's heart made the evening perfect.

Mom returns to the table with Ella. "Oh, you gave him the gift. Wonderful."

Caleb continues to study the picture on the box. "It is."

She turns to me as she helps Ella back into her chair. "It's getting windy out there. Do you all want to stay at the house?"

Audrey shifts her stare from Caleb to Mom and me. "I was hoping the kids would want to stay with me and I'd treat Caleb and Brynn with a room as my welcome home gift."

"Oh, Audrey—"

"Come on, Angel, it'll be fun. We accept, Mom, thank you." He ruffles Michael's hair. "That okay with you?"

"Can we go to the pool, Gramma?"

"Sure can."

"Yeah."

Caleb turns to Ella. "You want to stay with Gramma?" Her head bobs in agreement with her brother. "Brynn?"

In his gaze I read every decadent thing he has planned for me. I'm tempted to say no just to see his reaction, but with the kids around I'm better not poking the bear. "Thank you, Audrey. And Mom and Dad."

Dad chuckles. "Sure thing. There's no winning over a pool. You mind if we head over with you and watch the kids swim?"

"Not at all."

After a fight over who's paying the bill that my parents win, we step into the cool air and I lace my fingers with Caleb's. We fall back and let the grandparents and children lead the way the few blocks to the Harbor Inn.

A few boats in the harbor have Christmas lights around the lines or outlining the hull. I've thought of stringing lights on the lobster boat, but maybe next year. The wind has picked up and the waves slapping in the inlet lull me to a sense of peace.

Caleb keeps his voice low so only I hear him. "For a second, I saw my Marines' faces as they asked me to reenlist one more time. But when do the one-more-times stop?"

"I know. There are still times when on the wind I hear a Marine yelling *Doc*, and I think I should be there, there are Marines I could be saving."

"Now you're busy saving just one Marine."

"My favorite Marine."

"Or the one who got injured the most."

I hip check him. "That, too."

"You realize that dress is going to be ripped from you the second we're in the room?"

"I don't have to be psychic to know that. But may I suggest unzipping the dress and stripping me. You seem to like this dress and I'd hate to have it ruined."

"I accept that compromise. Lace underwear?"

"It *is* your welcome home party."

He groans. "You're killing me."

I hug his arm. "Did you really have a nice time tonight?"

"I did. They're amazing kids." He holds up the box with the still unassembled model. "I can't believe Mark didn't help him."

"Probably thought he would someday. We all tend to put things off thinking there's always one more day."

"Like getting married."

"Caleb."

He shrugs. "I don't care if it's Christmas Eve or New Year's Eve, but if you're hesitating about the day, I wonder if you're ready."

"I've been ready since we were fifteen. You're the one who didn't want to make that commitment while we were both serving."

"So let's tell the manager we're good for Christmas Eve."

We follow the family into the hotel, and Caleb starts to the desk, but I grip his arm. "Don't say anything tonight about the wedding."

He takes his arm from me. "You got it."

Ella pats my leg. "Momma, we don't have suits."

Before I can answer Audrey steps in. "I don't mean to overstep, but I brought their extra suits from the house when I packed."

I sit on my heels in front of the children. "There you go. I know you'll both be good tonight." I hold Michael's gaze, then encompass them both. "If your grandparents want to get you a treat, you can accept since we didn't have dessert."

"Thanks, Mom."

I wrap Michael in a hug and then drop a kiss on his cheek, before hugging and kissing Ella. "If you need us, you call."

Caleb steps behind me and then takes my place, dropping a kiss on Michael's forehead before sweeping Ella into his arms for a quick hug and then her slobbery kiss on his cheek. "Like your mom said, call if you need us." He turns to his mom. "And you call if you need us."

"We'll be fine."

"Thank you all for the dinner."

After a round of handshakes, hugs and goodnights,

Caleb and I step on the elevator up to our room. "You pissed we're not renting the space?"

"You know when I'm pissed, Brynn."

"True." It was not a sight anyone could forget. "Okay, angry?"

We step off the elevator. "I just don't get the hesitation. Fuck me, we've been talking about adopting the children. They call us Mom and Dad. You can't think I'm walking away from that?"

"It's not you, and I don't doubt you. Stop asking me that. I don't want someone else's wedding or reception. I don't want their flowers and decorations. Like I said, I've waited a long time for this, Caleb. I want my wedding; how I plan it.

He swipes the key card and opens the door. He steps in just before me, flipping on the lights, and his gaze sweeps the room as the door closes. "That I understand. Why didn't you just say so when Mom brought it up? He starts loosening his tie. "Start stripping, Angel."

I comply, but return to his statement. "Because I was a tiny bit ticked off. Did you see Audrey and Mom, they had the whole day planned? And it wasn't even on the day *we* told them we wanted to get married on. I spent ten years with someone else planning the next step. I don't want that with *our* family."

"I thought the dress turned me on, but it's you Brynn. Yeah, the dress is nice icing, but you are what makes it beautiful. So, a few people out to the lighthouse for a quick ceremony and ringing in the New Year?"

I let the dress fall to the floor. He traces every curve with his eyes. He drags the back of his fingers over the seams of the red lace bra. Then his hand drops and he outlines the V of my sex.

My voice is rough when I speak. "I like that idea."

His mouth flickers in a smile. "What idea?"

"The quick ceremony and ringing in the New Year."

"Then that's what we'll do." He traces my pussy again over the red lace.

I run the tip of my tongue over my suddenly dry lips and take my time letting my gaze wander over him. When I make it to his groin, I do a bit of tracing of my own running my fingertip over the ridge of his erection stretching his slacks. He's big already and not even fully erect. My lips part in a gasp when he drags his fingertip from the top of my thigh-high stocking up my inner thigh and under my panties.

He nips my lower lip. "Climb on the bed, ass in air."

"Is that an order, Staff Sergeant?"

"Affirmative."

"And you expect me to comply?"

My legs tremble as he slides two fingers into my soaking wet sex. "One hundred percent, if you want this ache to end."

I wrap my arms around him and press close. "Caleb."

He slides his fingers from me and into his mouth. "Like the finest Christmas candy. Taste." He captures my mouth and fills it with his tongue, forcing me to taste myself mixed with him. When he breaks the kiss, he nips my bottom lip, again. "On the edge of the bed, ass in air, Angel."

This time I don't tease, but climb on the plush bed and rest my head on the comforter, stretching my arms in front of me and wiggling until my ass over the edge of the bed. My fingers curl around hunks of the bedspread when he moves my panties aside and circles my clit with his thumb until my inner muscles contract around nothing.

A low guttural groan escapes from a primal place inside me. I feel his cockhead at my entrance. I know what's coming. I know it will be rough, and tonight it's exactly what I need. He rams his cock deep while gripping my hips. I whimper at the feel of him filling me, seated heavy and hot inside and throbbing as my inner muscles pulse around him. His strokes are hard, almost leaving me completely before ramming balls deep as I hold onto the bedding for purchase. The pounding seems to last forever and my body screams for release, but he's not going to let me go yet, and I'd be devastated if he did. He changes it up, burying himself deep and staying inside, caressing me as I work him with my inner muscles.

He reaches under me, molding my breasts and then smoothing his hand down my belly and pressing where his cockhead can be felt.

I slam my fist on the bed. "Enough! Let me come, Caleb, please." There's a cry of intense frustration in my voice.

Just when I think my mind will break from reality, he changes his strokes so each one blessedly hits my g-spot—and every other spot. With a deep push, he roars my name and I cry out at the feel of his heat filling me. He continues to ride me and reaches around, stroking my clit until at last I join him in the stars.

When he eases from me, he turns me on my back and settles between my legs. I open my lips for him when he presses his mouth to mine in a kiss that seals his claim. He lowers his body and the weight of him is like the warmest shelter in the harshest storm. Wrapping my leg over his, I run my hands over ever part of him I can reach and melt into his kiss.

He brushes kisses over my face and then down my neck before continuing down my torso. "You know my body better than I do."

He raises himself back over me, and his mouth curves in a wicked smile promising wicked good times. "That's because I've made it my course of study since we were seventeen."

"You've definitely earned your PhD."

He nips my chin and wags his eyebrows. "I'm going for a double major."

"Seriously, can I ask you something between rounds?"

"I was trying to get round two going, but shoot."

"How do you feel when Michael and Ella call you Dad?"

"There's still the initial gut punch, this isn't right, but then it's the sweetest sound I've heard next to you saying my name."

"Caleb."

"Yeah, just like that."

"That's how I feel, too, like a fraud, but they're so much a part of me sometimes it feels like they came from me, if that makes sense."

"I get it."

"And when I see you settle Ella in her chair and help with her ghetti, it's the sexiest picture in the world."

His forehead wrinkles. "You don't find Mrs. Phillapot sexy?"

I try to keep from laughing, but fail. "Mrs. Phillapot is hot as hell."

"It's the hat, right?"

"Definitely the hat." My laughter turns hysterical and I push against him when he digs his fingers into my sides, tickling me. Pressing my palms against his chest, I try to force a scowl even though I can't get rid of my smile. "Halt, Marine!"

Caleb rolls to his back, taking me with him, and cups the back of my head, and I bend to meet him for a decadent kiss. He breaks the kiss, but keeps me close enough his lips brush mine as he speaks. "Bring me home tonight, Angel."

CHAPTER NINETEEN

Caleb

BRYNN'S BODY IS heavy as she sleeps on me, but I wouldn't move her for the world. I inhale not for air, but to savor the scent of our bodies entwined. When we were younger, she used to wear the most arousing perfume, like the sea and lavender. She stopped after enlisting, even off duty. The first time I smelled her skin without it, I wondered why I ever thought the other scent was delicious. Brynn, just herself, encompasses the sexiest, spiciest scent. And she smells even better with me blended in.

I stroke my fingertips up and down her back, and then curl a silken strand of hair around my finger, before rubbing it between my finger and thumb.

"What time is it?"

"Nine."

"Just nine?" Her voice is raw from sleep, screaming, and taking me with her mouth. It's enough to get me ready for more.

"That's what happens when you go to dinner with two little ones so you're done eating by six. But it does make a longer night for fucking, so I'm not complaining."

She chuckles and snuggles closer. "I love you calling them little ones. It's sweet."

"Yeah, well, my thoughts aren't very sweet at the moment."

She lifts her head and her mouth curves in a smile that defines sexy. "I bet they're not. I can feel things are rising, or one very big thing."

My phone rings and I glare at the interruption. She nods to it. "Better look, could be the kids."

Grabbing the phone from the bedside table, I swipe answer when Mom's name appears. I frown when all I hear is screeching. "Mom?"

"I want Daddy!" It sounds kind of like Ella and kind of like a death wail.

"Mom?"

"Caleb, you and Brynn need to come quick. There's been an accident."

I shift from under Brynn and start yanking on clothes while talking. Brynn is tugging on her underwear and dress, too, either hearing my mom or taking her cue from me.

"Where?"

"By the pool."

"Why are you still by the pool? It's nine fucking o'clock." I lift the phone. "She hung up on me."

She scowls and tugs her hair into a ponytail and steps into her shoes. I shrug into my jacket and start toward the door, both of us grabbing our coats. "Is it Ella?"

We jog down the stairs. "She's the one screaming."

When we get to the pool, I sweep my gaze over the area, gathering information. While Ella is the one screaming, it's Michael who's hurt. No whining, screaming, or even a whimper. He's just sitting on a lounge chair with tears streaming down his cheeks. And I wish the kid wouldn't be trying so hard to look so brave. Brynn and I get to him at the same time, and she kneels in front of him, instant corpsman mode.

"What's wrong?"

He sniffs and his voice is a whisper. "My arm's broken."

She conducts a quick examination with as gentle a touch as possible, but when he inhales a sharp breath, she flinches. "I don't think it broke through."

Mom steps forward. "I'm so sorry. He slipped on the wet floor." She hands a howling Ella to me, who tucks her head under my chin and settles.

Brynn glances over her shoulder to me. "I need a first

aid kit."

Frank jumps to before I can move. "Got it."

"Make sure it's one with something for a splint."

None of us move toward Brynn and Michael, understanding her knowledge and skills are greater than ours. Frank hustles back and hands her the kit, then steps back."

"Caleb, could I get an assist?"

"On it."

I hand Ella off to Frank and kneel by Brynn, passing her the stiff plastic splint and tape to hold it on. I give Michael an encouraging smile. "You're going to be good to go, Michael. Your mom's fixed me up many times."

"She has?"

"Absolutely."

Brynn finishes the splint. "There we go." She stands and I straighten next to her. "We better get to the hospital." She turns her attention to her mother, whose face is ashen. "We'll need your car."

Rose nods, but doesn't take her eyes from Michael. "Of course. Frank already went to get it from the garage. He should be out front."

Thankfully, the children finished swimming and already put their sweats on. Lifting Michael, I start carrying him out with Brynn on my heels, carrying Ella. I'm barking orders and acting like I'm not shattering inside every time Michael sniffs and flinches.

"Sorry, Dad."

"Nothing to be sorry about. You hurting bad?"

"Yes, sir."

"Just hold your arm steady like your mom showed you."

"Okay."

Frank pulls up the SUV as we step out and Brynn slides in front with Ella, while I step into the back with Michael. Frank doesn't say anything, but the poor man looks like he might puke.

The twelve-minute drive from Camden to the Pen Bay Medical Center in Rockport feels more like twelve days. When he pulls up to the emergency room door, I fight against the instinct to launch out and step out with care for the precious cargo I'm carrying. "I'll go find a parking space."

"Thanks, Dad."

"Thanks, Frank."

With long strides, we step into the emergency waiting room. Walking up to the receptionist, I lift Michael slightly. "Our son broke his arm."

The nurse doesn't look up until she gathers some forms together. "Okay, we just need you to fill out these forms. We should be able to get him right in." Her smile is quick and drops when she sees Michael. "Poor guy."

Brynn shifts Ella to her hip and takes the paperwork on the clipboard. "Thank you."

As we take a seat, I adjust Michael so he can keep his arm straight. "Won't be long, bud."

"Okay." The weariness in his voice and hurt in his eyes tell me it's already been an excruciating long time to be a little one in pain.

Brynn amazes me by having the mother thing down, filling out forms around Ella on her lap. But when she glances up at me, I see a woman about to crack. Despite the fact she's dealt with wounds a thousand times more severe and in battle, those men weren't her son. "Do you still have my driver's license and insurance card?"

"Yeah." Reaching in my back pocket, trying not to jostle Michael, I tug out my wallet and hand it over. It's a good thing she gave me the ID and insurance card earlier, so she didn't have to bring a bag with her from the lighthouse, or we'd be hurting since the children aren't on my insurance yet.

I point to the line for relationship. "What are you putting there?"

"Guardian and aunt. We're not legally Mom and Dad yet." I nod even though she can't see, since her head is down. "Ella, sit still." She sounds like she's back on the battlefield ordering a Marine around. The little girl glances up at me and I wink even as my gut squeezes at her wet, red, puffy cheeks.

Michael is sitting like a statue. His cheeks are just as wet and red, but without the dramatics of his little sister.

When Frank comes in, Brynn glances up. "Dad, take Ella, please."

I expect a riot, but clearly Ella understands the tone Brynn is using is the one you don't argue with. I've seen Marines take a step back from that tone. Hell, I've stepped back from that tone. Frank settles with Ella, and Brynn takes the paperwork up to the desk.

When she comes back to the chairs, she stops and combs her fingers through Michael's hair. "It's gonna be okay, baby."

"I know, Momma."

"Michael Quinlin."

"Hold on, bud." I push out of the chair, and we finally get into an examination room. After setting Michael on the exam table, Brynn and I move out of the way when the doctor comes in.

"Broken arm?"

Michael nods. Brynn steps forward. "I think it's a buckle fracture. Seems bent, not broken."

The doctor inspects the splint. "You have medical training?"

I want to snort. Brynn nods. "Hospital Corpsman. Green."

The doctor huffs a laugh. "Definite medical training." He looks to me. "And you're…"

"The Marine she trained on, and Michael's uncle."

"I see." His forehead creases for a second. I smile at

the look of disappointment when Brynn takes my hand. *Yeah, asshole, this smart, brave, badass woman…she's all mine.* "All right, we're going to confirm it's a buckle, not that I doubt it, but we'll get some X-rays."

Through X-rays, where Brynn's diagnosis is confirmed, and getting the plaster cast from just above the elbow to over his hand, Michael weathers it all like a true Devil Pup. Brynn and I take turns holding his hand and cheering him on. The ride back to the hotel feels as excruciatingly long as the drive to the hospital. Stepping out of the SUV we mumble another 'thanks' to Frank and zombie walk inside.

Mom meets us in the hotel lobby as we enter much like we left. I'm holding Michael, but this time he's conked out, his head on my shoulder, and Brynn is carrying an equally zonked-out Ella.

Her eyes cut to the cast. "Poor boy. Sorry…"

"Not your fault, Mom," I interrupt. "And I'm sorry I was a shit to you about it."

"You were shocked." She hands Brynn a bag. "There's jeans, sneakers, and a sweater in there for you for tomorrow, so you don't have to ruin your dress."

"Thanks so much, Audrey."

"Sorry I don't have anything for you."

I shrug. "I'm not balancing on spike heels."

"You want to bring the kids to my room?"

"No, they'll want to be with us and we want them

with us too. We'll see you for breakfast at eight, though."

"Sounds good. Just text me if you need to make it later."

I lean down and brush a kiss on her cheek. "Goodnight."

"Goodnight."

The ride up to the room seems longer than the ride back to Camden. Brynn pushes off the wall when the doors open on our floor. I scan the key and nudge the door open. Finally, we can tuck the kids into bed. We switch children, and I press a kiss to Ella's cheek. The Little Bit snuggles farther under the covers. Brynn arranges a pillow under Michael's arm. "With the local anesthetic, he shouldn't hurt for a bit." She drops a kiss on his forehead and then Ella's cheek. Neither respond to the caress.

Once Ella and Michael are settled, I step behind Brynn and wrap my arms around her, tugging her close and dropping a kiss to her shoulder. "How you doing, Angel?"

"I feel like I'm crashing from a huge adrenaline rush. When I saw him…"

"Yeah, I know."

Her eyes meet mine in the mirror. "I think we have to face the reality—we need to move from the lighthouse. If this, or worse, happened there and it was storming, I just can't even let my mind go there. Hell, when you landed at my feet the other night, I should have demanded Brian take you to the hospital."

"No one can heal me like you, Brynn." She leans back into me. I wish I could argue with her knowing how much the lighthouse means to her, but I can't. If anything happened to her or the kids and we couldn't get to help... "But you're right. We'll stay through the holidays and then start looking."

She glances back at the bed. "I don't have anything for nightclothes."

"You can wear my T-shirt. It's not all that clean."

"It'll work."

Breaking from my embrace, she checks the children, then turns to me and steps back into my orbit. "You want to shower with me? Clean up, relax under some hot water?"

"Sounds good, Angel."

She takes my hand and starts walking. I grab the T-shirt I didn't bother with earlier in the rush to get downstairs, and follow her into the bathroom. She kicks off her shoes and unzips her dress. When it falls to the floor, this time there's nothing sexual, but almost the release of the last few hours. I hook my hip to the doorframe, watching her pull the band from her hair and shake out the thick waves.

She angles her face over her shoulder and keeps her voice low. "You're showering with your clothes on?" She peels off her panties and bra.

"Just admiring the view this room has."

"Caleb." The gold specks are back in her eyes.

"Showering together might not be the best idea."

Her mouth curves in a sweet grin laced with a lot of spice. "Come on, Caleb, don't be shy. Strip."

Pushing off the frame, I follow orders, and then step into the tub behind her. I adjust the water in the shower before sealing my lips to hers in a kiss. She is so sweet it lasts longer than I planned, and I break the connection before it leads to deeper contact. With the children just a thin wall away, and Ella's penchant for walking into rooms without knocking, we can't risk even a quickie. "Turn around."

She offers her back to me, and I empty the sample-sized bottle of shampoo, then start washing her hair. The soft moans have my mind and body reconsidering the, no-sex-because-the-kids-are-too-close, rule I imposed on myself before stepping into this steamy box of temptation. At the same time, I keep an ear trained to the other room for any calls for Mom or Dad. Watching the suds run down her back, I admire one of my favorite parts of her body, and those are the Venus dimples above her ass.

She rinses her hair and I repeat the process with the conditioner. Only this time I admire her body for the scars of a warrior. Tracing the long scar on her back, I feel her intake of breath, but continue to trace the white line where a piece of shrapnel sliced into her while she was making sure a young corporal didn't bleed out when his leg was amputated by an IED.

"What are you doing?"

"You are so fucking strong."

"It's nothing, Caleb."

"It's everything because you're everything. And I'm not just talking about Ramadi, Helmand, Syria, Africa or any other hell where you've saved Marines. I'm talking about you in four-inch heels and a tight red dress holding Ella while filling out forms and taking on shit like a badass."

She turns and shakes her head like she always does to diminish her skills. "As I recall, I had a big, hard, charging Marine by my side step for step, holding precious cargo."

"Fine, Brynn, if you don't want to admit it, I'm game, but you are the strongest person I have ever known."

"Tonight, I'm exhausted, and I'm regretting offering a shared shower when we can't make the best use of it." She reaches for the soap. "I'll scrub your back and you scrub mine."

I close my hand around hers. "Negative, Angel. If you touch me, either we're going to break the no sex rule, or I'm going to be in serious pain and we won't have time to ease it. We'll scrub our own backs tonight."

Without a fight, she starts washing down, and I grab another bar of soap and make quick work of getting hosed down and out of the sweltering box of lust as fast as possible.

Stepping out of the shower, I wrap a towel around my waist and hand her the other fluffy white towel. I'm barely into my skivvies and a small voice startles me.

"Daddy, I need water."

I pivot like a DI barked my name. Ella stands at the door rubbing her eyes; the breathing reminder of why I washed my own back tonight. "What did you need, Little Bit?"

She juts her tiny finger to the sink. "Water, please."

"You got it."

Brynn finishes tugging my T-shirt on and starts gathering our discarded clothes, then cups the back of Ella's head and kisses her forehead. "I'm going to check on Michael."

"Roger."

"Thank you, Caleb."

"Any time."

After handing Ella her water, I hold the cup, securing it as she tips her head back and gulps the liquid down. When Brynn comes back to the doorway, I meet her gaze. "He up?"

"Yeah, he's hurting pretty bad. I'm going to give him the pain medicine."

"Sounds like a plan."

She nods down to where my hand still holds the cup as Ella takes a moment to breathe. "See? Teamwork."

"You're still tough as boiled owl…" I glance down and back up. "Crap."

"Bad word," Ella mumbles, and I roll my eyes.

"Sorry, Little Bit. Let's hit the rack."

She frowns. "The rack?"

"Go to bed."

Swinging her into my arms, I carry her out to the bed and tuck her back in. My attention goes to Brynn and Michael. "You hurtin', son?"

His attempt at a smile turns south fast. "Some."

I know that dismissal of extreme pain. I've given more than I can count in an attempt to appear stronger than I was at the time. "I know when I broke my arm it hurt like a—well, it hurt a whole lot."

"It did?"

"Sure did. We're not made of steel."

He takes the pill from Brynn and washes it down. She raises her eyebrows at me like I helped her win some big debate. I feel like I won so much more; like I'm really their father beyond what any court document is going to say. "Do you think sitting up would help him?"

"I don't think so, but do you want to try that?"

The boy's eyes are already drooping and his lips part as he starts fading. "No."

She watches him and I watch her with equal amazement. The gentleness in her touch as she presses the back of her fingers to his cheeks and forehead, searching for fever, and then drops a kiss on his cheek and Ella's. She was born to care for others, to heal with a touch, a word, a whisper.

I spoon behind her after she joins the children under the covers and shelter her with my body. She exhales a deep breath and sinks as close as humanly possible to me, her hand linked to mine when she tugs my arm more secure around her.

I swipe send for the text. Eight o'clock breakfast with Mom wasn't happening this morning with as slow as we're moving. With a gentle pull, I bring the sweatshirt over Michael's head. "Okay, next the good arm." He nods and I smile. "I'm going to need verbal confirmation on that."

A brief smile is my reward. "Ready."

I help him shrug into that sleeve. Then I turn to the sleeve I cut up the seam earlier to accommodate for the cast. With a quick move, I get his arm in the open sleeve.

His shoulders relax. "Thanks, Dad."

"Sure thing. You gonna be okay to sit for breakfast or should I text your gramma again and call it off?"

"I'll be okay. And I'm hungry."

"We wouldn't call off the chow—just sitting in a restaurant."

"I'll be okay."

I ruffle his hair and look toward the bathroom where Brynn and Ella are stepping out after getting ready. I sweep my gaze over Brynn and smile. Her eyes narrow. "Don't you say a word, Caleb Quinlin."

"What, you in my mom's jeans and her—what is that? A reindeer sweater? Outstanding."

The kids giggle even as she gives us all the death glare. "It's clean."

"And that's about all it is."

When she advances on Michael and me, I prepare for a gut punch. Instead she tosses me one more glower before cupping Michael's face. "You okay, baby?"

"Yeah."

Any thoughts I avoided retribution are dashed when she leans closer to me. "You remember tonight when the kids are in bed and you turn to me on the couch, I'll be wearing your mother's jeans and her festive reindeer sweater."

I stumble back, adding a bit of dramatics by clutching my chest. "Knew you had a mean streak, but that was below the belt."

"And that's the only thing happening below the belt today."

"Vicious."

Ella plants herself in front of me with hands on hips. "She's not ish-ous."

I sit on my heels in front of the pixie, ignoring Brynn's chuckle. "No, she's not ish-ous. We're just being silly."

She tips her head back to check Brynn's reaction, and Brynn nods. Ella wraps her arms around my neck. "Okay. Up, please." And just like that all is forgiven.

Standing, I hook my arm around her legs. "Okay, let's move out."

As we start walking, Michael wavers. Without a word, I hand Ella to Brynn and pick him up. That he doesn't protest and try to convince me he's fine tells me he's not.

Like times on the FOB, or even in battle, Brynn and I communicate with only a look between us, deciding we'll cancel with Mom, grab breakfast to go, and get home.

CHAPTER TWENTY

Caleb

SLOWING TO A walk, I inhale the pine and sea air. I've been lax in my morning PT since moving back and that fact is driven home with rough breathing after a run of five miles, something I should be able to do without being winded. In the past few days, things have settled down; I can get back to regular exercise. Life is settling into a routine, and routine is good.

A shadow moves across the light in the lantern room of the lighthouse tower. After confirming his boat is there, I change course to meet up with Brian. I'm intercepted by a pixie in a puffy winter coat looking like a tick ready to pop. "Daddy!"

Unable to resist those little arms raised for me to pick her up, I swoop her into my arms. She snuggles close and reminds me just how little routine there is when there's a four-year-old and seven-year-old in your life. "What are you doing out here, Little Bit?"

"Momma said to."

"She told you to go out in the cold?"

"For you."

"Oh, that was nice of her."

"Come color with me."

"Oh, your dad should like that. Just don't let him eat the crayons."

The shit-eatin' grin Brian shoots my way says he knows damn well I can't respond like I want to because Ella will scold me for the string of profanity. I chose to ignore him, but Ella does not.

"Daddy doesn't eat crayons." She tosses back her head and laughs like it was the greatest joke.

I start walking toward the house. "Of course I do, green is my favorite."

She continues to laugh like she knows the joke. Brian falls in line next to us. I shift her in my arms. "I can't believe I'm asking this, but Brynn and I are planning to marry on New Year's Eve. Small deal. Would you stand as my best man?"

"Ella, can you go in with your mom?"

She looks to me and I set her on the ground. "Go on in, baby, I'll be right there."

When the back door closes after her, I turn back to Brian. "Something wrong?"

"No, for the first time in a long time I think things are going to be all right. When you first got back and had that letter, I resented Liz for doing this to Brynn. But now watching you all become a family, I understand. If she and Mark couldn't raise the children, you and Brynn together would be the best option. A team since you were born. I'd be honored to stand up with you when you finally marry my sister. It's about time."

"Thanks, Brian, I appreciate it. Man, I really do. And I agree, I should have married Brynn years ago." I nod to the door. "How about some coffee?"

"Perfect."

Brian and I step across the threshold; stepping inside the house, a rush of warmth fills me that has nothing to do with the heater or fireplace, but with candles in the window and greenery, holly berries and white lights up the staircase and more garland over the fireplace with four stockings hanging like a Norman Rockwell painting. The tree lights are glinting, and there's a sweet reason why the tree lights are on at nine in the morning. Michael's on the couch and Brynn thinks they'll cheer him up. I cut my gaze to Ella drinking a cup of cocoa at the kitchen table, coloring and singing a song she made up. It's the kind of moment a man cherishes for the rest of his life.

Footsteps on the stairs draw my attention and Brynn leans over the banister. "Hi Brian." Before he can answer, she turns to me. "Hey, Caleb, can you come up here for a second? I need your help."

"Absolutely." I wave to the counter. "Help yourself to coffee."

I don't wait for him to respond but take the stairs two at a time. I stop short as I step across the threshold to our bedroom. Brynn is shimmying off her jeans. "Shut the door."

I comply. "What—"

"Sex. Come on, we don't have much time." She kicks her jeans and panties over and shoves her hand down the waistband of my sweatpants. "I love you in gray sweatpants, by the way, almost as nice as greenies. Now strip, Marine." When she grabs my cock, I step back.

"What the hell, Brynn? Your brother and the kids are right downstairs."

"Yes, and Brian will keep Ella occupied. Michael is watching an Avengers movie. We just have a few minutes to jingle your bells. It's been three days and nights with one or the other child needing something. Three. Days. And nights. I'm burning up. So, start shedding those clothes and give me a present."

She's not the only one. I thought running in the freezing cold earlier helped, but the second I saw her on the stairs I needed to ice down my junk. This is a better option.

She yanks off her sweater and bra. My gaze rakes over

her and I snap out of my funk and start stripping. Why the hell was I arguing about having sex? Don't fight the fuck, it's my number one rule. Well, it wasn't until right now.

Brynn cups my face and brings my gaze down to hers. "Stop thinking and get to fucking."

Digging my fingers into her hair, I crash my lips to hers and drink from her like we're back in the desert. I turn her and press her against the wall, deepening the kiss. There's nothing gentle in the way I stroke her tongue or bite her lips. But this isn't about feelings or intimacy, this is about getting off. It is exactly what we both need, and because of who we are to each other, it transforms into something about the most intense feelings and most profound intimacy.

Tugging her hair arches her neck, and I drag my mouth down the sensitive column. She's pumping my cock, and I grip her hip and hold it high on mine, opening her for me. "Take me in, Brynn."

Her groan as she guides my cock inside her tight, wet heat is one of the purest sounds I've ever heard. There's no artifice, it's all lust and need, and I'm the only one who can sate that lust and meet that need.

Her eyelids flutter and she ropes her arms around my neck before her mouth curves in a smug smile. "That hits the spot."

I chuckle, then grip both hips lifting her. When her

legs wrap around me, I flex my hips, filling her over and over with demanding strokes. Her sex instantly starts sucking and pulsing around my cock, and her panted breath and moans work to bring me to climax.

She runs her tongue over her lips and I devour her mouth once more before I continue to give her what she begged for. I feel my body tighten and I'm going to blow my wad before I want to, but the feeling of her growing tighter and hotter has me teetering on the edge. When my gaze clashes with hers and all the golds, greens, and browns are on fire, it sends me over and I drive deep, emptying myself with every throb.

Reaching between us, I stroke her clit until her eyes roll back and her body shudders. The sound she makes is like a wail trapped in her soul, and she sinks her teeth into my chest, her scream of pleasure entering my heart.

Our breath comes in short pants, and she runs her tongue over her teeth marks on my chest, before she presses kisses, healing the pain. I hold still, as if I can stop time and feel her mouth on me and her sex around me forever.

She reaches up and kisses my neck, and I squeeze the thighs I'm holding. Finally, I ease my cock from her and smile at the hitch in her breathing. Lowering her legs, it's my turn to trace her lips with my tongue and replace pain with tenderness.

Resting my forehead on hers, I chuckle. "Fa, la, la, la,

la, Brynn. You got any more chores up here you need help with, because I am one thousand percent in the bell-ringing mood. Or, I could just deck the halls with you again."

She laughs and there isn't a carol with more emotion or joy. She skates her palms up and down from my chest to my abs and then back. "Mission complete, Marine, stocking stuffed. Plus, I'm sure we'll be missed soon."

"You could shower with me."

She rests her head against the wall. "What, no Christmas reference?"

"Nope, not even a chimney metaphor. Just want you in the shower wet with me."

She grins. "You are so tempting, Caleb, but you know there's going to be a tiny knock on this door in about five minutes."

I brush a quick kiss over her lips. "True. But damn, that was a hot fuck." She curls her hand into my biceps when I take a step back.

"It's not what we dreamed…this ready-made family. You have regrets?"

"Zero. I'm back with you. The sex is outstanding—being inside you always was, always will be—and yeah, we have to be more creative, maybe stop when all I want to do is stay in bed and inside you all day. But do I regret those kids…no fucking way. You?"

"Never the children. But sometimes I regret…" She

releases my arm. "Nevermind. Let me do a quick washup—"

I grab her hand, stopping her this time. "You regret we didn't marry right out of high school."

"Or at least out of training."

"I get that, and a part of me agrees, but if we had, we couldn't have served together. And I have to admit, I loved having you at my six and seeing you every day instead of a few months a year."

"I've thought of that, too. I'm not sure I'd want someone else taking care of you. It'll just be nice to have you officially mine." Her mouth lifts into a smile, but the gold flecks are missing from the mix of colors in her hazel eyes.

I caress her bottom lip with my thumb. "Marriage license or not, Brynn, I have always been yours and you have always been mine."

"Yes."

"Better go wash up—those aren't reindeer paws on the stairs."

"Momma?" A light knock on the door follows.

Brynn frowns. "Sneaky getting one more Christmas image in."

I wag my eyebrows. "I am firing on all cylinders, sweetheart." I holler through the door, "Go back downstairs, Little Bit, we'll be out in a minute."

"You sure?"

"Ella." I use my *I'm-not-fooling-around* voice.

"Okay."

Brynn kisses my cheek, before she steps around me and into the bathroom. "Oh, I do need you to reach the box on the top shelf of the closet. It's stocking stuffers I've bought throughout the year, and it slid to the back and I can't reach it."

"I knew this wasn't just about jingling my bells," I mumble loud enough for her to hear. I smile at the sound of her laughter.

Jogging down the stairs after my shower, I stop at the sofa, where Michael is. "How's the arm, son?"

He shrugs. "Mom said I couldn't do schoolwork today. I had to give it one more day."

"Then that's what it needs. Your mother knows her shi—stuff."

"I'm getting behind, though."

"Michael, you will catch up. It's been three days…" I go by Brynn's no-sex days count. "Don't put so much stress on these shoulders."

"I'll try. Will you play chess with me later?"

"Absolutely."

Brynn steps from the kitchen and my smile drops at her ashen face. "What's up?"

"Brian brought the mail." She holds up an envelope. "You need to see this."

Taking the envelope from her, I glance into the

kitchen. "Where's Ella?"

"Brian's building a snowman with her."

A rush of envy hits me. I instinctively know, I'd rather be outside with Little Bit building a snowman than reading whatever is in this letter. Shaking it off, I return to the mail and tug out the letter inside. I scan the document, rage drowning any other emotion. The sounds around me fade as I lift my gaze to meet Brynn's.

"The motherfucking asshole did it."

"Bad—" Brynn cuts off Ella's reproach with two fingers to the little girl's mouth. I hadn't even heard her and Brian enter.

Brynn's soft warning to the little girl registers. "Not this time, Ella. Go in with your brother."

"This is not your fault, Caleb."

"Yes, it is. If I wasn't a part of this family, he would have backed off." I hold up a hand to stop her. "But I am a part of this family so he can suck my—" Her frown halts me. "I'm going to end this right now." I lift my gaze to Brian. "Would you mind taking me into town?"

"Negative. I've gotta come back later anyway."

"Outstanding."

Brynn rests a hand on my arm. "This is not your fight alone. I'm their mother and I have every right to be a part of this."

"You have more right. But this is between him and me, Brynn, you know it's true. This isn't about you, or

Michael, or Ella, this is about me making a life for myself beyond his control."

"Then don't do anything that means you can't come home tonight."

"Roger that." After grabbing my coat off the hook, I bend and kiss her hard and hot before marching down to the dock with Brian.

I don't know if I thanked Brian or not for the ride. Blood is pounding in my ears, and all I can see as I march down Elm Street is Hal's obnoxious face. Tugging the door to his firm open, I wish I could yank it off and beat him with it.

The redhead I saw him with the other day stands as I storm by her desk. "Sir—"

Without even tossing her a glance I barrel into his office. "You son of a bitch! You are not getting my children."

"Sorry, Mr. Quinlin, he stormed past me," my father's paralegal and mistress rushes from behind me.

"That's all right, Alice, this is my son. His manners are more for a chow hall than office."

"It's mess hall, you asshole, and at least I don't have to worry about knives in the back from my Marine family."

He leans back in his chair and I want to pound the smirk off his face. That sums up the sad situation, because a son shouldn't want to drive his fist into his father's face. "You tried to set the rules about my seeing Michael and Ella. I'm simply reminding you, you don't set those rules."

"The hell Brynn and I don't. We are exactly who keeps them safe and you are the biggest threat to date. Now you won't see them ever."

"Keep pushing and I'll file for full custody."

"No, you won't, Hal."

My mother's voice keeps me from leaping across the desk and pummeling the shit out of him. "Sorry again—"

"Alice, the fact my husband is sleeping with you does not make you important enough to apologize for my or my son's behavior. Go back to your desk and shut up."

I suck in air at the calm manner in which my mom admits he's been cheating on her for years. The paralegal's face is beet red and moisture fills her eyes as she turns and leaves us. I'd feel sorry for her if she deserved even an ounce of compassion. The look of loathing she gives my mother as she passes her, confirms she does not.

My father's face is equally red, but not in embarrassment. "You—"

Mom stands between me and him and shakes her head. "Don't even say it, Hal, or I'll let Caleb beat the crap out of you. And you're not going through with this custody nonsense."

As if back in control, he steeples his fingers. "Really? Enlighten me as to why not."

"Because I will testify to what kind of father you really were to the boys. Then I will obliterate you, giving all the names of your past paralegals and what they really do for those nice paychecks. If that isn't enough, I'll let whoever will listen know that you hit on Brynn last New Year's Eve and you did the same to poor Liz the July before that. That's why she and Mark left the beach house early. He was so enraged and appalled he didn't drive safely and they got in that horrific accident. It was you who killed my son and my daughter-in-law and what makes me sick is I stayed with you."

I want to puke. He was worse than we ever knew. I can only guess he hit on Liz as revenge for Mark leaving the firm. And Brynn? Why didn't she say anything? Yeah, I know why, but fuck.

"What makes you think the judge will believe you?"

She places her hands on his desk and leans forward. "You really are an asshole. Who do you think got you this job, this office, any respect? My family name. You think the judges in this town respect you? They respect my father's name. It's over, Hal, you're over. I suggest you take your equally sleezy friend's offer and move to Portland."

"You wouldn't do that, Audrey."

"To protect Michael and Ella, in a heartbeat. I wasn't there for my sons; I won't let you hurt my grandchildren anymore."

Before I can say anything, Mom grabs my arm and leads me out like a child. When we step on the street, I realize she's shaking. "Mom?"

"I'm fine. Just furious."

"Well, you handled that like a badass. Kind of killed the tirade and threats I had planned."

"You want to go back in?" She lifts her eyebrow in question like she did when a principal wrongly accused me of cheating on a test and she ate his ass like she just had Hal's.

"No, I think your threats were better." I start walking, guiding her to a coffee house where she can let the adrenaline wear down.

"They weren't better, Caleb, each was as much a charge against me for staying with him. I'm sorry you had to hear about Brynn that way and the accident."

I scrub a hand over my face. "That was a gut punch. How could you not say something about him coming on to Liz?"

"I honestly didn't put it together until months later when he did the same to Brynn. It's no excuse, I should have said something then and about Brynn. Did you know about your father's affairs?"

I wish I could pretend. "I think everyone knows, Mom."

"I know. I've been so ashamed I stayed with him. I was weak and you boys paid the price."

I don't understand staying with someone who's abusing you and your children, but I've never been there and refuse to judge her. "Let's just go from here, Mom. Today you let loose with guns blazing to protect me and mine. Thank you."

She squeezes my hand, stopping me before I open the door to the coffee house. "Caleb, be careful. Your father is not the only snake in that den. Alice is different from his other mistresses, she fully intends to marry him and will do anything to make it so."

I'm instantly on high alert. "How do you know?"

"She's flat out told me. We struck a blow today, but I can't believe they'll let it go."

"Brynn and I won't let our guards down just yet. Now, come on let me buy you a coffee."

CHAPTER TWENTY-ONE

Brynn

DINNER IS ALMOST excruciatingly quiet after weeks of chatter and giggles. The children, picking up on Caleb's mood, are eating in self-imposed silence and shoveling in their chow as fast as he is. I could have served coal and it would have been appreciated as much as their tasting the homemade mac and cheese and baked ham.

His rage at Hal earlier had taken them aback. I'd seen that look in his eyes before turning them to pure ice, and it caused fear in the evilest enemy and strongest Marine. When I spoke to Ella and Michael, they, like me, knew he'd never turn it on them, but they were upset because he was upset.

"Are you two still playing chess this evening?" I try to get a conversation started with Caleb and Michael. Caleb grunts. Michael, still angry about me keeping him out of school, scowls. Fail. I turn to Ella. "Do you want to color after supper, Ella?"

"No," she mumbles. Epic Fail.

Their plates clean, I give up on any cheer. "Okay, then you two go upstairs and play, or watch T.V. in our room." Whatever it takes to get out of their funks.

Caleb and I clean off the table, the same stilted silence between us. When I start washing the dishes, he steps next to me and begins drying and putting them away.

"In the new place I demand a dishwasher." I chuckle.

"Sounds good."

I push his arm. "Come on, you said you thought Audrey scared the shit out of him."

"True, but there were a couple things she mentioned that hit hard."

I rest a hip on the counter and dry my hands. "Like what?"

"Like Hal's new mistress is batshit crazy and might be a threat."

"Then we'll keep vigilant. What else?"

He's squeezing the mug in his hand so tight I'm afraid he'll break it. "Like Hal came on to you last New Year's Eve."

The air rushes from my lungs and I can't inhale enough to respond.

He faces me waiting for a response. "Why didn't you tell me?"

I snatch the mug in his hand, before he does crush it. "It was nasty and humiliating and I didn't want you to kill him."

He nods. "Fair enough. Did you knee him in the nuts?"

"Wanted to. Instead I told him which part of hell was hottest."

"He also hit on Liz the night of the accident. Mom's convinced it was Mark being enraged that caused him to drive erratically. Could be."

I swipe at the moisture on my cheeks. "Poor Liz. That must have been horrifying."

He cups my neck and gently skates the pad of his thumb over my cheek. "Tell me the truth, Brynn—did he ever try something before with you?"

"No, I would have told you."

When he presses his lips to my forehead, I close my eyes. Not wanting to build a rift in the relationship he's building with his mother, I hesitate to ask the next question, but it's my sister. "How could Audrey know what he did to Liz, and the events following, and not say anything sooner?"

He steps back, but keeps his hand on me not breaking contact. "I asked the same thing. She says she didn't really put it together until he came on to you months later. She put it together with how things unfolded with Mark and Liz. I can't comprehend how she saw him do that to you and didn't go apeshit? I didn't ask though, there's not a satisfactory answer she could have given."

I relax against his touch. "No, there isn't."

He scrubs his hand over his face and then the back of his neck. "I don't want to break contact with her, but I won't be disloyal to you. If you want—"

I press two fingers to his lips. "No, I don't want to break contact either. She needs her family, and who knows what any of us would do after years with him." I trace his cheekbones and lips, taking pride when my touch melts the ice in his eyes, leaving a clear vibrant blue and a few naughty sparks. "Although you turned out outstanding."

"The Marines did that."

"Yes, they did." I force what I hope is stern corpsman frown. "Now there's just one more thing you need to do, Staff Sergeant."

He wags his eyebrows. "Go down your chimney?"

My laughter is more than what the dry joke is worth, but relief joins in humor as our world shifts back to the somewhat normal it's been. "Later, absolutely. But before that, you need to explain to Miss Ella that just because she was not allowed to correct your earlier string of impressive-by-Marine-standards cursing it does not mean she can ask her bulldog if he'd like more fucking tea."

Both his eyebrows rise in a mix of horror and pride. "Ella said *fuck?*"

"She did. And you know how she stumbles over some words and they're unclear…not so with the f-bomb, it was loud and clear."

"You sure she got it from me, not you?"

I give him a light shove. "Don't be an asshole, of course she got it from you. You were on fire earlier. Also, kind of scary, but super-hot."

"I'll talk to her. Now about your chimney…" He nips my bottom lip and I open for him as he traces my lips and teeth with the tip of his tongue before tangling it with mine. I melt into his kiss, and when he grips my waist and lifts, I assist by giving a hop before he sets me on the counter. I wrap my legs around his hips and my arms around his neck, pulling him closer and returning his kiss with all I am.

His hands mold my ass and he tugs me closer so I can feel his erection against my sex. I rub against the hard length until we're both moaning. His kiss turns harder and more possessive, and I give everything right back lost in the feel, taste, and scent of him. His erection grows against me and I reach for his waistband.

"Momma? Dad?"

The small words break over us like water on rock. The feel of Caleb's erection still fit against my sex, hard and large, tells me he isn't turning around any time soon.

I angle my head around his broad form and smile doing my best to act as nonchalant as possible. "Yes, Michael?"

Michael doesn't seem phased to see me wrapped around Caleb like an anaconda and smiles. "Would you watch a movie with us?"

"Absolutely. Do you have one pulled up already?"

"Not yet."

"Okay, you go do that and we'll be right up."

"Great."

When Michael's feet hit the staircase, I frame Caleb's face and rub my nose against his. "You're not getting smaller."

"Your pussy is still tight against me. It's not going down without a fight."

I chuckle and he makes a pained sound as I unwrap my legs. Sliding down his front to tease him is a bad idea as it teases me, too. Gathering my hair together and putting it into a somewhat organized ponytail, I step out of his space.

"I'll make some popcorn and try to get my cock to stand down."

Lifting onto the balls of my feet, I drop a kiss on his chin. "You're a good dad."

"Yeah, yeah, yeah. Tell me that when I'm not harboring uncharitable thoughts."

"Whatever." I start walking to the stairs and turn. "And don't forget to talk to Ella."

"I'm on it."

As I walk up the stairs, I keep my gaze on Caleb in the kitchen until a half wall blocks my view. Despite the ominous cloud of his father over our lives, I have a peace I haven't experienced since I was seventeen. Being a Devil Doc is a reward I wouldn't give up for the world, but years of patching up Marines—or worse watching them take their last breath—left me with a hole in my heart and soul. I chose the lighthouse, hoping the seclusion would be my salvation.

Instead, if I'm finally honest, the seclusion brought the worst of the nightmares to life and there was no one to fight them with me. Even after Michael and Ella moved in, single motherhood added to the loneliness of the one-woman fight.

I stop halfway down the hall. The image of Hal approaching me the previous New Year's is like a cold draft down the passageway. I've never cared for Caleb's father, but always assumed it was more about the way he treats Caleb than the creepy crawlies I feel when he's around. I forced a smile, and then he touched my ass and asked if I needed company. My bones chill at the memory. I'd been hit on by a hundred men; you can't be around thousands of horny guys twenty-four seven and not have at least one try his luck. But none made me feel as scared and alone as that encounter had. That it happened in my parents' home made it all the worse, and the feeling of wanting to puke, knee him in the groin, or knock him to the ground overwhelmed me.

The long, hot showers I took for days after while pretending around the children that nothing was wrong while secluded out here. I should have told my parents, or Brian, or even sucked it up and Skyped Caleb. That Liz went through the same thing…she must have felt devastated. He was her father-in-law. Her children's grandfather.

I startle at the feel of a warm hand on my lower back. "Angel?"

The scent of buttered popcorn and Caleb rips me from the nightmare. I open my mouth to lie and say everything is fine, but instead I lock my gaze with his. "I was thinking about that party." I lower my voice so the children don't hear. "About him touching me, his words."

"I'm so sorry, Brynn. Whatever you need to do, I'm there for it."

"I don't know yet. I think Mom, Dad, and Brian need to know about me and about Liz. I don't want to hurt you, though, in telling them."

"I can't say it's not embarrassing, and if Mom's right about Liz and Mark, I don't know how she and I will face your family. Fact is, if Michael and Ella weren't part of all this, I'd suggest we'd hold off marriage until you could fully process it."

"Don't. Don't you ever think that I put any of this on you. He was responsible for your brother's death, too, if Audrey's right. We're allies, not enemies, you and me. Like always. I don't need to process anything to know how much I adore you and want to marry you. Do you want me to keep this from Mom and Dad?"

"Absolutely not. I think they have a right to know. They'll need to know all about this custody thing anyway. Just don't be surprised when they're not as thrilled to have me as family."

"Don't you be surprised when it doesn't change how they feel about you at all."

"*Come on*, you guys, you can adult talk later. *The Grinch* is starting."

Michael's plea, said with such pain at having to deal with us, lightens the air in a flash. We share a chuckle at being chastised, then walk into our bedroom, where Ella is propped up on the pillows on Caleb's side of the bed. The bells of the opening of *The Grinch Who Stole Christmas* are just starting.

It seems everyone wants to be close to Caleb and the popcorn. With all four of us on the bed, it becomes clear we might need a bigger bed for movie nights. I nestle close to his side and he plops Michael between his legs with a pillow to prop up Michael's arm. Ella's eyes grow misty looking for a space. Solving the problem, I sit her between my legs and swipe the popcorn from Caleb, holding the bowl for her as she takes a chubby fistful.

Caleb narrows his gaze at me and takes back the bowl, setting it between his leg and mine where we all can reach it. "Community popcorn. No bogarting."

Michael and Ella giggle at his false anger. Time is ticking down to Christmas, and between Michael's arm and Hal's threats, it might not be the perfect holiday I planned.

I scan my little family and smile. It's so much better.

CHAPTER TWENTY-TWO

Brynn

MY DAD WRAPS his hand around his coffee mug absorbing the warmth. "Why didn't you tell us, Brynn?"

"Like I told Caleb, it was disgusting and I was shocked. I wanted to act like it never happened."

He releases the mug and smoothes his hand over the red tablecloth. "And Liz?"

"It's a theory Audrey had after he did the same to me. I guess Hal confessed when she laid it out, or at least he didn't deny assaulting her, or me."

Mom is almost vibrating in anger. "It's just so shocking. He's been to our house a million times. And then to treat our daughters like…"

Caleb clears his throat and I hate the red I see on his cheeks like he has anything to be embarrassed by. "I think it was more about myself and Mark. Mark wasn't going to join his firm, and he's always hated me. To embarrass the two people we love most, it's a win for him. I'm sorry Brynn and Liz had to get caught up in his loathing for his sons. I wish Mark would have pounded the son of a bitch instead of driving away."

Mom's mouth drops open in shock. "You have nothing to be sorry for, and neither does Mark. I'm sick for all four of you having to deal with this insanity."

"I'm hoping it's over now. Mom came in with some good shock and awe. But I noticed there were lights on in his office as we drove by, so he hasn't run off to Portland."

Dad pushes up his glasses on his nose reminding me of Michael. His voice is calm, but the too calm of a storm raging inside. "And the custody hearing?"

I take Caleb's hand. My voice doesn't hide the fury. "He dropped that. We were notified two days ago. He did include an offer to buy custody of the children. We've given a negative response to that offer." I didn't expound that the language used would get us in trouble with Ella for years, especially after Caleb was done explaining in a very staff sergeant manner why she should stop dropping the F-bomb immediately.

I expected questions, but it's getting tiresome. Mom lobbies what I hope will be the last. "Does Brian know?"

"We told him yesterday. He was not as calm as you

both."

Mom rests a hand on Caleb's arm. "He didn't blame Caleb or Mark?"

I exhale a breath. "No, his target is Hal."

Dad leans back in his chair, his coffee cold and untouched in front of him on the table now. Mom went all out with the Christmas decorations like every year. Greenery and holly berries are on mantles and up the banister. Only our tree rivals hers for lights and ornaments. Even her dishes were changed out from the everyday to holiday fare including ugly Christmas sweater wraps for the mugs.

When I look at Dad, though, the bright colors and lights fade staring in his hollow eyes and pale face. "We should have waited until after Christmas to tell you."

He waves a hand. "No, you shouldn't have waited one more second than you did. I'm glad you're home, Caleb—you two were always a strong team."

Caleb's jaw flexes. "If I wasn't home, sir, my father wouldn't be pulling this crap with the children."

Frowning, I squeeze his hand. "I told you to stop saying that."

"Brynn, I can stop saying it all you want, but it's true."

Dad takes Mom's hand and leans forward. "I'm not sure about that, Caleb."

"What do you mean?"

"I can't believe a man would hate his sons, and it pains me to agree you and Mark are a part of this. I'm just not sure it's how you think."

"You don't think he's trying to hurt Caleb?"

"I think that's a bonus, as it would have been with Mark. But I think he's been trying to replace you with the children."

"Frank, you don't think he wanted Liz or Brynn as a wife?"

"If it meant the children came with them. Think about it. He hits on Liz after Mark tells him he's leaving Camden and starting his own firm. He'd never come on to the girls before…"

Mom whispers. "Before they had Michael and Ella."

Caleb's gaze collides with mine and I read my own shock and repulsion in the depths as they turn to ice. "He thought I'd ever be with him? Even if you and I didn't connect, he'd have to know…I don't even like him."

Dad shakes his head. "Hal's always thought money and prestige could buy anyone."

"Not always." Mom's comment turns all attention to her. "There was a time he cared more about family, and you, Caleb, than anything. After Mark was born, he was obsessed with his sons joining him and no one could tell him otherwise. Lord knows Audrey tried to. She told him a million times they should encourage you both to follow your path, not to be like his father and hers. He started resenting her, and that was the beginning of his twisted heart."

"And I should have died on the battlefield rather than come back."

"Who said that?" Mom sounds like she just took an incoming round.

Caleb just lifts an eyebrow. Dad and Mom inhale sharp breaths. "With that and Brynn and Liz, he's more twisted than I thought."

My lungs burn and I release the breath I've been holding. "Brian will be bringing Michael and Ella back soon. They know that they won't be seeing Hal again. Neither was brokenhearted, but of course they don't know the details. We've decided not to speak of him…hopefully he'll just fade away, but we're not letting down our guard."

"There's no use in talking about him. Your father and I plan to enjoy the day."

I smile. "Good. But could you enjoy the day here? We don't want the children downtown without one of us in case he's there. Oh, and could you not do Christmas cookies? I'd like to do that with them."

For the first time since they greeted us, my parents smile. Mom's eyes glint with the thoughts of a retired kindergarten teacher and what crafts can be done. "We can do that. Ornament decorating all right?"

"Yes. We've already done that, so you're good to go."

"And don't let Michael work on math. He's still upset about missing a few days this week, but this is Saturday and he needs to have fun."

Dad returns Caleb's smile knowing the order was aimed at, him, the retired math teacher. "Got it, no math, and no cookies. Can we sled down the hill in the backyard?"

"Oh…" Caleb and I harmonize, and my parents belly laugh.

His hand tightens around mine as we join their laughter. My muscles unwind from the tension and Caleb's shoulders relax.

Dad leans forward. "Now we have some orders for you two. You're going to leave now, so you can't give orders to the children, and you're going to have a fun day together Christmas shopping for your little ones. It really is a special event, and we want you both to enjoy every minute."

We shrug and stand without argument. I hug Mom. "Thank you for watching them."

"We love it."

Dad winks. "And we'll do our best to stay within the parameters of the mission."

"Aye, aye." Caleb salutes my dad.

Grabbing our coats and hats, we step out into the bluebird day, where the sky is a cloudless blue and the sun shines bright off the white of the snow. I hug his arm as we walk to the SUV Mom and Dad are loaning us for the day. "Where to first?"

"Thought we'd hit Planet Toys."

I stop and inspect the vehicle before turning to him. "We might need a bigger car."

His chuckle is almost joyful, and I hope to get it back to full on by the end of the day. "We are not going to spoil our children."

"Come on, a little spoiling. They're so cute. Admit it, they're cute."

He shakes his head and rolls his eyes, but I see the fight he's putting up not to smile. He opens the door to the passenger side, and as I step into the car, he mumbles, "They are cute. A little spoiling."

When he settles into his seat, I wink and win the fight when he smiles. His smile is more deadly than any weapon, especially when it reaches his eyes and those tiny lines form. "This is going to be a fun day."

He starts driving to the parking lot on Washington Street. "Should be—I'm with you."

"Wow, that's sweet."

"I mean it. You could make a war zone fun…well, not when I was being shot at."

"Thank you."

He doesn't respond and I don't expect him to, but after the sour-tasting discussion with Mom and Dad, his words are a frosted sugar cookie. After he parks the SUV, we meet behind the vehicle and lock hands.

Stepping into the toy store, he stops short. I scan the store filled with books, puzzles, games, as well as socks and what seems like a million other items, including slime. It's like Santa's toyshop on steroids. "What's wrong?"

"We needed to whiteboard this out, so we don't get sidetracked from the mission."

I give him a light push and he smiles. "Oh, look they have Pet Vet. Ella would love it for her 'medicine bag'. Let's get her one." I drag him over to the box and he lifts it, examining the contents from stethoscope to 'cone of shame.' "She'll have her stuffed bulldog in the cone STAT."

He huffs a laugh. "Yeah, this looks good." He keeps the box, and tugs me over to another shelf. "Look Legos—let's get a set for Michael. And we'll get him some slime. That boy's going to be a kid whether he likes it or not."

"Look at this, it's called Cobra Claw—we could play as a family. Ella will need some help."

His gaze drops to the tile game like it holds the key to some magical land. "Let's get a few family games. We'll get a couple she won't have a problem with."

Swallowing around the lump of emotion, I nod. "Absolutely."

He is full throttle into toy shopping. "We need to get a couple toys for Toys for Tots, too."

"Definitely."

He sits on his heels to examine a book that claims it stretches out as long as a tyrannosaurus, and I wander a few steps away. I've always known Caleb has a tender heart. The Marine with the hard candy shell and the gooey center. But watching him shop for not only Michael and Ella, but a couple other children in need of Christmas, I'm falling in love with a man I didn't know, or the man I knew before all the deployments and war changed us both. My Caleb.

"You see something, Brynn?"

I laugh when I turn to find his arms overflowing.

"Can I put those behind the counter for you, sir?" A kind employee saves the day.

Caleb hands over his treasures and then turns back to me. "You find something?"

I realize I didn't answer his question. "Sloth socks." I grab the first item in front of my face so I don't have to explain what I was thinking.

"Sloth socks?"

"Sure, I think Mom would love them." She'll hate them, but I'm going with it.

"Okay. Maybe I'll grab Mom a pair."

Great, now both mothers can discuss amongst themselves about why they were given sloth socks.

"How about books?"

"Mom and Dad have that covered, remember?"

"Roger."

"But that does remind me, I need to stop at Sherman's or Owl and Turtle and get Mom a gift card."

"You don't know what she reads?" He sounds appalled.

"I know exactly what she reads. She reads romance. What I don't know is all the books she's already read, because she reads all the time."

"Understood."

"I think we've bought this place out." As we walk to the cashier, I notice he's getting his wallet out as I'm digging a card out of mine. "How do you want to split this?"

"I'd like to get it, Brynn, you've fed, clothed…well, fucking everything for a year. Let me handle this Christmas."

"All right." I put my wallet back in my purse. When I lift my head and meet his gaze, his eyebrow is raised.

"That's it?"

"I think it's nice and I'm too happy to argue, but right now I'm getting a little pissed off—"

He raises his hands, waving the stupid sloth socks. "I got it, I got it. We're good."

Bag after bag is handed over the counter. "This is more than we carried on a ten-mile hike."

He grunts and hands over his card before gathering half the ruck. Without a word, we start back to the SUV to drop off the loot. The town of Camden could be in a Dickens novel. Perfect for a holiday romance.

"So off to get your mom's gift card."

We start down Main Street and then turn onto Bay View Street. Less crowded than the Christmas by the Sea days, we can enjoy the walk and Christmas decorations a bit more without feeling pushed along. He rests his hand on my lower back, and the warmth from his hand seeps through the cold and my clothes, straight to my heart.

"I read a couple romances in those boxes they send to servicemembers."

"What brought that up?"

I shrug. "Talking about Mom and then walking with you." Caleb, being a voracious reader, must have stumbled across some when digging through the donations. "Did you ever read a romance?"

"Once."

"Didn't like it?"

"It was a good story. Historical, took place in Wyoming. Loved the description of the places and the characters were interesting. Then it got to a sex scene, and I mean, not the best thing for a man in the middle of a combat zone and no relief in sight. Plus, it just made me think about how good you feel when I'm inside you and…"

"I get the picture. I'm guessing if I would have been there…"

"We both would have been kicked out of the service, because the things I'd do to you would be legendary."

"What would you do to me?"

"The same thing I did last night and will be doing tonight." He opens the door to the bookstore.

The low rumble of his voice, memories from the previous night, and the promise of his words could melt Maine. Dropping my gaze before I combust on the scene, I duck under his arm and into the store.

CHAPTER TWENTY-THREE

Caleb

CLIMBING THE LADDER up to the deck, I'm still chuckling at Michael and Ella. When I join Brynn in the wheelhouse, she tosses a look over her shoulder. "What's going on?"

"They're down there looking through the bags but—thurt because all they're finding is food and supplies for Christmas goodies and dinner."

She tosses her head back, laughing. I step behind her, soaking up the joy and joining her laugh. "Outstanding plan to leave the gifts in your parents' car."

"The true test will be tomorrow when Brian brings them and we have to get them to the house."

"I was thinking about that. Why doesn't he just leave them in the tower and I'll run over when the munchkins go to bed?"

"Well thought out, Marine."

"I'm not just good looks and charm." I grip her hips. "I've always loved watching you behind the wheel of a boat, or even better, sailing like some sexy pirate queen."

"Sexy pirate queen?"

"One thousand percent."

She leans back into me. "It's good to be on water again."

I can't see her gaze, but I feel it move to the lighthouse. The distinctive green light shines from the beacon and touches the water, creating a path and illuminating the danger of the rocky shore. I shift my gaze to the small white two-story keeper's house. It's drafty, the floor squeaks, and the heater has to go through a series of clinks and bangs before it finally coughs up heat. But the Christmas tree lights sparkle in one of the windows, while light from LED candles flicker in the others. I'm going to miss it almost as much as Brynn.

"You know when the Nor'easter kicked up I kept my gaze fixed on the light?"

"The beacon?"

"No, Brynn, you." She rests her head back on my chest. "The house is nice, but it's you, and Michael, and Ella that make it home."

"When I bought it, I thought it'd be a safe harbor. When the images of mangled bodies plagued my mind, I could listen to the water against rock and soak in the green light of the tower. Now the images don't plague me as much, and I listen for Michael explaining the anatomy of a dinosaur, or Ella giggling, or you laughing with them, loving on me. The three of you are my heart and safe harbor."

"I wish I would have been a year ago."

"I was so pissed at you, Caleb, for breaking up with me and not leaving the Marines. But you might have had it somewhat right, though I don't think we needed to break up. I think I needed to see what I was without you, and I pretty much hated it. I think if you'd dropped everything two years ago and moved in, you'd resent it because it wasn't what you wanted."

"You have always been what I wanted."

"With two kids in Camden?"

"Maybe not Camden, but I'm starting to appreciate my hometown now."

She steers the boat like she was born to it, and she was. She uses short bursts of throttle, then cuts the throttle and backs into the slip with as much ease as pulling a car into a garage. No one would know she'd gauged the wind and current while talking to me.

I hop off and tie the lines, then climb back on. "Bets on if we're carrying the kids?"

She adjusts the white knitted hat on her head; I'd bumped it off-kilter standing so close. "There's no doubt. It's way too quiet down there."

Climbing down the ladder behind Brynn, I'm surprised when I hear Michael talking to her. Ella is trying to stay awake, although her eyes are at half-mast.

I tune into Michael and Brynn's conversation. "What sounds good?"

"I don't know, just hungry."

"Let's get the groceries in, and we'll see what we can do."

"Okay."

I nod to Ella. "Help your sister onto the deck, but don't get off the boat. Your mom and I will help you when we get this unloaded."

"Yes, sir."

We work in silence unloading the grocery bags from the boat, then helping the children, before grabbing the bags and walking up to the house. When the groceries are unloaded, I turn to find Ella continuing her fight with sleep and losing. "I'll get Little Bit tucked in if you want to feed the growing boy."

Brynn gives a sympathetic glance to Ella and nods. Lifting Ella, I realize how tired she is when there's no fight to stay with her brother. Instead she wraps her arms around my neck and rests her head on my shoulder. Her small body grows heavier with each step up the stairs until she's more hundred-pound ruck than forty-pound child. It's a sweet weight though; a sleep born of pure trust I won't drop her, or hurt her, or let anyone else hurt her.

I flip on the light to her bedroom and flip it off again when her tiny body jerks like a vampire facing the sun. "Sorry about that."

She mumbles something and her mouth remains open as she drifts back to sleep. After laying her on the bed, I undress her and slip one of the princess nightgowns Brynn bought over her head, then smile when the static from the nightgown causes strands of her hair to stand on end. Tucking her under the covers, I drop a kiss to her cheek. She nestles farther under and I stand over her, watching in fascination. The complete trust she has that Brynn and I will keep her safe is both humbling and an honor.

Pain squeezes my heart as my mind goes to thoughts of Mark and how excited he was when his children were born. When I talked to him, the conversation was filled with Michael's first words and later Ella walking. I understand his need to work hard and find a place for his family away from Hal, but it rips me up he ever let Michael believe there was something wrong with him for not being good at sports. Or that Ella missed knowing how much Mark melted when she took his hand. I feel sorry for my brother, and a touch of the old guilt rears its head when I think of the things he'll miss and I'll enjoy.

Ella turns and flops on her stomach, spreading out as if claiming the whole bed as her domain. The guilt disappears replaced by a love and protectiveness I've never known I could feel. I'm her and Michael's dad now, and I couldn't see my future playing out without them in it.

I walk out of the room before I disturb her and head downstairs. Michael looks up from a sandwich. "What did you decide on?"

"Peanut butter and jelly sandwich."

"Good choice."

Brynn lifts the jar of peanut butter. "You want one."

"No."

She continues loading the PB&J ingredients back in the fridge. I sink into a chair across from Michael. "You and your sister are good kids, Michael. I'm proud to be your dad."

The boy's eyes go wide and he pushes his glasses up. "Thank you, sir."

"Sir?"

"Dad."

Brynn brings over a mug of tea and sets next to me. Always on the same page as I am, she knows where this is going.

"You believe me that you're a good kid?"

"I believe you think so, but I did something you won't forgive."

"You told your dad, my brother, you wish he'd never talk to you again."

Pools form in his blue eyes. "You know?" His gaze shifts between Brynn and mine.

"Yes, we know," she confirms, her tone holding no judgment, only love.

"Then you know I'm not good."

"No, son, your mom and I know you're a human. We all have said things that hurt someone we love." I refuse to meet Brynn's gaze; this is about Michael, and she and I already hashed out our shit.

"But he didn't come back and neither did Momma. Grandad said—"

"Your grandad…" I almost choke on the word. "Was more wrong than you for saying what he did. Who do you believe, us or him?"

"You."

"Good. Know this, Michael, there isn't a soul who knew your dad better than I did, and he understood why you said what you did and forgave you the second you said it. All he was thinking that night was how much he loved you, and your sister, and your mom."

He locks his gaze with mine and searches my eyes for the truth. When he finds it, the tears he's holding onto fall. He crawls into my lap and hugs me close, sobbing. Brynn wipes at the tears on her cheeks and rests her hand on Michael, connecting us all in our grief over loss and thankfulness over the new family we've created.

BRYNN RESTS HER hip against the doorframe to the head while I'm brushing my teeth. "That was tremendously handled by you."

I shrug, then spit and rinse. "Needed to be done. I didn't want him feeling guilty about every gift he got."

"It did need to be done and you did an outstanding job."

I stop at the door and press a kiss to her forehead. "Thanks, Angel." I slip by her.

Sitting on the edge of the bed, I soak in the sight of her, from the cascade of thick, dark waves to the frown over her hazel eyes—now more green than brown or gold. I visually follow the curves I've mapped a million times, and molded my body to, marking her and receiving the brand of her body on mine. She's wearing one of my green Marine T-shirts that stops just above her knees. Brynn could make anything from desert utilities, to dress whites, to a fancy red dress look sexy as fuck, but this look is my second favorite.

"Why don't you take off that T-shirt and let me admire the view?"

Instead she stands between my legs, and I tip my head to make eye contact. "Because something is wrong."

"Something is always wrong, Angel, you know that. I'm sure you have a good idea what the wrong is tonight. I want to make something right." I roll up the hem of the shirt with my palms. "Something so fucking good.

Wrong can wait." I trace her bellybutton with the tip of my tongue and her belly flexes under my touch. I inhale the scent of her arousal and feed off the soft sigh of my name.

"We'll talk later, right?"

I smile against her skin. "Promise."

"Why do I feel like it's going to be hours before we talk?" I hear the smile in her voice and lift my gaze to hers again.

"Because you know me better than anyone, Brynn."

The gold flecks are back in her eyes that now match the green stone in her ring. She tugs the T-shirt from my hands and lifts it over her head. I smooth my palms over her hips and belly and cup her full breasts.

"Lie back, Caleb."

"No, I want to feast on you."

"But I want to suck you."

"Then let's both get what we want."

She tips her head and one side of her mouth curves in a sexy smile. "It's been a while since we've done that."

I wag my eyebrows. "Then by my clock it's time to do it again."

She steps from between my legs, and I stand and strip off my skivvies then stretch out in the middle of the bed. Her hair falls on both sides, framing her face as she crawls towards me, her lips already parted. She straddles my face, and I don't hesitate—the second her pussy is in my face, I rim her vagina with my tongue before sucking her clit. She gasps and her body shudders over me.

"Wait, Caleb! Please." Her voice is an octave lower and each breath is a pant.

I give one lick and then stop as she settles over me. When she grips my hard cock and sucks the head between her lips, my grip on her thighs tighten and a primal groan is ripped from my lungs. I slake my elemental appetite, kissing her sex like I would her mouth, shoving my tongue deep and savoring every last drop of her essence like honey.

I inhale a sharp breath when she starts sucking me hard and strokes my balls. I dig my fingers harder into her thighs, holding her steady, and suck her clit. She moans around my cock with her first orgasm, but I'm not done with her and return to sucking and licking as she continues the same with me.

One of my favorite things about oral with Brynn is she is not quiet. She slurps, and moans, and whimpers until it combines with my grunts and gulps. The erotic sounds fill the air. She drops her sex until all I can taste and smell is her over my face, and the feel of her mouth on my cock as her nipples scrape over my belly with her movements. Her legs tremble under my hands and I feast on her through her second orgasm. Every muscle in my body is drawn taunt, warning me I'm not going to last much longer even as I pull every ounce of control together to make this last as long as possible.

Her mouth leaves me for a second. "Caleb."

I recognize the hesitation in her eyes. "If you don't want to swallow say now, Angel."

I hold my breath and release it on a groan as she returns her mouth to my cock. Flexing my hips, I lap at her sex as I come inside her mouth and feel the hum of her climax around my sensitive flesh. I know my grip is painful on her thighs, but I hold tight as my neck bows. "Brynn! Holy—"

She continues to suck me through my orgasm and I return to her ultra-sensitive nub to give her one more climax until she slaps my shins, signaling me to let her go. I kiss and suck her inner thighs, leaving my brands before dropping my hands from her flesh, cringing at the new bruises.

When she rolls to her back, I shift to my side and propping my head up with my hand. Her eyes are as dark as the small forest behind the house and her cheeks are flushed. I drag a fingertip from her swollen lips to her bellybutton and back up. "We should definitely do that again soon."

"Definitely." She cups the back of my head and I take the hint. Bending I seal my mouth to hers. The kiss is slow and easy. She opens for me and I slide my tongue along hers. When she sucks the tip of my tongue, a low rumble emanates from my throat.

She opens her legs, and I take my place between them. For what seems like hours we stick with kissing; good old-fashioned making out. I skate my hand over the curve of her hip, then torso, and finally pinning her hands above her head. She breaks the kiss, when her neck arches as I ease my hard cock inside her soaking wet folds. Her inner muscles start working me instantly and she sighs; a sweet ethereal sound like she's truly a heavenly being.

She locks her gaze with mine before raising and lowering her hips. She moves in the rhythm I've set; slow and steady, a cadence to keep us connected as long as possible.

Her fingernails dig into my hand. Her chest rises and falls with deep breaths. "I love you."

"I love you, too, Angel."

"Make me fly."

Releasing her hands, I rock in and out of her harder and deeper and she moves to meet me stroke for stroke. She locks her legs and arms around me like I'm the anchor holding her to earth. Her lips part as if she needs to call out, but she doesn't. Like a string pulled tight then released right before it breaks, her body trembles and then relaxes. Her inner muscles close around my cock and work me. She peppers kisses on my neck and shoulder and chest as I continue to ride her until I flex my hips, driving deep in a mind-numbing climax.

As I drift back to earth, Brynn traces my face with the tip of her finger. I brace my weight on my arms and hover above her.

"Do you know how sexy you are picking out toys?"

Thinking I must have popped a few brain cells with the last orgasm, I laugh. "What?"

"You are so hot picking out toys. It's the intensity; every one has to be perfect."

I shake my head. "You're crazy."

She gives my shoulder a shove and her nose wrinkles. "You are. Extremely sexy. I want a dozen babies so I can watch you pick out all the toys every Christmas."

"A dozen babies won't give you much time to do much about how sexy I am after we pick out the toys."

"True. Okay, two more."

I tug her more securely under me. "I am crazy in love with you. I will give you all the babies you want, Brynn. And I will pick out all the toys if it turns you on. And I swear I will wipe noses, help with math assignments, and even be Mrs. Phillapot for tea, whatever it takes. I will adore every child that comes from your body. And I will continue to adore the two down the hall that come from the heart."

"Caleb."

I kiss her forehead. "No more talk tonight. I want to worship you for a few more hours, because it doesn't take you doing anything to turn me on. Just you being on this earth does that."

CHAPTER TWENTY-FOUR

Brynn

I JOLT AWAKE when a tiny finger nudges my shoulder. I feel the large form surrounding me tense as Caleb wakes, feeling the change in my body. Mentally calculating and confirming he and I aren't naked and the covers are up, concealing where he's hiked up the T-shirt I wore to bed and rests his hand on my thigh. I turn my attention to the owner of the finger. My gaze collides with ice-blue eyes in a pixie's face.

"Momma, Santa came. You and Daddy have to come."

Groaning, I try to sink farther under the covers. "Baby girl, ten more minutes."

Her smile turns to a stern frown. "He brought lots."

We know he brought lots, though we didn't give Santa credit for much when we started spreading out the loot. We commented on it the night before when we were still wrapping it all at midnight, but Caleb insisted each thing be wrapped separately no matter how small. Following the wrapping, we then sat down to eat the sugar cookies and drink the milk left for Santa. It really was the perfect Christmas Eve.

When I close my eyes, she turns to the big gun. "Daddy, please. It's hard waiting."

He shakes my hip and I know the battle is lost. "Come on, Angel."

I want to remind him, he's the reason I'm exhausted and questioning if I'll be able to walk. Since the other night, he'd made it his personal holiday mission to unwrap me every night, all night.

"Is your brother up?" I grasp for my last hope.

"He's downstairs."

"Okay, baby, we'll be down in a minute."

She hops off the bed and from the top of the stairs screams, "They're coming!"

I join Caleb chuckling and try to slide to the edge. Caleb holds me tight. "No Christmas kiss?"

Shifting in his arms, I narrow my gaze. "Wasn't it just supposed to be a Christmas kiss last night?"

"You're safe—we've got kids waiting." He presses his mouth to mine and gently adds pressure until my lips part. The kiss is tender and sweet. "Merry Christmas, Brynn."

"Merry Christmas."

"Are you coming?"

"Ella, leave them alone."

I shake with the laughter I'm trying to keep silent. Caleb scrubs a hand over his face and swings his legs off the bed, pulling on his sweats and a T-shirt. "You know that promise I made about as many kids as you want…"

Tugging on my sweats and a cardigan, I wag a finger at him. "No takebacks, Caleb Quinlin."

He assumes a façade of anger, but his eyes spark before we trudge down the stairs.

The second I enter the living room, thoughts of sleep transform to the joy of Christmas. The scent of pine fills the room and the glow of the fairy lights against the snowflakes on the other side of the window paints the perfect-picture of Christmas. Ella and Michael are adorable in their Christmas pajamas, Ella's with reindeer and Michael's with snowmen, and the enthusiasm is contagious.

"Merry Christmas!" Caleb and I harmonize.

Michael hugs me. "Merry Christmas, Mom."

He hugs Caleb next, and Caleb ruffles his hair after the hug. "Merry Christmas, son."

I grunt when Ella practically jumps in my arms, and I set her on my hip. "It's Christmas!" she announces.

"Yes it is, Little Bit." Caleb chucks her chin. "Let's get started."

"I'll hand out gifts," Michael volunteers, and takes my hand. "Come over here and sit."

Setting Ella on her feet, I follow Michael's lead. She doesn't stay grounded for long and goes to Caleb, who swoops her up. I sink onto the couch where Michael gestures and Caleb sits next to me, his focus is on Michael, and he looks almost as excited as the boy.

Michael steps next to my legs and holds out a small package clearly professionally wrapped in silver paper and with blue ribbon. "Michael?"

"Open it, Momma."

All eyes in the room are on me, and I feel like the only one not privy to what's in the box. After taking the gift, I tug off the blue ribbon. Michael leans closer and rests a small hand on my leg. Unwrapping the paper, I lift the lid of the box off and swallow the boulder of emotion in my throat. On a bed of cotton sit silver snowflake earrings so delicate and lacy they almost look too fragile to wear. The first warm tear cuts down my cheek.

His fingers curl around my sweats. "Do you like them?"

Lifting my gaze to his, I smile. "I couldn't love a gift more, Michael." Caleb rests his hand on my back, knowing I'm not just talking about the earrings but the one who gifted them too.

"Put them on," Michael orders, then his cheeks turn

red. "Please."

"Absolutely." I take one of the earrings and start putting it on.

"Dad helped me pick them out. But I paid for them all by myself."

I cut a look to Caleb then back to Michael. My dad told me he gave each of the children ten dollars the day of Christmas by the Sea, thinking they'd spend it on themselves. These are not ten-dollar earrings. But under torture, Caleb and I would both confirm Michael paid for them all by himself.

"He sure did."

I fasten the other earring and pull my hair back so he can see. "They're beautiful." I hug him and drop a kiss to the top of his head. "I love them, and I love you."

He nods to his sister, who is staring at the earrings and the wrapping paper, and it's not hard to read her disappointment that she doesn't have a gift for me. "I forgot they're from Ella, too."

Ella smiles and I give her a hug. "Thank you, Ella, for the beautiful gift. I love you, too."

Caleb rests a hand on Michael's shoulder. "Proud of you."

I wrap an arm around his waist and give him a quick squeeze. "Okay, I am not the only one getting presents today. There is a pile over there, so we better get to unwrapping."

"AW, MICHAEL WINS." I laugh, then take a swallow of my peppermint tea, choosing the soothing brew to the children's hot chocolate or Caleb's coffee.

Caleb and I are getting our asses kicked at Rat-a-Tat-Cat, one of the family games we got, and what's sad is we're not losing on purpose.

I lean back in my chair. "Okay, kiddos, I'm pulling the sore loser card. You guys go play in the living room for a bit."

They both start cleaning up the cards with pictures of cats and rats on them. Caleb stops them. "Go ahead and play—your mom and I will clean up."

"Okay." Michael and Ella say in unison.

They push off their chairs around the table and scamper into the living room. My stomach roils when I stand, and Caleb waves me down. "I'll get it." He cleans up the cards and puts the lid on the game box. "Nothing like a game suitable for a four-year-old to reinforce that you suck at math and have no memory."

I laugh. "You're a math genius."

He huffs a laugh. "Yeah, right." He glances over my head and out the window. "Still snowing."

"Good thing we decided to have our Christmas with just us out here."

"You still all right with that?"

"I am. It was nice both yesterday and today doing what we wanted, fixing a small turkey dinner and having more time enjoying the children instead of sharing them." Saying the word *turkey* turns my stomach, and I take a quick gulp of tea. "Plus, the way I'm feeling I don't want to be in a crowded house."

"Shit, Brynn, you okay? You need to go to urgent care?"

"No."

"Why is it the corpsman is always the last to take care of themselves?"

I frown over my mug. "I'm not. I have medicine here if I need it. I think I just ate too much dressing."

"Right. You want more tea to settle the *dressing?*"

"Yes, and don't be an ass. It's Christmas."

"Roger that. Initiating Christmas cheer even though you're about to puke."

"I'm going in the living room to join the happy elves. You can bring the tea in there."

"Yes, ma'am, Mrs. Claus." He stops me before I get to the archway between kitchen and living room. His smile fades as he cups my cheeks. "You have a fever, Angel."

"I took Motrin."

"Go ahead and change into sweats, sprawl on the couch. I'll see to supper."

It sounds like a command, but it's an offer I can't refuse. "Aye, aye."

"So stubborn."

"Yes, sir, Mr. Claus."

With each step up the stairs my good humor fades. Operation Perfect Christmas did not include feeling like crap. I step into the bedroom and start taking out the earrings Michael gave me. My gaze drops to the tactical MOLLE stockings Mom and Dad sent the other day with Brian for Caleb and me, each pocket filled with a small gift, candy, books, and gift cards. Michael and Ella had more fun watching us unload our stocking than looking in theirs.

Thinking of their faces as they opened their gifts, and even more so as we opened ours, I adjust my attitude. It wasn't the Christmas I envisioned, but it *is* the perfect Christmas.

After changing into my sweats, I grab a blanket, which happens to be Caleb's poncho liner again, and head back down the stairs. Caleb's voice stops me at the second to last step.

"Mom doesn't feel good, so we're going to suggest Christmas movies instead of more games."

"Okay," their small voices harmonize.

"And we're going to eat our turkey sandwiches in the kitchen instead of living room so she doesn't smell them."

"Okay."

My heart. They are all so sweet.

Walking by the kitchen, I almost melt at the scene of

my family around the table eating their turkey sandwiches and potato chips. Michael watches Caleb, trying to mimic him, but can't grip the sandwich the same due to his cast. Ella is trying her best to get her small mouth around the stacked turkey.

Before I'm spied, although I'm sure Caleb knows I'm there, I head to the couch. It seems he and I will need another talk about how much Ella and Michael can eat compared to a full-grown Marine.

I'm settled on the couch with the poncho liner tucked around me and almost asleep when a tiny hand wakes me for the second time today. "Momma, I'll sit with you."

Caleb sweeps her up. "No, Little Bit, we don't want you to get sick, too." Her frown mirrors mine, but he's right and his raised eyebrow challenges me to fight it. His gaze then drops to the poncho liner and I swallow my argument. "You ready for more tea?"

"No thank you."

He settles in the recliner with Ella on one side and Michael on the other. I sit up and try to follow the animated Christmas story. I cut a glance to the recliner to find two elves fast asleep using Caleb for a mattress.

"Did they brush their teeth?"

He smiles and huffs a laugh. "Yes, Mom, when you were sleeping earlier."

"I didn't sleep."

"Really? They ate, we got ready for bed, and they brushed their teeth and washed their little pumpkin pie–covered faces all before Ella served as alarm clock."

I scowl at them, noticing for the first time they are in their pajamas and Caleb in sweatpants and a T-shirt. It's clearly time to come clean. "I'm sick."

"I know, Angel."

"It sucks. You never get sick."

"Is getting blown up a fair trade?"

"Don't even joke about that." Changing the subject is my only defense. "You never told me what the wrong was the other night."

"You want to talk about that on Christmas?"

"Christmas is the best time, because on Christmas everything is right even what's wrong."

"That's some twisted reasoning, but I'll give it to you. I worry about Hal."

"About?"

"I can't imagine he's given up without a fight. And with what Mom said about Alice. It's like wading into a minefield."

"What does Audrey say?"

"She hasn't heard from him for a few days, since he told her he was moving to Portland. Then she saw him going into his office today when she was headed to your folks' house."

"What can we do?"

"Live our lives, but keep situational awareness until he's gone."

I don't respond, lost in thought. The popping of the fire and movie lull me back to my previous peace.

"Sorry you asked?"

I rake my gaze over him and the children. "No, everything is still right. You're holding them and they couldn't be safer."

"Today was the best Christmas of my life, Brynn."

"Mine, too, even being sick."

"You ready for New Year's Eve?"

"Yes. I'll try not to puke on you."

"That'd be a bonus, but even if you do I'll still say I do."

"I always have and always will."

"You sleeping in bed?"

The thought of lying down flat makes my bones ache. "Negative."

"I'll sleep down here in the chair then."

"That's sweet."

"No way I'm sleeping in that bed alone." He nods down to the kids. "Should we let them sleep under the tree like they've been asking?"

"Looks like they already claimed their spot."

"I wouldn't need a blanket, they're like hot lava. Is that a kid thing, that your body temperature rivals the sun?"

I chuckle at his feigned irritation. He'd let them sleep on him and love it even as he grumped about it.

"Merry Christmas, Caleb."

"Merry Christmas, Angel."

CHAPTER TWENTY-FIVE

Caleb

"HEY BRIAN, MERRY Christmas a day late." I walk toward his truck in the parking lot to Hannaford's Store and Pharmacy.

"Back at ya. Mom sent this for Brynn." He lifts a cooler. "It's enough turkey soup for everyone and her homemade rolls."

"Thanks, man."

"Sure. How's she doing?"

"She's wicked sick. We've passed the alien trying to break free stage, but it's not the sound of carols coming from the house."

Brian steps back like I might be contagious. "I'll skip visiting the house this afternoon."

"Wise choice" I lift the bag from the pharmacy. "Now, I better get the elixir of life home." My phone buzzes and I lift a hand in a bye to Brian as I swipe the answer button. "Yeah, Mom?"

"Caleb, you need to get home. I just saw your father's boat heading to the lighthouse."

My heartrate skyrockets and a wave a nausea to rival Brynn's flu hits. "Got it." I disconnect. "Brian!"

"Yeah?"

"Mom spotted one of Hal's boats headed to the lighthouse. I'm heading there STAT! I need you to get whatever authorities needed and get your ass out there."

As I'm issuing orders, I'm climbing in the truck. I pull out of the parking lot, not waiting for confirmation; Brian will take care of it. I turn down Elm to Bay View. When I get to the dock I barely stop the truck before bursting out and double-timing it to the cruiser.

Brynn

WITH A GROAN, I shift on the couch and force my heavy eyelids open. Michael is building a ship with Legos and Ella is checking her bulldog's heart and fitting him for a cone of shame.

Michael lifts his gaze. "Did you need something, Mom?"

To have my insides put back into place. "No. You?"

"No, Dad said we'd have lunch when he got back."

"Good."

The roar of a speedboat's engine getting closer to the

island raises my hackles. "Look outside and tell me who's in the boat, please?"

Michael nods and steps around the Christmas tree. "I don't know. He's big, though, and driving one of Granddad Hal's boats."

My blood freezes and Caleb's concerns about Hal cause a flood of adrenaline to push me forward. "Michael, get away from the window." I push up and grab their coats, hats, and gloves from the coat rack. I yank on my coat and go to Ella, giving Michael his outerwear as I pass. "Put that on, hurry."

"Momma, I don't…"

"Shhh, Ella. There isn't time, we've got to go." I finish bundling her up and stand.

I weave and a rush of nausea slams into me, but the crunch of heavy boots closing in push me on, and I lock and bolt the front door. "We're going to the lighthouse and you're going to be very quiet."

"Yes, ma'am."

Herding them to the door my heart races and sweat drips down my face. I count the seconds, waiting for the boots to fall on the first step to the house, so we'll be hidden from him as we run. I wish I had time to get my 9mm, but I wouldn't chance running up the stairs, and I won't send Michael.

When the bottom step creeks, I open the back door just enough for us to get through. Then, even though I want to slam it, I close it gently so I don't alert the man.

There are three thunderous knocks on the front door, and I push Ella and Michael on, thankful neither is aware enough to cry out.

"Open the door, lady, it'll go easier on you if you do!"

Michael casts a glance at me over his shoulder and I shake my head. For a second, I doubt my choice of the lighthouse and almost turn to one of the outhouses, or into the forest. There'd be no protection in the barn, and not knowing how long we'll have to wait him out, I can't risk the children out in the subzero temperatures.

We slip inside the door to the oil room, and I continue to herd them into the tower of the lighthouse right before I hear the crash of him breaking down our front door.

"Climb," I order. We start the winding climb and my mind goes to all the times I chastised characters in books and movies for going upstairs instead of outside.

When we reach the anteroom, I stop them. "What's going on, Momma?" Michael whispers.

"We need to hide from that man. He's not good," I whisper back.

Taking my phone from my pocket, I try Caleb's phone. "Yeah, Angel."

"Hal sent someone. I don't know who. He's in the house. We're in the lighthouse."

"I'm almost there. Hold tight."

Either he disconnects the call or the signal ended. Swiping at the sweat on my brow, I paste what I hope looks like a smile of encouragement on my face. "We'll be okay." I wrap an arm around each of them and hold them close.

It seems like hours pass as we huddle together. Maybe he'll give up when he can't find us in the house.

"You better hope I don't find you, bitch!"

I should have known. Still, there's a resurgence of hope when I hear the faint motor of a boat and a helicopter. The Marine has landed and he's brought the Coast Guard.

Letting the children go, I cut between their gazes. "Get up to the lantern room and don't you come out for anyone but me or your father." They stare at me, and I raise my voice. "Now!"

They scurry past me and start climbing just as the door below bangs open. I search the room for a weapon and find a piece of pipe. There's the low rumble of a laughter that is nothing but evil, as he has to hear the children's feet on the iron stairs.

"So here you are." The voice doesn't sound familiar. "Now you've pissed me off and I'm going to fucking rip you apart before I take those kids."

Stepping from the anteroom, all I see is a tall, dark shadow lunging for me. I swing the pipe for all I'm worth and take satisfaction when there's a low grunt of pain as I make contact right in his belly.

As I lift the pipe again, a bout of dizziness sends me off kilter, and I grab for the railing. The man recovers and, and with a snarl, grabs the pipe. He stands in the light, and I can finally make out his features. He's about Caleb's height, but not as fit, but what catches my eyes is the hate twisting his face.

He raises the pipe over his head. Lifting an arm to fend off the blow, I lower it when nothing falls. Instead there's a bellow echoing from the stone walls and the man is disappearing down the steps, being dragged out by Staff Sergeant Quinlin. My Caleb—the Caleb the children climb over—is gone, replaced by a mountain of granite forged by the Marine Corps for one purpose.

When that purpose comes to mind, I hold tight to the railing and make my way down the stairs in triple time. Caleb is picking up the intruder and pounding him with his fists once more. Already, the man can't stand as he flops to the ground, blood coming from his mouth and nose.

"Caleb, halt!"

He picks up the man I once thought was big, but now appears small and timid. Caleb raises his hand, but I grab his arm with what little strength I still have. "Caleb, please, no more!"

The man weaves and then hits the ground. Caleb

turns to me and cups my face, his eyes slowly adjusting back to the blue of calm waters. "Did he hurt you, Brynn, touch you?"

"No, no. I got a good wallop in, but this stupid fever."

He turns back to the beaten form, and I wrap my arms around his waist and hug him close so he doesn't start the beating again now that he remembers I'm sick. His arms embrace me and squeeze tight. A moan from the stranger breaks us apart. "Caleb."

He sits on his heels next to the fallen man. "I'm just going to ask a question."

I keep a close watch. He pushes the man's shoulder. "Who are you?"

"Fuck you."

"You're the one who's fucked, man. Whatever he promised you—well you'll have years to talk about as roomies in the state prison."

"You two all right?"

So, intent on making sure Caleb didn't kill the man, I didn't hear Brian arrive, but now I see the helo hovering over the dock. "Yes." I grab Caleb's hand. "The children. I have to go get…"

"You get your pretty ass back in the house. I'll get the kids."

I turn to complain to Brian, but he's already hauling the stranger down to the dock. I halfway comply, retreating to the back porch steps. Caleb emerges from the tower with the children. Michael runs to me, wrapping me in a tight hug as Ella sits perched on Caleb's arm like a queen.

"That's not in the house, Brynn."

"I'm going in…now."

I cringe when we walk inside, hoping he didn't tear everything apart. Surprising both of us, the only damage is the front door. But knowing he was in the house and touched things makes my shoulders shake in a shiver of disgust.

"You want to go to town? Stay in a hotel or with your parents?"

I ruffle Michael's hair. "Do you?"

"Not really. This is where Christmas is."

I look to Ella. "You?"

She shakes her head and rests in on Caleb's shoulder. Caleb holds my gaze with his. "I'm asking you, Brynn. The children and I will go where you need to."

I look to our tree and the sad bulldog in the cone of shame, and shake my head. "We'll stay. This is where Christmas is."

"Then sit your ass down."

Ella must sense this is one of those times correcting Dad's language is not cute or funny. Before I can comply or tell him where to go, I dash to the bathroom and empty what little is in my stomach.

A strong, warm hand rubs circles on my back as I suck in deep breaths. "You are so fucking badass, Angel."

"I don't feel badass."

"Come on, you're like the living dead and still you manage to get our kids to safety and land a pipe to the gut of some son of a bitch."

When I stand and flush, he lifts me in his arms. "You were pretty badass yourself."

He starts walking to the couch. "Well, that goes without saying." He winks and I roll my eyes.

"Who was that, Caleb?"

He sits without setting me down first so I'm cradled on his lap. "No idea. Someone Hal hired."

The children are back to their toys, but not really playing with them, just sitting by them. "And?"

"And Brian is taking care of that. I didn't want to go back to town and leave you all alone. We might have to go in and give a statement to the police. Brian said he'd talk to them, figure out jurisdiction and all that crap."

"Did you want to stay at a hotel?"

"Negative. I don't want to see Hal yet either." His eyes turn cold before he presses his warm lips to my ear and whispers, "I'd kill him.

"Understood." I tip my head toward the children. "Maybe some hot chocolate is needed."

Two sets of eyes swing to us, and they answer unanimously. "Please."

His body shudders under mine as I feel the tension and rage ebb. He sets me on the couch and tucks the poncho liner around me. "Rest. I'll grab your medicine after I get their hot chocolate and fix the door."

I nod and accept his kiss even if my breath rivals a corpse. When he and the children leave the room, I focus on the tree and try to bring back yesterday and all the warmth and joy. There is only one time when I have been as scared but forced to act as today, and I push back that memory before it can even unfold, for fear of nightmares.

The adrenaline is draining and with being ill no matter what I want I'm going to crash any minute.

From the kitchen there are giggles and a deep, gruff laugh. Maybe the dreams will be sweet after all.

Caleb

I EAT UP the pavement to Hal's office. For weeks I've refused to even call him father, and after yesterday I know why. I hesitated to leave Brynn and the children again so soon, but this time I left them with Brian.

Like a few days before, I walk through the door and straight back to his office without stopping, only this time when I get into his office, I steamroll him and slam him against the wall. "You're going to die, old man."

"What the hell is this?"

"What the fuck was that yesterday with Brynn and

the kids?"

"I don't know what you're talking about."

"The police might have believed your bullshit, but I don't. Brynn told me he only mentioned her. You saw me when I first got into town and knew they were alone. What was the fucking plan?"

His face drains of color and I'm ready to ground him to a pulp when he admits it. "I didn't know, Caleb, I swear to God, I didn't know. She asked if she could borrow the boat. Were the children hurt? Was Brynn?"

I search his eyes for the lie, the hidden sneer behind his question about Brynn's welfare, but it's not there. I don't see a lie, just fear. Releasing him, I stay close in case I'm wrong. "Who asked?"

"Alice. She acted strange on Christmas. Said she had a late gift for me and I'd get it yesterday. Then she asked if she could borrow the boat to pick it up. She didn't come back to work yesterday or this morning."

"It wasn't Alice in that boat."

"I don't know who he is. I have done some horrible things to you and Mark and the women you love. I've been forced to admit every charge against me is true. But this...I wouldn't take the children by force and I would not hurt Brynn."

At least he wasn't hypocrite enough to include me in the list of people he wouldn't harm. "Just file for joint custody."

"Yes, I did that and, like I said, many other things."

"Where is she?"

"I don't know. She must have fled when her accomplice was caught. Let me get you her file. There are the addresses of her emergency contacts there; maybe she went to one of them."

He staggers to the file cabinet and digs through folders until he pulls out one. "Here it is. I'm leaving for Portland at the end of the week. All you had to do was join me at my firm. Was that so hard to do?"

I hold his gaze, the only love I've ever seen there is for power and money. "Yes." I take the file to pass along to Brian not trusting he would. He nods. "I would like to see the children someday, if at all possible."

"At this point, Hal, I don't see that ever being a possibility. Wrong day to ask, but then I don't see a day when that will be a good question."

"Understood. Would you at least tell Brynn, I'm sorry?"

I can't tell if he's sincere or if this is more of his manipulation. I ignore the request. "If it's ever proven you were involved with yesterday, I'll hunt you down."

"I don't doubt it."

Before I turn to go, I stare at the shell that was once a man I respected, then one I feared, then one I loathed, and finally one who meant nothing to me.

Without another word, I pivot on my heels and walk

down the hall and out the door. There are some things even Christmas can't fix.

I stop at the bookstore and pick up the romance book I read in Syria for Brynn to read while she recovers. Then I keep walking to the docks. I'll give the folder to Brian, and the Coast Guard and police can decide who hunts Alice down. If neither do, I will.

Climbing onto the boat, I search the buildings and streets before me. It's a pretty little town, I have to admit. I ignored as much of it as possible any time I was back, and now I see it through Brynn, Michael, and Ella's eyes.

"Happy Holidays, Caleb!" Mr. Worthington, my high school lacrosse coach, waves from the street.

"Happy Holidays!" I shout.

"Good to have you home!"

I feel my smile grow. "Good to be home!"

CHAPTER TWENTY-SIX

Brynn

I DON'T KNOW what Mom and Audrey are talking about, but they seem happy with my occasional uh-huhs, so I don't try to keep up. I lean back, trying to catch sight of my new husband in the kitchen.

This day is exactly what I wanted. My house, my decorations, our children standing with us. If there was one misstep it is in the number of people invited. While small by any standards, it's not as intimate as I imagined. But when Rafe Manelli and Collin Hanson showed up, there is no way I wasn't going to invite them to stay. They did drive all the way from Jacksonville, North Carolina, after all. And honestly, it is fun talking "shop" again with Manelli; making sure he's caring for my Marines. Then Mom and Dad invited a couple people, Audrey did the same, and Brian brought a date. The small keeper's house seems almost overflowing, but so full of love, I wouldn't want it any other way.

Mom, Dad, and Audrey talked Pastor Hayes, a man who gets seasick by looking at water, into crossing the bay on a cold night to perform the ceremony. How they did it, or what they traded, is something Caleb and I don't want to know so we won't have to testify. But the pastor seems to be having a good time now since he survived the ride over, he's thawed, and is reconciled to the fact I'm wearing a red dress instead of white.

The red dress wasn't planned, but is perfect for us. With everything going on and me being knocked on my ass the past week, I didn't even consider needing a dress. I wanted to wear something he hadn't seen. Thinking of how much Caleb liked me in red, I tugged out this dress two days ago, praying it still fit.

When I bought it, it was for another special occasion three years ago, the Marine Corps Birthday Ball. We received orders the day after we'd be deploying a few days before and spending the Marine Birthday in Afghanistan.

The front has a jewel neckline, and long sleeves. Caleb is a bit chagrinned the back isn't low-cut, but rallied once I exposed the thigh high slit in the side.

With one more, "yes, uh-huh," I slip away from our mothers' conversation. Dad and Brian are deep in conversation about hockey; I smile and wave as I walk by. Hanson and Brian's date are talking, and I cringe at how far south the situation could go knowing Hanson's reputation and Brian's temper.

I step into the kitchen, sure I'd find Caleb and Manelli, but a sweep of the area shows the rest of the guests but no Caleb.

"You looking for me, Angel?"

I lean into Caleb's hand when he rests it on my lower back. "As a matter of fact, I was."

He draws circles in my back with his thumb turning my blood to fire. "Good. I've been dying to get back to you. Have I told you how gorgeous you are?"

I tip my head to the side to watch his mouth curve in a smile that promises wicked delights. "Yes, you have, but I could hear it again."

My hair is styled in an updo, so there's open access to my neck and he takes advantage, pressing a kiss to the sensitive skin. "You look fucking outstanding, Brynn," he whispers in my ear. My body responds to his touch and his words.

I skate my gaze over him in his navy suit. "So do you."

"Yeah, but remember the plans for a chapel, me in dress blues, you in white lace?"

"I like this better. This fits us. Simple vows spoken for the state of Maine and our families. Because really our vows have been spoken a million times with our bodies, words, and actions."

He caresses my cheek with the back of a finger. "True. You've been mine forever."

"And I'll be yours on this side of forever, too."

He nips my earlobe, and there's something about the fact that he really doesn't care who sees him that makes it all the more arousing.

When he lifts his head and straightens to his full height, I see everyone decided to give us some privacy and are deep in their own conversations.

His gaze sweeps the room. "Where are Michael and Ella?"

I nod to the recliner where they're curled up, sleeping. "So much for staying awake until midnight."

He chuckles, and like always it feels like I've won something making him smile or laugh. How are you feeling?"

It takes me a second to process the change of subject, but when he lifts an eyebrow I answer. "A little tired and I'm avoiding the kitchen so I don't smell the food anymore than I have to."

He cups the back of my neck. "Maybe we should have waited?"

"No way, needed or not, I would have stood up in my pajamas and spew bucket and said I do."

"Nice image, Angel, but I appreciate the enthusiasm."

Mom flips on the TV just as the countdown in New York begins. We all join in ten, nine, eight, seven, six, five, four, three, two, one. "Happy New Year!"

I tip my head as Caleb bows and captures my mouth. His kiss isn't a sweet, short welcome to the New Year. It's a hot, decadent, all-consuming welcome to the New Year where I am his. I break the kiss when I need air.

He skates the pad of his thumb over my bottom lip. "Happy New Year, Brynn."

"Happy New Year, Caleb."

The spoken words are simple, but the emotions and hopes and dreams we share without words are complex and will take us a lifetime and then some to fulfill. When the low rumble of conversation breaks into our space, I give him a lopsided smile and turn back to our guests.

TUCKING MICHAEL IN, I smooth back his bangs and kiss his forehead. He's been cast-free for a few days and cleared by the doctor, but I check his arm anyway before pulling the covers over him.

I meet Caleb, who was tucking in Ella, in the hall and we walk into our room. He unzips the dress and slips his arms under it and into the sleeves, tugging them over my arms.

"Caleb."

"I know, Angel. I'm not such an ass I'd expect sex when you're still sick. I simply love touching you."

I turn and caress his cheek with the back of my fingers. "I know you're not an ass. I'm sorry for both of us that I'm not up for an all-nighter, or even an all-hour."

"No need to be sorry. We have a lifetime of all-nighters and afternoon quickies, and morning delights. A few more nights until you're one hundred percent is nothing in a lifetime."

I continue to undress and he starts stripping. "I can sleep in the bed again, though, so at least there's that."

"I'll take it. I used to be able to sleep anywhere, but a few weeks holding you and I haven't slept worth shit without you in my arms."

"Agreed and agreed."

Once I have his T-shirt on, I wrap my arms around his waist and rest my head on his chest. His arms are heavy and solid and amazing as he holds me close.

I nestle closer. I'm where I belong. Where I'm needed. Where I'm valued. Where I'm desired. Where I'm safe in the harbor of his love.

EPILOGUE

Caleb

New Year's Eve, Two Years Later

FROM THE ARCHWAY between the kitchen and living room I watch those who have become my life. As it should be, Brynn stands in the center and everyone revolves around her. She's wearing a red dress, and I smile thinking of how I'll remove it later. She's deep in conversation with our mothers, but she could tell anyone exactly where each of her children is, where I am, and how to care for anything from flu to flesh wound.

On her hip, sits our one-year-old daughter, Ruthie. She is by far the most adorable one-year-old on the planet. I'm not biased at all—it's fact. Okay, maybe not fact, but I dare someone to tell me different. Brynn has her dressed in a fluffy green velvet dress, her chestnut hair the shade of her mother's and pulled into two small pigtails, only enhancing the cuteness.

Ruthie catches me staring, and her mouth curves in a grin. Her ice-blue gaze collides with mine, and her tiny hand opens and closes in her version of a wave. I wave back, but don't move. There are two more lights shining I focus on.

Michael sits with Brian and Frank around a card table, playing a game. Since going back to school in Camden, he's found his footing. He's a typical kid, sometimes too typical and Brynn and I have to remind ourselves it was us who pushed him to be just that. He and I have played lacrosse, and tossed a football, but neither are his thing, and I'm just as happy spending time with him over a game of chess.

"Daddy, can Mia and I have another cup of hot chocolate?"

"What did your mom say?"

"Not right now."

"Then that's your answer and I told you not to play your mom and me against each other."

"Yes, Dad."

And then there's our kindergartner. I hold onto my chuckle as she walks back to the friend from school we allowed her to invite. They don't stay disappointed for long, and find a place near the Christmas tree where they sit and begin playing with a miniature doll set she got for Christmas. Ella, when she's not angling to get her way, is every ounce my Little Bit. She melts my heart. She's also one hell of a hockey player, a sport she picked up after Brian got her, her first pair of skates.

We didn't need a court to tell us we were a family, but it sure felt good when all the paperwork was signed, and Michael and Ella became ours legally a year and four months ago. I shake my head remembering when Brynn and I figured it out and the goosebumps we got thinking of Mark and Liz having a hand in the journey.

I meet Brynn halfway when she hands Ruthie off to her mother and walks toward me. "Happy anniversary." She lifts on her feet, and I bend sharing a brief kiss with my wife.

"Happy anniversary to you, Angel."

"What are you doing standing over here by yourself?"

I scan the room again. This time I don't narrow my focus on Brynn and the children, but Frank, Rose, Mom, and even Brian. I wouldn't admit it to him, but I'm going to miss Brian barging in on us when he takes a temporary post off Bath.

I caress her cheek with the back of a finger. "Taking inventory of my blessings." I take her hand and guide her over behind the tree for a little privacy. I glance out the window at the green light touching the water. "When are we selling the keeper's house, again?"

Her eyes spark as she laughs. "I thought we decided the twelfth of February thirty of never."

I chuckle. "I'll plan on it."

She hugs my hand. "The Marine with the plan."

I rub my chin between two fingers. "Not that many of those panned out."

"Like how, because I want to be with Ruthie, you're now getting your degree in education before I finish my nursing course?"

"Yeah, like that one."

"And we started Michael in school earlier than planned and Ella right away instead of homeschooling for a bit?"

I try to frown, but smile. "Exactly like that."

"And—"

I brush my lips over hers. "I get it. The plan is usually not what's executed on the field."

She takes a step back and the sparks in her eyes and curve of her lips promise mischief. "And that brings me to another plan of ours that has gotten a little off course."

I narrow my gaze. "What plan is that?"

Her smile grows. "The plan where we wait until Ruthie is three to have another baby."

Stunned isn't even close to how I feel. The air rushes from my lungs. Her smile falters. "Not happy?"

I recover and cup her cheeks, peppering her face with kisses. "I'm overwhelmed at what you've given me, Brynn. Holy shit, another baby!"

She presses her lips to mine, wrapping her arms around my neck. "Shhh, love, I don't want to tell anyone else yet."

Roping her waist with my arms, I hold her close and

bury my face between her neck and shoulder. "How long have you known?"

"I took the test this morning, but wanted to wait until tonight to tell you."

I lean back to make eye contact. "When did you suspect?"

She chuckles and shakes her head. "I didn't really. I've been feeling off for a couple weeks. This morning I saw the pregnancy test in the medicine cabinet from when we were trying for Ruthie. I thought, *what the hell.*"

I swallow the *Rah!* I want to bellow. Picking her up, I bury my face again and kiss her neck as I squeeze her tight. Her body trembles, and when I set her on her feet I confirm it's in laughter.

"We might reach your dozen, yet, Angel."

I can only imagine my smile is as big as hers the way my face feels stretched. "I love you, Caleb. You're my heart."

Resting my forehead against hers, I inhale the scent of pine, cinnamon, and all the good things of the holidays, but then it narrows to her. Like everything in my life, every small moment in my life, every major event, it all comes down to Brynn.

"I love you, Brynn. You are everything I've ever wanted. You are my home."

SHORT LIST OF MILITARY TERMS

MEDEVAC: Medical Evacuation

CASEVAC: Casualty Evacuation (more serious injuries;
    any aircraft can respond)

FMF: Fleet Marine Force

2/8: 2nd Battalion, 8th Marines (out of Camp Lejeune)

3/7: 3rd Battalion, 7th Marines (out of Twentynine
    Palms)

Hi Readers!

Since writing the historical romance GILLIAN: BRIDE OF MAINE a few years ago, I've wanted to write a contemporary story taking place at a Maine lighthouse. Caleb and Brynn raised their hands and offered up their story. A Marine and Hospital Corpsman…I was absolutely giddy to start writing this story. I fell in love with not only Caleb and Brynn, but with the children Michael and Ella. I hope you, too, will fall for this family born from the heart.

When using a real location, I always try to be as authentic as possible. Sometimes as an author we have to change things so they fit the story we want to tell. The Marines in Helmand Province and the firefight, while based on real Marines and real actions in Afghanistan are of my own making. The main alteration I made was to the lighthouse. Curtis Island Lighthouse is an operational lighthouse in Maine. However, it is owned by the Camden Historical Society. I re-opened the keeper's house as a private residence for Brynn. The inside of the keeper's house is also altered some to fit the story. Any other small alterations are for the same purpose. I hope you will look over these and enjoy the story.

Thank you for reading THE MARINE'S HOLDAY HARBOR! I hope you enjoyed Caleb and Brynn's story! And stay tuned for more from Maine…Brian is headed to Bath, Maine…just saying.

Wishing you all the best,
Kirsten Lynn

ABOUT THE AUTHOR

Historian by day, romance author by night. Kirsten Lynn lives in Wyoming and uses the rugged terrain and small-town settings as a backdrop, and sometimes character, in many of her stories. She loves first loves, second chances, and happily ever afters. When she's not lost in writing a sexy story about a swoon-worthy Marine, cowboy, or firefighter meeting their match, you can find her with a cup of coffee by her side buried in history books, or finding inspiration in the mountains close to home.

MORE FROM KIRSTEN LYNN

4 MARINES FOR HISTORY SERIES
CHERRY PICKED
CHERRY HOT
CHERRY ICE
CHERRY WINE (COMING IN 2020)

TEN SLEEP DREAMING SERIES
CHOCOLATE COWBOY
IRON COWGIRL

HARBOR LIGHTS SERIES
THE MARINE'S HOLIDAY HARBOR
THE GUARDIAN'S LIGHT (COMING IN 2020)

For links and information about these and other titles
please go to:
Website: www.kirstenlynnwildwest.com/books.html

www.ingramcontent.com/pod-product-compliance
Lightning Source LLC
Chambersburg PA
CBHW030832110726
47900CB00006B/1856